About Rolan
and *Bloody Mer*

Few individuals are better qualified to create and depict those characters, scenes, settings, actions, and atmospheres that made the Old West a place of legends and heroes as long-time guide, Roland Cheek. When the robust sexagenarian isn't hiking, climbing, riding, and rafting through the still-wild parts of the Northern Rockies, he writes about the places he's been and things he's seen.

With two decades of newspaper columns, hundreds of magazine articles, and six previous books depicting the West as it is today, why wouldn't the man qualify to write of the West as it was?

He does. And with his previous historical Western, *Echoes of Vengeance*, Roland proved it. Now comes *Bloody Merchants' War*, the second in his **Valediction for Revenge** series of six novels depicting the life of Jethro Spring, a man born of an Indian mother and a white father, a man who passes through both worlds without feeling at ease in either.

Bloody Merchants' War is set in Lincoln County, New Mexico. It includes, as any tale of that era and place must, Billy the Kid, John Chisum, Alexander and Susan McSween, John Tunstall, and the Santa Fe Ring.

In retrospect, Lincoln, New Mexico Territory, was not the place to be on August 6, 1877, especially for a man wishing to avoid trouble, as happens to Jethro Spring....

Other Books by Roland Cheek

(non-fiction)
Learning to Talk Bear
Phantom Ghost of Harriet Lou
Dance on the Wild Side
My Best Work is Done at the Office
Chocolate Legs
Montana's Bob Marshall Wilderness

(fiction)
Echoes of Vengeance

BLOODY
MERCHANTS'
WAR

BLOODY MERCHANTS' WAR

Roland Cheek

a Skyline Publishing Book

Copyright 2002 by Roland Cheek

Cover design by Laura Donavan
Text design and formatting by Michael Dougherty
Edited by Tom Lawrence
Copy edited by Jennifer Williams

Publisher's Cataloging in Publication
(Prepared by Quality Books, Inc.)

Cheek, Roland.
    Bloody merchant's war / Roland Cheek: author ; Tom
Lawrence, Jennifer Williams: editors. — 1st ed.
    p. cm. — (Valediction for revenge ; 2)
    ISBN: 0-918981-09-3

    1. Frontier and pioneer life—West (U.S.)—Fiction.
    2. Ranchers—West (U.S.) 3. Farmers—West (U.S.)
    4. Lincoln County (N.M.)—Fiction. 5. Western stories.
    I. Title.

PS3603.H445B56 2002   813'.6
                             QBI33-485

Published by   Skyline Publishing
                  P.O. Box 1118
                  Columbia Falls, Montana 59912

Printed in Canada

Dedication

To my father who taught me to read... and think.
And to a mother who taught me to work.

Acknowledgement

I suppose some might consider it overkill if I wish to give additional credit to the professional individuals who bring our Skyline Publishing books into being; the editors and designers who hone the craft and bring cover and pages to life. But this is *my* book and they're essential elements to *my* team and I want to pay a little extra homage to their skills. So Laura Donavan, Jennifer Williams, Narelle Burton, Michael Dougherty, and Tom Lawrence—thanks.

Thanks, too, to Bill Lepper, the jet captain who keeps our computers operating. And to Brandon Norack, the twelve-year-old who's virtually responsible for helping us to enter a more comprehensive virtual age.

CHAPTER ONE

They came from the Capitans, a gaunt, sweat-streaked sorrel mare and her grimy rider. Topping a low ridge, the man gave the mare her head.

Without pausing, the horse plunged down the rock-strewn foreslope, squatting on her haunches like a dog sitting on a porch stoop, sliding amid a cloud of pea gravel and dust until she leveled out above a sandstone bluff. The rider checked her there and sat staring at a sluggish stream and the scattering of buildings shimmering through heat waves beyond.

The mare was so fine-lined that few owners would've ridden her into such an unforgiving land as the desert at their backs. The man straddled a hand-tooled Visalia saddle that, from its weathered appearance, had seen misuse.

The man's clothing was also badly worn: a faded blue-cotton shirt ripped at an elbow, patched canvas trousers, a high-crowned hat so battered and dusty its original shape and color were hardly decipherable. Worn, moccasin-style boots completed the ensemble.

Like the once expensive California-style saddle and the well-bred mare, a lined face beneath the hat's floppy brim hardly squared with the raven hair of youth. Nor did the eyes: startling gray, set deep in a face shaded darker than the well-oiled leather holster hanging midway down his thigh. The rider unconsciously slapped dust from that holster, then wiped the darkened walnut buttplates of a polished and oiled Colt revolver until the worn grip reflected a late afternoon sun.

A bead of sweat trickled from the hatband and coursed down his grimy face as the man slid a scarred Winchester carbine from its scabbard and, with a twist of his wrist, checked the action and magazine. Satisfied, he slapped the lever shut, then thrust the rifle back beneath his leg, clucking to the mare, reining her to a break in the bluff and down to the water flowing between hill and hamlet.

A chicken squawked and a dog barked from farther upriver as the mare quenched her thirst. When she lifted her head, the man clucked and pointed her up the far bank to the row of adobe houses beyond.

Two vaqueros leaned against a building on the left, staring vacantly at the newcomer. A hand-lettered sign over their heads read:

STORE—JOSE MONTANO, PROP.

Above a door on the building's far end was another hand-lettered sign:

SALOON.

No music or laughter drifted from within.

Back from Montano's store stood a larger one-story stone building. Above its double doors hung a better crafted sign:

COURT HOUSE—LINCOLN COUNTY, NEW MEXICO TER.

A new building with a fresh-painted sign proclaiming J.H. Tunstall & Co. stood on the right. A large corral half-circled the building at its rear. Both store and corral were constructed of adobe. A white-haired gnome of a man, his skin wrinkled and dark as a shriveled prune, tilted a rickety chair against the store's porch wall. The rider acknowledged the old man's fluttering wave by inclining his head.

Beyond Tunstall's store was a sprawling whitewashed home, encircled by a picket fence. A scattering of smaller adobes squatted beyond, blending with the beaten earth of the road.

The man reined in at the last building, dismounted and using his shapeless hat, slapped dust from his trousers. Inside, the newcomer paused until his eyes adjusted to the cave-like gloom of a one-story hotel, then poked a tiny desk-top bell. A calendar advertising barbed wire hung from a wall. Each day was crossed off until this one: Sunday, August 6, 1877.

"Yeah?" Only a fringe of white tufted over the ears of a ferret-faced little man who shuffled into the lobby, wiping his hands on a flour-sack apron.

"I need hay for my horse. And oats, too, if you got any."

"This ain't no stable. It's a hotel. Only horses we put up are ones belonging to people what stays here. You try Murphy's store, 'cross the street. They put up drifters' horses provided they got money."

"I want a room, too."

Ferret face frowned. "You got any money?"

The newcomer nodded.

"Well, let's see it. Four bits for the room, two bits for the horse, a nickel for oats. I ain't movin' nowhere 'til I see you got that much."

A silver dollar flipped through the air and a toothless

smile fractured the vertical lines of the old man's face. "Put your hoss in the stable, boy. I'll make change."

———◆———

"Poured you coffee there on the table," ferret face said as his newest boarder returned through the rear door. "Case I didn't tell you, meals is extra. Two bits apiece and you got to be here on time to get 'em."

"And when's that?"

"Comes at seven, mornin' and evenin'."

"Seven would be near sundown this time of year, wouldn't it?"

The old man paused from rolling bread dough. "You may be trainable, after all."

The stranger sipped his coffee. "You Wortley?"

"That's the name o' this hotel, boy. You need to know more?"

The stranger shook his head, then asked, "Where's my change?"

"Out on the desk, by the register. Don't forget to sign in, hear? If you can't write, mark an X and tell me your name."

Even white teeth flashed in the bronzed face, then faded. "A bath—how much?"

Ferret face's nose wrinkled. "You need one, that's sure. Be a dime. And you'll have to wait 'til I heat the water."

"Fair enough. I'll leave the dime by the register. How long will it take to heat the water?"

"Hour, more or less. I'll call you."

The stranger started on, then paused to ask: "Stores don't close on Sundays in this town?"

"Murphy's, across the street, don't. Reckon Tunstall's won't neither if they figger to run Murphy's out of business. Them's the only two that counts. Rest of 'em are Mex.

Them two's the only ones white folk ..." The old man's voice trailed off and the pale face reddened. "You're white, ain'tcha? Them eyes look it."

The stranger ignored him. "You said Murphy's, across the street. Sign says J.J. Dolan & Co."

"Was," ferret face said. "Was Murphy's until a couple of months ago. Still is, you ask me. Murphy, him and Dolan, they run this county."

The gray eyes flicked to the open door. "If Murphy and Dolan run things in this county, how is it Tunstall's is going to put 'em out of business?"

Ferret face worked furiously at his bread dough. "Your room's second on the left, down the hall. No key. Remember, you can't write, mark the register with an X."

Jethro Spring picked up his change and a quill pen. After dipping it into the ink jar, he turned the register to face him, then swiftly wrote *Jack Winter, Laramie, Wyoming.* Seconds after he walked out into the brilliant sunshine to cross Lincoln's single street, the hotel's proprietor spun the register around to read.

"*Quien es?*"

Wandering slowly along an aisle of garden implements at J.J. Dolan & Co., the newcomer appeared not to hear the clerk's question.

Behind, another deeper voice said, "Follow him, Bill. Them damned Mexes will steal us blind, we don't watch."

"*Quien es?*"

Still ignoring the clerk, Jethro Spring moved to shelves jammed with pots, pans, kettles, crocks. Idly, he ambled up one aisle, down another, followed by the Dolan & Company clerk.

"Goddamn it, Mex, you buyin' or ain'tcha?"

The newcomer paused at a shelf heaped with denim trousers, pawed through them until he found the right size, jerked out a pair, looked at the price, then replaced them.

"Shit," said the clerk. Then, "You speak English?"

"Sometimes," Jethro replied, shuffling through a pile of blue cotton shirts. "Most of the time, in fact, when I'm addressed civilly."

"I'll be damned. You Injun?" The question hung there. "Well, dammit, you buying, or ain't you?"

"Prices seem a little high." Jethro threw the folded shirt back on its stack. "Fifty cents for a bottle of saleratus, seventy-five for a pound of green coffee, fifty cents a pound for loaf sugar? Makes a fellow want to check out the other stores."

"Okay, *mestizo*. That does it—out! Get out!"

A tall, ruddy-faced man with a full, sandy-colored moustache stood near the door as Jethro Spring, followed closely by the clerk, ambled to the exit. "Found nothing you wanted?" he asked.

"Your prices are a little high, Mr. Dolan. Leastways they seem that way to me. But that's not why I'm not buying, for I surely do need some new pants and shirt and maybe a hat."

"My name is Riley," the tall man said, smiling affably. "John Riley. And why is it you're not buying here?"

"Normally if a man is going to pay these kinds of prices, he'd prefer not being insulted while doing it."

"Damn you ..."

John Riley knocked away his clerk's hand just before it reached Jethro's shoulder. "If an apology is in order, I'll offer one. I'm sure Mr. Burns meant nothing."

Jethro nodded, then pushed out the door. As he did, John Riley murmured to his angry clerk, "No, Bill, there's no profit in it."

The ancient Mexican, sombrero at his side, still tilted in his chair, just as he had when Jethro rode into town. "*Buenos tardes*, senor. A wonderful day, no?"

"It sure is, pardner," said the newcomer as he entered J.H. Tunstall & Company's store.

A clerk peered over his spectacles. "What can I do for you today, sir?

"Looking for a shirt and pants. These I'm wearing is near tuckered."

"Follow me and I'll show you what we have."

Jethro Spring slid out a chair at a boarding house table heaped with an assortment of food. A stocky, mustachioed man across the table asked without looking up, "You Winter?"

"News travels fast."

"My business." The stocky man pulled back a shirtpocket flap to expose the star. "I'm sheriff here. Name's Brady. You travelin' through?"

Jethro shrugged and reached for a bowl of boiled potatoes.

"I like a quiet peaceful town," Brady said.

The stranger's gray eyes met those of the sheriff. "Me too."

Two Negro soldiers came in from outside, both still chuckling from some private joke. There was no expression on Jethro Spring's bronze face, but he tensed. The soldiers pulled out chairs on his right.

A fort, he thought. *They've got to be stationed around here!* He willed himself to relax, then said to the nearest soldier, "I'd like a touch of that gravy if it'd not be too much trouble."

The ferret-faced man shuffled in from the kitchen. "All right, you what ain't paid, shell out."

Groans met the hotel-keeper's dun, but the bronze man heard none of it. *Is there anyone at that fort who might know me—know I killed an officer?* Jethro Spring snapped to the present as one of the soldiers chuckled, "That Mist' Wortley, he sho' don' miss no tricks."

Later, Jethro Spring strode outside to breath deeply of the night air, drinking in its clean sweetness, marveling at the difference between its evening essence and the hot, dusty, daytime air of this high desert country. He stretched hugely, the starched newness of his shirt scratching his neck and shoulders and elbows. Beside him, one of the soldiers said, "Bes' time of the day."

Jethro nodded into the darkness, murmuring, "It is that." Then the sound of laughter and murmur of voices drew him inside.

Sam Wortley drifted down the length of the rough plank bar. "What'll it be, Winter?"

"Your beer as hot as your tank water, old man?"

"Could be. That what you want?"

Jethro shrugged. "Bring it on."

"Cost you a nickel." Wortley drew the beer.

"See you found clothes—I trust at prices better than ours?"

Jethro turned to see John Riley smiling down at him. "They were better."

"I must apologize for my clerk, Mr.—Winter, isn't it?"

"I should have hung the name outside so everybody could take a look."

"It's a small town, Mr. Winter. Besides, one should not be ashamed of one's own name."

Jethro turned back to his beer.

"What brings you to Lincoln, Mr. Winter?"

"People here ask a lot of questions, but nobody answers any. Why's that?"

"I really couldn't say. Do you wish to ask me a question?"

Jethro shook his head, then said, "Yeah, maybe. Sign over your store says Dolan and Company. You said you're Riley. Yet your clerk called you 'Boss' and everybody calls your place 'Murphy's store'. I don't follow."

Riley grinned. "Easy enough. Major Murphy started the store, retired and sold it to Mr. Dolan and me. I'm the 'company' part of Dolan and Company."

Jethro pondered, grimacing as he took a swallow of tepid beer. Riley continued: "Murphy's is far and away the largest trading company between the Texas border and the Rio Grande Valley. Actually, the largest this side of Santa Fe. We're understandably proud of that fact."

Jethro nodded, drained his beer and set the mug down. As he slipped from his stool, Riley asked, "Will you be in Lincoln long, Mr. Winter?"

"A wandering man, Mr. Riley—he seldom knows where he'll be, one day to the next."

Riley pointed at Jethro's low-slung revolver. "Do you know how to use that, young man?"

"Could be. I'm not real sure myself. But I suspect we'll both be better off if neither of us finds out." Jethro turned away, then spun back. "It's not for sale, if that's what you mean."

Amusement glinted in John Riley's eyes, then Jethro Spring was gone.

Later, as Jethro tugged off his moccasin-soled boots and lay fully clothed upon a sagging, squeaking bed, his revolver's handle prodded his side. He saw its discomfort as a grim reminder of the day when he'd not had the Colt close to hand; a day his Chinese laborers were swept up and massacred in a senseless riot along a distant railroad right-of-way.

CHAPTER TWO

He leaped to his feet at the first gunshot. Distant shouting followed by more gunshots sent him fumbling for his boots. More gunshots and he collided, cursing, with the chair he'd propped against the unlocked door.

As he groped his way to the entry desk, Jethro Spring had the sense of other people in the dark hallway. Boots clattered on the boardwalk and a man burst through the door, leaving it swinging in the moonlight. "Senor Brady! Senor Brady! *Por favor.* Ees Senor Brady within?"

Hands grasped the white shirt, bunching it. "What is it, Romero? What's going on?"

"Senor Freeman! *El Diablo*, he is back! Senor Bowdre is with him. They tear up Montano's store. Now they come here."

"Sonofabitch!" a third man shouted down the inky hallway, "Freeman's back! And he's heading this way!"

"Where in the hell's the sheriff?" someone near Jethro muttered.

"Somebody's got to get Brady," another said.

A fusillade rattled from down the street. Another white-clothed figure burst into the hotel. "My father's store—it is in ruin. Please, will not someone do something?"

Everyone babbled like coyote-stalked geese. More gunshots momentarily quieted them. Someone struck a match and lifted a lantern shutter. The match was struck to the floor, fluttering out. "Are you crazy!"

"They are wild with drink, they steal from my father!"

"Is Brady deaf? Why ain't he doin' something?"

"Ha! Brady? You don't think he's fool enough to go up against Freeman or Bowdre? Not without the Ninth Cavalry."

"What the hell is going on?" Jethro Spring's voice cut the sudden hush after another fusillade. "Who is Freeman? Or Bowdre?"

"You must be new, you don't know about Freeman," a quavering voice replied from behind.

"For God's sake, there's two. Two goddamned men are out there. How many are in this room?" Jethro demanded. "Ten? Fifteen? How many does it take to quiet down a couple of drunks so a body can sleep?"

"You sure as hell don't know nothin' about Freeman—meaner than a rattlesnake with a broke back, even sober."

"Drunk, he's pure poison," another murmured. "I'll put a twenty gold against ten silvers he's already killed somebody."

Another rattle of gunfire sputtered—all from revolvers, Jethro thought. He wondered if Freeman and Bowdre were the only ones firing? Probably. A couple of drunks treeing an entire town. "What about the sheriff?" he asked. "Hell, I'll go get him."

"You're out of your mind, stranger. Freeman or Bowdre'd cut you down, sure."

"Where's Brady live?"

"Other end of town. Past them crazy bastards."

Someone almost as black as the night itself loomed in the doorway. "Oh Lawdy," the soldier moaned. "He done killed the sergeant."

Jethro shouldered forward, took the man by the arm and led him into the lobby. The soldier collapsed into a chair, covering his face with his hands. "They shook hands. They shook hands like friends. Then Freeman, he lays his gun agin the sergeant's ear and ..." The soldier began sobbing.

Gunfire crept nearer. Someone darted in. "I think they're going to McSween's. I heard Freeman holler something about calling Chisum out."

"Chisum's there all right. I saw him pull up today."

"There's women in that house!"

No one stirred.

Jethro Spring dashed through the kitchen, cursing as he collided with chairs and tables amid the darkness. Outside, gun in hand, he sprinted to the stable. More revolver fire roared in the street, definitely near the white adobe with the picket fence. Angle and movement indicated Freeman and Bowdre were on horseback.

"Chisum! Y'all don't come outta there and talk to me'n Charlie, we'll come getcha." The man fired at the house and roared with laughter. "Chisum! You gutless bastard."

Jethro slipped near, low to the ground like a stalking cat. The riders, black against the starry sky, reeled in their saddles.

"Chisummmm! You mangy yellow dog! Y'all are hiding behind a woman's petticoat!"

Both men reloaded, still weaving, laughing, and shouting to each other. Jethro raised his revolver, then wondered why a stranger should take part. The larger of the two silhouettes fired twice into the sky and spurred his horse toward the western edge of town, Jethro's gun trained on the rider as he sped by. The other reveler continued to blast steadily at the McSween house. Tinkling glass reminded Jethro of ice breaking on the Montana ponds of his youth.

The rider to the west fired at several buildings, then galloped back crying, "My name's Frank Freeman! Ain't no twenty men can arrest meeee!" His revolver flashed again and again at the shuttered McSween home. "I'm Frank Freeman and I'll kill any man I don't like!" The drunken rider spurred his horse over the picket fence and into the yard. "Here I come, Chisum, ready or not."

His companion followed and the two fell from their horses, laughing and shooting randomly. One shutter fell askew. Freeman wrenched it off.

"Chisum! You come out, or we come in."

Without waiting for an answer, the black-bearded man broke out the remaining shards of glass and crawled through the window, followed by Bowdre. Seconds later, a lamp flared.

Jethro eased forward to peer inside.

Freeman roared, "If Chisum ain't gived to me in five minutes, I'll burn this house down." He staggered to front a sewing machine and began shooting into it. Bowdre joined him.

"Ain't nobody got no guts in this town, Charlie." The two paused to reload. In the lamplight, Freeman's full black beard and the two revolvers in his waistband and another thrusting from a pocket of his heavy leather chaps combined to make him appear fearsome. Bowdre cackled like a setting hen. Cartridges spilled from his fingers.

Jethro Spring stepped through the broken window and said, "Party's over, boys."

Both men staggered around to face him. Freeman gaped at the cartridge clamped in his fingers, then at his revolver's open loading gate. "Who the hell are you?"

"Easy does it, big man. I'm a friend. Just a friend come

to tell you to tone the party down so's a body can sleep."

Freeman blinked. "I ain't got no friends what ain't white, mister butt-in. Y'all ain't too smart if y'all come in here to arrest me. His left hand inched toward his belt.

"If you're thinking about trying for another one, don't."

Bowdre stooped to pick up the cartridges he'd dropped. Jethro's eyes followed. Freeman hurled his empty revolver and launched himself at the newcomer.

Jethro bobbed aside, grabbing the man's outflung arm, twisted, then jerked Freeman around and slammed him into the adobe wall. In the same motion, he sent Bowdre spinning with a well-aimed kick.

"You sonofa ..." Freeman's snarl died as Jethro's revolver barrel snapped a mule's kick behind his ear.

The party's latest-comer holstered his Colt and sat on Freeman. He was cleaning his nails with a pocket knife when a door squeaked open. Jethro saw a round face with a drooping moustache. "Who are you?" round face asked.

"I could ask you the same thing."

"Indeed you could. But your grounds are not as impeccable as mine. You see, this is my house."

"On the other hand," Jethro replied, turning back to his nails, "it likely wouldn't be if I hadn't taken a hand. I figure that gives me some squatting rights."

The other chuckled. "I'll concede that, sir. I'm Alexander McSween, and I'm indebted."

The seated man rose and shook hands. "Name's Winter. Jack Winter."

Others crowded in. One, a thin, bandy-legged man with a craggy laugh-wrinkled face and wearing an expensive broadcloth suit shoved through the group. He grasped Jethro's hand and pumped furiously. "A pleasure, sir. Did I hear `Winter'?"

Jethro winced as the other squeezed.

"Most everybody around New Mexico knows of me,

boy. Name's John Chisum. I own the biggest cow spread in the territory. Down on the Pecos."

Jethro drew his Colt and said, "Excuse me." Then he knelt and poked the barrel into one of Freeman's ears. "I wouldn't," he whispered.

Freeman grunted and pushed the gun he'd been palming from beneath him.

"Now the rest."

"Can I turn over first?"

"First the guns, then the comfort."

The bearded giant pushed out another revolver.

Jethro plucked the small revolver from Freeman's chaps pocket and said, "Now you can roll over."

Freeman did so, then scooted up, his back against the wall. He glared at Jethro's Colt, then at the dark-faced man holding it. "You, I'll remember," he snarled.

"Best if you did, big man. Likely you'll not get hurt if you do." He kicked Freeman's loose weapons into a corner, glancing at Charlie Bowdre who blubbered into both hands.

"Well, gents, it's way past my bedtime. What do we do with these two?"

After McSween left to fetch the sheriff, a voice reminded Jethro of the tinkling of wind chimes: "I don't know how we can repay you, Mr. Winter."

He spun to see a pink silk robe belted tightly around a tiny waist. Ruffles from a nightgown swept the floor. Pink slippers peeked from beneath. He stared at the slippers until one of them stamped, then his gaze ratcheted up to a pale oval face, framed in disheveled, light brown hair. He blinked at a pert up-turned nose, full cherry lips, and broad lines of unplucked eyebrows that matched the color of her hair. As he stared, the eyebrows arched. Then he fidgeted under her direct gaze until she smiled and said, "I'm sorry. I've not introduced myself. I'm Susan McSween."

His eyes fell.

She asked, "You are new here?"

"Yes'm. I rode in this afternoon."

Her gaze was disconcerting. "Yet you had the courage to broach Frank Freeman in a drunken fit. You are unusual, Mr. Winter."

"Maybe lack of fear is nothing more than ignorance, Miss McSween."

"Missus," she corrected. "No, Mr. Winter. I do not believe your courage comes entirely from ignorance."

"Nor do I," boomed John Chisum. "I like your measure, boy. The Jinglebob can always use a hand of your cut."

"Jinglebob?"

"My ranch. The Jinglebob, that's my earmark."

"Oh? I'm not much of a cowhand, Mr. Chisum. I ride well enough, I guess. But I don't rope worth a damn." He glanced quickly at Susan and whispered, "Darn, I mean."

When Alexander McSween returned with the sheriff, Brady stomped over to the still-crouching and sobbing Charlie Bowdre and kicked him sprawling. He wheeled toward Freeman. The bearded man snarled, "You try that with me, Brady, and I'll tear out whichever leg you use and feed it to you heel first."

The lawman wrenched out his revolver, cocked and pointed it at the big man. "Charlie Bowdre and Frank Freeman," he intoned, "I'm hereby arresting you in the name of the sovereign people of New Mexico."

"On what charge?"

"Malicious destruction of private property for starters," the sheriff growled. "That and attempted murder if that sergeant presses charges."

"He didn't die?" Jethro broke in.

"Naw. Even sober, Freeman can't do nothin' right, let alone drunk."

The bearded giant roared. "Shoulda knowed better'n to shoot a nigger in the head."

"Get up, Freeman."

Curious men filled the doorway. All carried guns at the ready.

———•◦•———

Greetings and congratulations came thick and fast as Jethro entered the near-filled Wortley Hotel dining room the following morning. Men waved from the table's far end. John Riley slid out an empty chair, pointing at the newcomer. "We saved that chair for you, Mr. Winter."

Jethro took the seat, noting that Brady sat across the table.

"A noble piece of work last night, lad," Riley said, holding out his hand.

Jethro took it, shook it. "I hardly think it was noble. They were both too drunk to pee straight."

Riley chuckled. "I think I can vouch for the fact there are few in Lincoln County who'd care to brace Frank Freeman, drunk or sober."

Jethro nodded, reaching for a plate of pancakes and staring pointedly at the sheriff. "Wasn't any at all, I could see."

Brady flushed. "You don't live here, Winter. You don't know how things are."

"How are they, sheriff? Two drunks tear up a town, shoot up a house with women in it, shoot a soldier, terrorize everybody else including a cattleman who has dozens of cowboys riding for him back at the ranch. There's a bunch of able-bodied men here in this town, all armed and touchy as cornered polecats. Even the store clerks carry shoulder guns. Yet nobody takes toys away from two mad dogs who're so drunk they can't keep their pistol muzzles from dragging in the dirt. So, go ahead, sheriff. Tell me how it is. And while you're at it, tell me again how you like to keep a nice quiet town."

Brady's face was scarlet.

"You may be a little hard on him, lad," Riley said. "You must remember, sheriffs are human, too, and Freeman's rampages are a thing of note here in Lincoln County."

Jethro recalled how others besides Brady had been fearful of Freeman. Riley's logic made sense. Besides, what did he care about this place and these people? "I'm sorry, sheriff. That was uncalled for."

A man next to Riley said in a high-pitched voice, "He's apologizing, William. Give him that. Accept it, please."

"All right, Winter. Let's forget it."

"Pay up, them as hasn't." Wortley passed Jethro. "Not you, Winter. You got a free day for last night. Ever'thing you and your hoss can eat and drink is free. So's the room."

Riley laughed aloud. "Be damned! You'd ought to feel honored, boy. To my certain knowledge it's the first time that old skinflint ever passed a chance to get into someone else's pocket. Isn't that right, sheriff?"

Brady nodded and Jethro felt the awkwardness of his outburst drifting away amid the general feeling of good will surrounding the morning table. He was half through with his breakfast when Riley pushed his empty plate back and said, "Mr. Winter, if I can intrude for a moment, there's someone here I'd like you to meet." Riley indicated the small man on his right who'd insisted Sheriff Brady accept Jethro's apology. "This is Jimmy Dolan. He's my friend and business partner."

Dolan leaned forward. He was a dapper man wearing an embroidered dress shirt with a freshly starched linen collar and a black satin bow tie. "The entire community is indebted to you," Dolan said. "What you did was a courageous thing."

Jethro's mouth corners drooped. To a man who'd once lived by his fists, who'd learned the way of Oriental fighting from a Chinese friend, it was indeed nothing.

"You are too unassuming, Mr. Winter," Dolan said. "Frank Freeman is a desperado of the worst sort, and Charles Bowdre is but a notch below. No, you deserve every accolade, sir."

Jethro shrugged and addressed Brady. "What's to become of your prisoners, sheriff?"

"They'll be bound over for the fall term."

"And when is that?"

"Sometime around the first of October—ain't been set yet."

"That's a long time to hold them, isn't it? That is, if they're as bad as I hear."

Brady nodded. "That's why we asked Fort Stanton to let us transfer Freeman to the stockade."

"So that's why the soldiers. Where is the fort?"

Riley waved a hand. "Nine miles west, up the Rio Bonito. Headquarters for the Ninth Cavalry."

"And this Ninth Cavalry. They're stationed in the country for what reason?"

"Mescaleros," Riley said. "Their reservation lies to the southwest. The Ninth more or less watch-dogs the Apaches."

"Wilson is to set bail at nine o'clock," Brady said. "He'll make it plenty high, mad as everybody is about last night. Will the cavalry detachment be in for Freeman today, for sure?"

Riley nodded. "For sure."

Jethro's head pivoted with the conversation. "You mean you asked for the stockade for one, and not the other?"

No one replied. Instead, Riley said, "Mr. Winter, Jimmy and I would like a word with you. Do you mind?"

"Guess not. Here, my room, or your place?"

Dolan stood. "I believe it would be more appropriate if we talked in my office."

Jimmy Dolan, John Riley, and Jethro Spring trooped

across the street from Wortley's Hotel to the huge, two-story brick building of J.J. Dolan & Co. It was Riley who unlocked the door and held it open. Dolan led the way down narrow aisles, past shelves laden with merchandise. They entered a rear office where Dolan drew aside blue print window curtains for more light. His partner entered and closed the door. The small man turned from the window and in his high-pitched voice asked, "How long do you propose to stay in this country, Mr. Winter?"

Jethro shifted his back to a wall and flicked the thong from the hammer of his Colt, taking some satisfaction that Riley and Dolan exchanged glances. "Why?"

"Because if you remain, we'd like you to work for us."

"Doing what?"

"We really haven't decided that. We do have a wide assortment of work—stock ranches, the store, a freight out-fit. We make cattle drives ..."

"Because of last night? Because I slapped a couple of drunks around and took their toys? You're joking."

Riley's deep voice cut in, "I assure you, we're not."

Dolan nodded and said, "Can't you just accept the fact we'd like to have you associated with Dolan and Company?"

Riley added, "We admire your courage and decisiveness, Winter, and we'll pay sixty a month and what you need from the store at cost."

Jethro shook his head in wonder. "I've been in town one night and already I've received two job offers."

"May we inquire as to your other offer?"

"Sure. Chisum. Last night. Said if I wanted ..."

"We'll pay you eighty dollars a month, Mr. Winter."

"That's war wages, Mr. Dolan. I already told Mr. Riley my gun's not for hire."

The small man's smile held as much warmth as an open door on an empty stove. "We have no intention of hiring your gun, Mr. Winter. Our only concern is that we retain able, hard-working men. We both agree that your demonstrated ability to think and act clearly and courageously warrants prime consideration.

An awakening bluebottle fly tapped and buzzed at the window.

"And if I say no?"

"Then we must ask you not to stay long in Lincoln County."

Jethro's thoughtful nod hid the sudden rush of anger. "And how long might I consider your proposal, gentlemen?"

Dolan's reply came too quickly: "We want it now."

"Jimmy!" Riley exclaimed. "We can give him some time."

Jethro Spring's gray eyes narrowed as they swept the dapper Jimmy Dolan from head to toe, then he brushed past John Riley to stride down a narrow aisle to the front door and on into the dusty street.

⇒ Chapter Three ⇐

Outside the J.J. Dolan & Co. store, Jethro Spring secured the thong over the Colt's hammer and crossed the street deep in thought. The ante went up right after he'd told the partners of Chisum's job offer. Jimmy Dolan had also given an ultimatum—take their job at twice the going rate or clear out of Lincoln County.

Sam Wortley was in the kitchen when a pensive Jethro wandered in looking for a cup of coffee.

"There's a note for you in your key slot."

"I thought you said my room didn't have a key."

"Don't. But it's got a key slot—number three. Behind the register desk. That's where your note is."

Jethro started toward the lobby, then returned. "I don't suppose you could shed any light on what's going on around here?"

Wortley wagged his shiny head. "What I don't know would fill most of a book, sonny. Maybe two or three."

.

Jethro took the note from the slot marked "3" and opened it.

> We'd like very much to talk to you at your earliest convenience.
> Alexander McSween
> John Chisum

Jethro left his hotel room around mid-morning. The broken shutter of the McSween home was already repaired, but the glassless window stared like a blind eye.

Susan McSween opened the door. "Oh I'm so glad you could come, Mr. Winter. And I do hope you'll stay for dinner."

"Well, yes'm," Jethro murmured, twisting his weathered hat. "I guess I could."

A white blouse with button-up collar and billowing sleeves set off her piled light-colored hair and oval face, while a beige taffeta skirt with its black velvet piping accentuated the tiny waist. "Please come in. The men are in the drawing room."

As he shuffled past, his face reddened at her nearness. She smiled sweetly. "May I take your hat?"

Entranced by her faint perfume, Jethro was only dimly aware of the home's lavish furnishings as he followed Susan McSween down a long hall. She opened a door at the end and stepped aside for him. "Ah, yes, Mr. Winter. So good of you to come." Alexander McSween strode forward, extending his hand. John Chisum, standing behind, waited with a cavernous smile. Then Jethro's own mouth fell open at sight of a disheveled Charlie Bowdre, slumped at a small serving table, sipping steaming black coffee. Bowdre never looked up.

"Of course you remember Mr. Chisum," McSween said. Jethro nodded.

"And I believe you've met Mr. Bowdre, but have you been formally introduced?" Bowdre's mouth corners drooped and he shut his eyes, but made no other motion.

McSween gestured to an overstuffed armchair. "Please have a seat, Mr. Winter." The door behind them closed with a click. "I'd like once again to tell you how grateful we are for your timely assistance last evening, and to assure you we'd like to turn our gratefulness into something more tangible than mere accolades."

"I'm asking for nothing."

McSween's easy smile looked as if it was pasted in place. "Of course not—we realize you seek nothing. By the way, would you stay and have dinner with us? Did Susan ask ...?"

"Yes I did, Alex. And Mr. Winter already agreed to stay. We'll merely have something light, but I'm sure the fine companionship will more than make up for the meal's lack of substance."

Her voice again reminded Jethro of wind chimes. But his eyes stayed with the lady's husband. "Why did you ask me here, Mr. McSween?"

"Hell, boy," Chisum interrupted, "we wanted to talk to you. Get to know you."

Jethro came out of the overstuffed chair as if on springs. "I don't play in a game where I can't see the cards."

McSween asked abruptly, "How long do you plan on being in the area, Mr. Winter?"

Jethro glanced first at Chisum, then at Susan McSween, and Charlie Bowdre, at last returning to Alexander McSween. "You'd like to hire me. Right?"

"That's our thought."

"Mr. Chisum already offered me a job."

"That's true," McSween said. "But daylight places things in better perspective. John's ranch is sixty miles away. Upon reflection, we think you might be of more value if you weren't so far from Lincoln."

"And what would I do for you?"

When McSween hesitated, Jethro softly added, "You don't know, do you?"

"Well, we haven't gone that far," McSween replied. "But believe me, there's plenty to do. If you wish, we'll keep you busy."

"*If I wish!* Mr. McSween, you have a different idea of work than I do. If I hire somebody, they'll work at my pleasure, not theirs."

"Fine. Fine. All the better. Will you consider it?"

"No."

"Why not?" It was Chisum this time.

"Because," Jethro said evenly, "you're trying to buy a gun, aren't you?"

"Absolutely not," McSween said. "Both John and I are committed to peaceful means in matters legal."

"Uh-huh," Jethro said, rolling his eyes in a manner not lost upon the others.

Alexander McSween said, "Do you know what my profession is, Mr. Winter?"

Jethro shook his head.

"I'm an attorney. There's every reason in the world for me to support and defend the law. I've never carried a gun. Neither has John. What do you say to that?"

"Two things, Mr. McSween. First of all, a man's a fool not to carry a gun. I'll never again be far from my own Colt. I ride with it, walk with it, eat with it, even sleep with it. Once, I needed it and didn't have it. Since that time, I've spent a lot of time and a lot of cartridge money relearning what a Texas Ranger once taught me: that just because a man carries a loaded gun don't mean he has to shoot himself."

When he fell silent, McSween murmured, "You said you had two things to say about us not carrying guns, Mr. Winter?"

Jethro nodded. "You said you don't carry a gun. But you never said you don't hire men who do."

The pasted smile vanished from McSween's face. "I wish you'd give some consideration to our offer, Mr. Winter."

"Just what *is* your offer?"

"We'll match today's earlier offer, Mr. Winter. That really should be sufficient if you'll stop to consider our long term benefits."

"Which are?"

"That we'll be here in Lincoln County when the people who run the Murphy 'house' are behind bars."

"Do you know how much they offered?"

"No, and I don't care."

"I do," Chisum interrupted. "I want to know how much they offered. What was it?"

"Eighty a month and wholesale store prices for personal stuff."

"Eighty a month! They must want you bad. You got to know that's gunfighter pay."

"I told them the same thing I told you, Mr. Chisum. But they said the gun wasn't part of the offer."

"Bullshit!" the cattleman exploded. "Sorry, Sue."

"Did you accept?" McSween asked.

"No."

"Will you accept our proposal?"

"No."

"Please, Jack—Mr. Winter." She took a step nearer and Jethro swam for a moment in the liquid of her green-flecked eyes.

"Why?" Chisum demanded, breaking the spell.

Jethro shook his head to clear it, squaring to face the rancher. "My reasons are my own and I don't think I'm called on to explain 'em to God or anybody. But I will tell you it's because there's some things going on here that I don't understand."

"Can we explain them to you then?" Susan asked, brushing her hand lightly on his forearm. Again her faint perfume engulfed him.

Jethro jerked, shook his head once more, then nodded at Bowdre. "You can start by explaining that."

"Easy enough," Alexander McSween said. "Judge Wilson set his bail at five hundred dollars. I made it."

"Why? After he wrecked your home and shot up the town? You made his bail. That's crazy!"

"He was merely drunk."

"Hell, I know that. But so far, this town has showed all the wrong kind of tolerance for a drunk. First thing the sheriff did last night was kick this man down when he had his head in his hands. Why the sudden kindness now?"

"Because he is one of ours, Mr. Winter."

"One of *ours?*"

McSween shrugged. "Charles has a small farm on the Rio Ruidoso. He's suffered the oppression of Murphy's yoke for too long. Like most of the rest of the county, he's ready to throw off that yoke."

Jethro stared at the floor, stroking his chin. "What about the other one? Freeman. What about him?"

"Let Murphy's bunch take care of their own."

"You mean Freeman is one of Dolan and Company's men?"

"Precisely."

"He's one of their hired guns, all right," Chisum agreed.

"Then what was Bowdre doing with Freeman?"

"Poor Charles," McSween said. "Freeman got him blind drunk."

"But why?"

"A Dolan plot, of course. Think, Mr. Winter. Freeman is a Dolan man. If he came in alone and shot up the opposition, everyone would know Dolan put him up to it. But if one of our men drank with him and both of them did it, who could blame whom?"

Jethro seemed absorbed by Bowdre. "Is Freeman out on bail, too?"

"No. His bail was set much higher."

"I heard a cavalry detail was to transfer him to Fort—what was it—Stanton?"

McSween nodded. "I heard that, too."

"So justice serves one side and not the other. Is that it?"

"You have much to learn, Mr. Winter. You don't think Freeman will be held for long, do you?"

"You're not suggesting the U.S. Army's in this, too?"

McSween's moustache danced as the pasted smile returned. "Let's wait and see, shall we?"

Chisum pounded a fist into a palm. "Look, Winter, we want you to work for us. Will you?"

"I answered that."

"Scared?"

"Scared? Of whom?"

"Of 'The House'. The Santa Fe 'ring'."

"The Santa Fe *what?*"

"Never mind, Mr. Winter," McSween cut in smoothly. "It's not important at this time. What is important is that you consider our offer."

"To hell with that," Chisum said. "We want him to work with us. Or we want a reason why not." The cattleman's face wore the merest hint of a smile, but the wide-set eyes held no warmth.

A grandfather clock ticked loudly in the ensuing silence as Jethro cold gray eyes collided with Chisum's green ones. "Good day, Mrs. McSween, Mr. McSween. Thank you for the dinner offer, but I'd best not stay."

She took a deep breath, then smiled sweetly. "I'll get your hat, Mr. Winter."

"We almost had him, John," McSween said as the door clicked behind his wife. "You pushed too fast at the end."

"Sometimes you gotta rope 'em instead of ask 'em, Alex."

The attorney shook his head. "Not that one, I think." Then he asked, "Do you really think he's worth eighty a month?"

Chisum shrugged. "Sure wish I had seen him in action. I don't like buyin' no pig in a poke."

"That's just it," McSween murmured. "Nobody's seen him in action. Why is Dolan ..." The attorney saw Bowdre as if for the first time. "Nobody saw him in action except ...Bowdre!"

The Ruidoso farmer muttered, "I don't 'member nothin'. But I'll tell you this—next time I see him in action, it'll be while I'm cutting the black Injun bastard down to size."

Jethro Spring paused in Lincoln's only street. A puff of wind raised a dust devil at his feet as if from the earth's bellows. He cursed and kicked at the dust devil, started for the hotel, then spun on his heel and stomped toward Tunstall's store.

The ancient Mexican, sombrero at his side, leaned against the store wall in his rickety chair exactly as the day before. The wrinkled old-timer waved as Jethro thought better of Tunstall's and wheeled for Montano's, throwing a perfunctory salute.

A crude "closed" sign hung across the door to Montano's. Jethro twisted the knob, found the store unlocked, and entered.

"I am sorry, Senor, but our store is not open at the moment." The man held a broom. The boy Jethro had seen at Wortley's and a woman almost as broad as an inside aisle struggled to set up fallen shelves.

Jethro nodded. The room lay in shambles. Scattered canned goods, broken bottles, dishes and earthen pots, pans and kettles, bolts of yard goods and spilled flour, corn, sugar and salt littered the plank floor.

"May I help?"

Jose Montano shook his head. "No, Senor. My wife and my son, they will help. It is but a matter of time."

Jethro shrugged and turned to leave. As he did, the store owner said, "*Gracias*, Senor Winter—for what you did last night."

Jethro trudged back up the street to Tunstall's store.

"*Buenas dias*, Senor. A nice day, no?"

Jethro glanced at the gnome, took in his rickety chair. He said, "Old man, I think every day is a nice day to you."

The old man chuckled, head bobbing as if on a string.

Jethro entered the store, emerging moments later, tucking a handful of cigars into his shirt pocket and squinting into the sunlight. He saved one, biting the end from it while staring at the distant skyline.

Two factions vied against each other in Lincoln County. But why? Who belonged to each side? Both wanted his gun without knowing if he could use it. The senselessness of both job offers made him growl. Remembering the unlit cigar, he fumbled for a light. After patting his pockets, he glanced at the store's open doorway and was turning to re-enter when the old man said from his rickety chair: "I have a match, Senor."

Jethro took the extended sulphur match, struck it on a porch post and touched his cigar, then blew the fire out and tossed the spent match into the dusty road. "Thanks, old fella."

The ancient Mexican bobbed his white head. "Si, Senor. A small favor to repay for what you did last night."

Jethro sucked in his breath. "Old man, if I hear another time about how I did a great and noble deed by taking the guns away from a couple of falling-down drunks, I think I'll puke my guts out into the street."

The gnome cackled like a setting hen.

Jethro leaned against a post and again stared at the distant ridge. *Dolan and Riley represent the Murphy "faction." Chisum and McSween must be their opposites. But why are they fighting? What was it Sam Wortley said? "Tunstall figures to run Murphy's out of business." What does that mean? What has Tunstall to do with Alexander McSween and John Chisum? I need somebody to explain what's going on around here.*

"The Senor, he chooses not to work for those who offer him work, no?"

Startled, Jethro glared down at the wrinkled face. "What did you say?"

"The Senor Winter, he will no work for Senors Dolan or Chisum. Is that not right?"

"How did you know that, old man? How *could* you know that?"

"One who keeps his eyes open learns much."

Jethro's back slid down the porch post until he squatted on a level with the white-haired gnome's charcoal eyes. "Tell me what such a one might learn, old man."

A soft chuckle again cracked the sun-dried face. "It is easy, Senor. After you go in with Senor Dolan and Senor Riley, you come out soon, no? You walk like you are angry. You stop in street ..." The old man's eyes fell to Jethro's worn holster and the butt-plate of the Colt. "...and you put loop back on *pistola's* hammer. You would not do this thing if you had not taken loop off in Murphy's store, eh?"

Jethro lifted the cigar and puffed, peering through a

smoke ring. "Go on."

"Senor Chisum and Senor McSween, they see you go with Senor Dolan and Senor Riley. Senor Chisum, he go to hotel while you are not there."

"And?"

"You go back to hotel. Then you go to Senor McSween's casa. Senor Chisum leaves note, no?"

"And?"

"You no stay long. You come out and kick little puff of dirt in street. If you work for Senor McSween and Senor Chisum, you would eat with them, no?" The old man squinted at the sun. "Is time for *frijoles*, no? If you work for them, you not kick dirt in street, eh?"

Jethro took another long pull on his cigar. "I'll bet an old man like you—one who sees much and thinks much— I'll bet he has a handle on most everything that goes on in this town, doesn't he?"

"Big eyes, Senor. Small village."

Jethro shifted against the porch post. "Nobody talks, old man. Do you?"

Gnarled brown hands fluttered in a dismissive gesture. "Would an old man who sits in the sun and drinks only water have something to hide?"

"What have others to hide, my friend?"

The hands fluttered again and the charcoal eyes fell away. "*Quien sabe?* Perhaps they have much to lose. A store. A hotel. Perhaps life. Who knows?"

"But you?"

"I am but an old man, Senor. One who has lived to see trees grow; through three *esposas* and many *muchachas*. Since all this belonged to the Indios. Now I have only my chair and my sombrero. One who has nothing cannot fear to lose what he has not. One with a long life behind does not fear death as one with much life ahead."

"Are we talking life and death, my friend?"

"Death many times stalks Placita, Senor Winter."

"Placita?"

"Ah, yes. Placita. Gringos come, change name to honor our great presidente."

Jethro stared in silence at a spot over the old man's head as smoke curled upward from the corner of his mouth. "Your name, my friend?"

"Antanasio Salazar, Senor. At your service."

Jethro nodded, imprinting the name in his memory. "Mr. Salazar ..."

"Please, senor, you would do me an honor if you talked of me as an equal."

"A deal, Antanasio—if you will call me Je—Jack."

"That, too, would be an honor—Senor Jock."

"Antanasio, two camps struggle here, right?"

"Si."

"What for?"

"Money, Senor Jock. What else?"

"But I don't get the connection. A store against a lawyer and a big cattleman?"

"Trade, Senor, trade. Murphy's, they have long controlled all trade in this part of New Mexico."

"Their prices are high, Antanasio—that I can see. But trade from the few settlers and the people of this village isn't enough to fight over. I can't even see how they could justify a big store like that one up the street." Jethro nodded behind him at Tunstall's. "Or this one, either, for that matter."

"You come from the north, Senor Jock. Is that not right?"

Jethro's chin dipped.

"From the north is few people. Past El Capitan Mountains is desert—only cholla and perhaps some yucca. Water is difficult to find, no?"

Jethro nodded again.

"There is only a little tabosa and grama for the cattle to eat."

"Chamiza brush, too," Jethro said. "I'm told that's good cattle feed."

"Si. And Chamiza. But mesquite, she grows low to the ground and will barely shade a lizard."

"That's true. I didn't let my shirttail touch my back until I was across it and into the mountains."

"But it is not like that to the south, Senor. Or to the west. To the west is Sierra Blanca, the tall one that has snow much of the year. It lies in the mountains your people named for it—the White Mountains. To the south, the Sacramento Mountains. From both flow many streams. The Rio Bonito, itself, comes from the slopes of Sierra Blanca. Is it not a pretty river, Senor?"

Jethro Spring grinned. The huge rivers of Montana—the Missouri, Yellowstone, Flathead, Clark's Fork of the Columbia—made the Rio Bonito appear little more than a trickle. "Yes, Antanasio, it is a pretty river."

The Rio Bonito looked damned good when he rode down out of the Capitans, he had to admit. But up in Montana it probably wouldn't even have a name. Instead, it would merely be a branch of any of dozens of rivers: The Stillwater and the Judith, the Bitterroot and the Blackfoot, Powder and Marias. Then there was the Medicine where he was born, and the Milk, the Bighorn, and the Musselshell.

Jethro Spring paled. The bloody goddamned Musselshell where his mother and father were butchered. Along with an entire unsuspecting Indian village. Tucked against cutbanks, during one of the most bitter winters in memory....

"...and along this Rio Ruidoso, many small farmers and ranchers struggle to live. Also, many people are on the Rio Hondo, beyond where the Rio Bonito and the Rio Ruidoso flow together."

Jethro, snapping back to the present, said, "So many people, Antanasio, that traders fight to see who serves them?"

"Oh no, Senor. They fight because of the army and *Indios*."

"The army and the Indians? Well, that's nothing exactly new. They've been fighting for years."

"No, no, no, Senor. The *Indios* do not fight with the army. The traders, they fight to see who serves the *Indios* and the army."

"Aha!"

Antanasio Salazar continued: "At this fort are many, many *soldados*. They are there to watch the Mescalero Apache reservation. Perhaps there are two thousand *Indios*? They must eat. The soldados are all young and strong and eat much. And have you ever before know of a single *Indio* who could not eat a buffalo by himself?"

"Then it's a trade war over government supply contracts?"

"Si."

"And Chisum, he's got beef?"

"Si."

"What's the problem then? Chisum's close. He ought to be able to underbid others."

"Si. But for years, Murphy's have all contracts. For cattle. For flour. For all things. Even salt."

The gray eyes narrowed. "Beef—that's the big one, isn't it? Maybe flour's got some money in it, but cattle is where the real money is."

"Si."

"So Dolan and Riley have the beef contracts and Chisum wants them."

"Si, Senor."

"Flour and salt are on the line, too. Is that it?"

"Si, Senor."

"And that's where the J.H. Tunstall and Company comes in, eh? They compete with Dolan and Riley for general supply contracts."

"Si. *Es verdad.*"

Jethro wallowed this new information around, then asked, "Where does McSween fit in? He's a lawyer."

"Si. Senor Chisum's lawyer. And Senor Tunstall's, also."

"Who is Tunstall, Antanasio?"

"Senor Tunstall is young, perhaps the age of Senor Jock. He is from England and *muy* rich. He has a ranch—perhaps two ranches—on the Rio Feliz and the Rio Penasco. He does not like the grip of Murphy's store around our people's throats and has sworn to ruin them. I believe Senor Tunstall to be a good man, Senor."

"Has Murphy's been that bad, Antanasio?"

"*Muy malo*, Senor Jock. They cheat poor people forever. Most of all, they cheat their own government. They cheat army and Indios and grow rich beyond a simple man's dreams."

"How have they done that?"

"They deliver flour to three, maybe four times more Indios than on reservation. Same with cattle. Flour is poorly ground. Lard is spoiled. Cows are thin and have little fat, many bones."

"And you say they've cheated the army, too."

"It is said they take money for goods of high quality and bring goods of poor quality."

"How can they get away with this?"

"Perhaps they have friends in high places."

"The Santa Fe ring?"

Antanasio nodded. "I have heard of such a thing. Perhaps is true, perhaps not."

Jethro's cigar was dead. He dug through his pockets, then accepted another match from his new friend.

"You know, Antanasio, you're talking about one hell of

a lot of crookedness, requiring a hell of lot of cooperation from a hell of a lot of sources. If it's true, and the people are fed up enough, sounds to me like change is in the wind."

"Let us hope, my friend. But people lack courage. Courage and a leader. Remember also, Murphy's has many friends in high places. This battle for power and money, it will be long and bitter. No man can predict its end."

"How do things stack up right now, Antanasio?"

"Who could say, Senor? Most of my people favor Senor Tunstall and Senor McSween. But Senor Dolan and Senor Riley have no mercy. It is said they have many *pistoleros* from the nearby hills."

"Outlaws? Thieves?"

"Si, Senor."

"You believe that, Antanasio?"

"I know it is true."

"So Dolan and Riley have gunfighters and influence at high levels. How can Tunstall, McSween and Chisum hope to win?"

"The Murphy store, they cheat so many for so long, Senor Jock, that many small rancheros and farmers from the Rios Bonito, Ruidoso, and Hondo also are against Senor Dolan and Senor Riley. Many are *malo hombres*, senor, and are not afraid to use the gun."

"Charlie Bowdre?"

"And others. Do not underestimate Senor Bowdre, my friend, for he is *mucho malo*."

Jethro puffed on the cigar. "Then there's Chisum. He's big, isn't he? What of his cowboys?"

Antanasio smiled grimly. "Senor Chisum would indeed hold the balance, Senor Jock. But I, Antanasio Salazar, would not trust my back to his defense."

"I don't understand. Doesn't Chisum have the most to gain from this?"

"Si. But Senor Chisum is ver' good with having others

to fight his battles."

Something sparkled on the road from the west. Jethro squinted, saw reflections from silver conchos studding the band of a sombrero, and the headstall and saddle of a showy dark horse that trotted their way.

"Where do I fit in, Antanasio? Why do both sides want me?"

"Perhaps both wish the services of your gun, Senor."

"They say not."

"Then perhaps, Senor, they each wish to keep your gun from the service of others."

The vaquero pulled his prancing black horse to a stop before the Tunstall store's porch. He was lithe, with black tight-fitting pantaloons tucked into knee-top black leather boots. Silver spurs trailed savage three-inch Spanish rowels. Two silver-handled revolvers hung low from full cartridge belts. A particularly long, curved knife hung from the silver-mounted saddle. Expressionless black eyes met Jethro's, then swept to those of Antanasio's. "*Hola, mi padre.*"

Antanasio turned to Jethro. "Permit me to introduce my eldest son, Senor Jock. Eugenio Salazar, one of whom I am proud."

"Eugenio," Jethro nodded, rising to extend a hand up to the showy rider.

"An honor, Senor," the horseman replied. Then he returned to the elder man. "It is as you expected, father. Senor Freeman 'escaped' from the cavalry patrol only three miles from town."

Antanasio turned sadly to Jethro. "Then it is you, Senor Jock, who may suffer. Senor Frank Freeman does not forget one he hates.

CHAPTER FOUR

Jethro Spring glided behind the sorrel as a shadow fell across the open doorway. Susan McSween peered into the gloom, waiting for her eyes to adjust. She saw the mare, then smiled as Jethro stepped from behind the animal, currycomb and brush in hand.

"There you are! Mister Wortley said you might be caring for your horse."

He said nothing.

The woman came closer. "A beautiful creature, Mr. Winter. Is she gaited?"

"Sometimes. When she's fresh and on smooth ground."

She stroked the mare's shoulder. "What is her breeding?"

He shrugged. "She's got some kind of walking horse in her. And judging from her withers and hind-quarters, I'd guess maybe a little thoroughbred."

"She's very pretty."

"She's got some bad habits, though."

The full lips puckered. "All ladies are alike."

Jethro blushed. "I wouldn't know, ma'am."

"Does she have a name, Mr. Winter?"

"Tanglefoot."

Her laughter was infectious and he laughed, too. "I think Tanglefoot is a fine name, Mr. Winter. Is that her bad habit?"

"Partly, maybe. She tends to get a little flighty if things don't go to suit her."

"Just like a woman."

Jethro hung the brush and currycomb on nails studding the stable wall. "Why are you here, Mrs. McSween?"

"Please, can you call me Susan? Or Sue?"

"I don't think so. I know you're Mrs. McSween and it don't feel seemly to ..."

She stamped her foot. "I'm not the kind of woman who's suggesting an affair, Mr. Winter—Jack—just because I'm suggesting we forego formal address."

He blushed again. "You still haven't told me why you are here—Susan." Her tinkling laughter sent shivers along his spine.

"Much better. I came to ask you to reconsider my husband's offer. I desperately wish you would do so."

"Why?"

"My husband is a dear, Mr.—Jack. An extremely able man and a quite successful attorney. But he is from the East. He knows little of the West or western ways. Though he has an inner courage that may or may not be laudable, he is not a violent man. As you no doubt by now know, circumstances lead him into opposition to entrenched and ruthless adversaries. Violence, not alien to them, is actually part of their creed."

He again smelled her faint perfume as she moved closer and peered up with disarming green-flecked eyes.

"My husband needs a man like you, Jack—someone with courage and ability. Someone who will dare act."

"And I'm that person?"

"I believe so. My husband believes so. The people from Murphy's apparently believe so, or they would not have attempted to employ you."

"I thought I made it clear, Mrs. McSween—I'm not signing on anywhere for gunfighter wages."

She sighed and turned, trailing fingers along the mare's rump. Then she spun back to lay a hand on his arm. "Mr. Winter—Jack—it is not your gun that is wanted, or even needed. It is leadership. There are many determined men who are already willing to fight, but they lack a leader. Even more, they lack leadership that avoids rash and impetuous action."

"I don't understand."

Her hand fell to her side. "Surely you do. You didn't kill Frank Freeman and poor Charles."

"Kill them!" He drew away, shaking his head in dismay. "Kill them? Why should anyone have to kill a drunk when he can bat sense into his head?"

She followed him. "Exactly! You not only saw a need, determined to act, and did so, but you did it properly, correctly. That has impressed people, Jack. You used only the force necessary to disarm two crazy-mean drunks, and you held them for the proper authorities. That's commendable."

She was near enough for him to again smell her unnerving fragrance. "And that makes me a leader? You people in this town have a low threshold for leadership."

"Jack, affairs have progressed to the point where ordinary citizens are afraid of merely offending one side or the other. They know Dolan and Riley are ruthless; they know the small farmers and ranchers have been pushed to the wall and are very, very angry. Everyone knows Lincoln County might explode. To take either side is to court death. Beyond that, emotions are intense. Violence is often the only considered means."

"You should be on stage, Mrs. McSween. Or a lawyer yourself. You cast a convincing image."

"Jack, it's all true. If any other man—or group of men— had tried to stop those two, it would have been by gunning them down, full of whiskey or not!"

"More stage playing, Mrs. McSween?"

"Susan!"

"Susan."

She sighed. "Perhaps it is a bit of melodrama, Jack. But you're badly needed here. My husband, all Lincoln County, needs you. *I* need you." Her hand brushed his sleeve once more.

The gray eyes narrowed and bored into hers before he said, "If you will excuse me, Susan, I believe supper is being served in the hotel."

Her eyes fell. So did her hand. "Of course. Please consider what I said, Jack. It was not intended as a stage performance." Her skirt brushed against the stable door and she was gone.

All eyes were upon him as he took an empty chair in the half-filled dining room and reached for the potatoes. Brady slid into a chair next to Jack. James Dolan moved his plate down the table to sit opposite.

"Evening, Mr. Winter," Dolan said.

Jethro nodded. "How do. You, too, sheriff."

Brady grunted and reached for the stew.

"Have you had a chance to think more about our employment offer, Mr. Winter?"

"All day," Jethro said, taking a slice of bread. "Way I got it, though, the offer wasn't good after this morning."

"You'll reconsider then?"

"Nope."

The pinched face across the table became expressionless. "Did they offer you more, Mr. Winter?"

"It's not a matter of money."

"What is it, then, Winter? Is it the beautiful temptress, Susan McSween? We can hardly match her offer, can we?"

The room fell still—so still the mere act of Jethro laying his knife and fork to the tabletop sounded thunderous. "If you meant what I think you said, that'll require an apology."

"Hold on a minute," the sheriff broke in, "Dolan's just a little guy."

Jethro glanced from one to the other, then around the room. A jumble of heads were all turned his way. All motion ceased—Sam Wortley was in mid-stride. Even their breathing stopped. Riley's face appeared, dim in the hotel lobby. *Boxed*, he thought. *They're trying to hold my feet to the fire.* He smiled broadly at Dolan, then turned to Brady. "Yes, he is little, sheriff. But he don't have to be little through and through."

Dolan scrambled to his feet, knocking over his chair and a glass of water. "Are you calling me out?" he cried in his high-pitched voice.

Jethro grinned up at the storekeeper. "Your ears work better than your mouth, mister. Unhook the slur you made on Mrs. McSween and I'll take back what I just said about your size.

A second hush fell over the room. Dolan boiled. Anticipating Winter would react violently to his slur on the McSween woman, he'd staked Riley and the sheriff where they could intervene. He'd become angry instead. At last Dolan wheeled and stomped from the room.

Jethro picked up his knife and fork. "Nice quiet town you have here, sheriff."

"You're getting awful big for your britches, sonny," Brady grunted.

Riley ambled in, straightened the overturned chair and sat down. "Jim sends his apologies, Mr. Winter."

"Then you may carry mine to him. You may also consider one of as much value as the other."

"You are an obstinate man, Mr. Winter."

Jethro shrugged.

"No doubt others have filled you with lies about the J.J. Dolan Company.

"No doubt."

"May I ask what they were?"

"You can ask."

After a moment, Riley, too, thrust back from the table. "My advice to you is not to plan on staying in Lincoln."

The bronze-faced man scooped out a cup of stew. "I'll keep your advice in mind."

Later, Jethro whistled tonelessly as he grained his mare. Dolan had made his decision for him. He *would* accept McSween's offer. He waited in the stable until full dark, then glided through riverbottom cottonwoods and willows until he approached McSween's home. The evening was warm and pleasant and he paused to listen to the river's murmur. Instead, he heard voices:

"I don't like it, Alex. I don't like you in John's store. We can't afford the ten thousand dollars. Besides, you're a barrister, not a storekeeper. I don't even like John in it. He came here from England to go into ranching. He didn't come here to get into a trade war with the Murphy thieves."

Jethro moved nearer to the open window. The next voice was Alexander McSween's:

"The opportunity is too great to miss. Someone will replace Murphy's and profit by it. It might as well be us."

"This is just a beginning, isn't it, Alex?"

"Oh yes. Now it's mostly John's money and his experience in trade. But he'll eventually tire of it. When he sells, I want him to sell to me. A Lincoln County trading monopoly can be a springboard to greater things. Who knows, perhaps all New Mexico will be ours. My name is already being bandied around for political office, you know."

"You're talking about replacing Murphy's monopoly

with one of your own."

McSween chuckled. "You'll have to admit, my dear, that Murphy's has done well. They became too greedy, that's all."

"I still don't like it," Susan McSween said stubbornly. "Dolan and Riley won't go down easily."

"Of course not. But with Chisum on our side, the balance of power favors us. With the right man leading our malcontents, we'll win."

Jethro Spring tiptoed down the riverbank and drifted into the willows.

Antanasio Salazar regarded him somberly as Jethro Spring tied his mare to the hitchrail in front of Tunstall's store. "It is sorry I am to see you leave, Senor Jock. This old man had selfishly hoped you might stay and keep him company through the twilight of days remaining to him."

Jethro squatted before the ancient Mexican. "I do not leave from fear, Antanasio."

"That much I know, Senor."

"Instead, I leave because I find it difficult in my heart to trust any of those who wish power."

"Si. Everyone knows about Senor Dolan and Senor Riley. And I myself have told you about Senor Chisum."

"Yes, but you did not tell me about Alexander McSween."

The old man's black eyes narrowed. "What is this of Senor McSween?"

"You did not tell me he seeks to replace the Murphy trading empire with one of his own."

The frail shoulders lifted and the gnome heaved a sigh. "Then, Senor Jock, you know everything." The dark eyes flickered and closed, then popped open to study the floorboards at his feet. "Si, it is as you say, Senor. Senor McSween does plan another empire."

"How can you support him, Antanasio? What good is it to trade one monopoly for another?"

"What can we do, Senor Jock? The Murphy's store, they have stolen so long and will do so as long as we live and they live. Is it not wise to support another in the hope it will be better?"

Jethro rubbed a hand across his face.

"Besides, Senor, we are helpless in the iron grip of these Murphys. Once that grip is broken, it will be easier to break a second grip." The old man leaned forward to grip the squatting man's shoulder. "Who knows if Senor McSween will survive? Or if he will command the trading store that is here after others are gone? Is it not better to seize an opportunity when it comes?"

"I reckon," Jethro murmured. "But I hope you can understand why I want no part of it."

The old man's hand fell away and he nodded. "Where will you go, Senor?"

Jethro shrugged. "One place is as good as another."

"Si. But will you then do a favor for an old man—on your way to nowhere?"

"Certainly."

"Visit Senor Tunstall on his ranch along the Rio Feliz. Tell him Antanasio Salazar asked you to stop and tell of him. Be sure to give this message only to Senor Tunstall."

"Is that all? There must be more to the message."

"That is all, Senor Jock. Senor Tunstall will know what is meant."

Jethro nodded and entered Tunstall's store to purchase coffee, beans, salt, and cigars. Outside, he stuffed them into his saddlebags, then swung atop the mare.

"Goodbye, Antanasio."

"*Adios, amigo.* Take much care."

CHAPTER FIVE

San Patricio shimmered amid heat waves as the sorrel mare topped a rise and singlefooted to the half-dozen adobe buildings squatting at the junction of the Rio Bonito and the Rio Ruidoso. Jethro Spring tied the mare in front of a weathered mud hut with a CANTINA sign, dusted his clothing with his hands, and pushed open the door.

Planks spread across two barrels comprised the cantina's bar. Jethro hesitated for a moment, framed by light from the doorway. It was very dim inside, but he could see a man at the far end of the planks.

"Well, I'll be damned!" Frank Freeman drawled. "Christmas comes more'n once a year, don't it half-breed?"

Jethro nudged the door closed with a boot heel, gray eyes sweeping the rest of the gloomy room. There was only the big man and the bartender. "Howdy, Freeman. I'm surprised to find you this close to Lincoln."

The black-bearded man slapped his belly and cackled.

"I was looking for you, runt. I want to talk to y'all about this welt over my ear."

The bartender's knuckles stood out like hen eggs as he gripped the bar planks, almond eyes darting like marbles spilled to cobblestones.

Jethro willed himself to relax, hooking thumbs into his cartridge belt. "Is talk all you want, Frank?"

Freeman's eyes widened. "Guns? Is that what y'all are 'fear'd of?"

Jethro's teeth flashed.

Freeman tossed off his amber drink, grimaced and shoved from the bar to better face his enemy. "Naw, runt. I wouldn't gun you down just 'cause you slapped me with a pistol barrel. Hell, that ain't no killin' offense. All's I'm gonna do is rip out your right arm and feed it to you, joint by joint." The bearded man stalked forward.

"You don't look like you're drunk this time, Frank. Be hard to use that for an excuse, won't it?"

The crooked smile on the giant's face appeared nailed into place. "You got more sand than sense."

Jethro stuck out an arm, palm outward. "It's not too late to break this off, Freeman."

The giant launched a gigantic roundhouse.

The one-time prizefighter, then named Kid Barry, ducked beneath the wild swing, glided in and stabbed a short, hard right into Freeman's kidney.

The big man roared in surprise and swept around, both arms outstretched, grappling for his smaller quarry.

Jethro seized one extended arm at the wrist, planted both feet, twisted and pulled at the same time, jerking the bigger man off balance. Still gripping the arm, he shifted, threw out a hip and levered the other's bulk across his body.

Freeman slapped into the plank door, ripping it from its leather hinges. The bearded man shook his head, rolled over and clawed for his gun. A moccasin-toed boot kicked the gun from his hand. Freeman cursed, rolled to his feet and charged. Three straight lefts hammered into his nose. Blood spurted. The big man cursed again and bored in. Fists flailed as Jethro backpedaled agilely around the small room, his own left fist flicking with a surgeon's skill at the bloody, flattened nose. Abruptly, Jethro set himself and drove a powerful right through the wild hands and into his adversary's belly. Freeman grunted and doubled over. His tormenter moved to one side and the edge of the right hand chopped wickedly down at the base of the out-sized neck.

Freeman folded to the floor and lay still.

"*Madre de Dios!* Never have I seen such hands," the bartender breathed. "That ..." he pointed down at the still heap, "... is Senor Frank Freeman!"

"How much farther down the road is the Rio Feliz fork?"

"Si, Senor." The bartender's eyes shifted again to the beaten man, then widened.

Jethro spun to see Freeman coming to his feet, an ugly ten-inch blade clenched in his fist. The other fist swiped blood from the bearded man's smashed nose.

"Y'all are dead, half-breed. I'm gonna carve out your heart and nail it to the top o' your head with this knife." The snarl ended with Freeman's rush.

Jethro's boot drove the man's right knee away, spoiling the savage thrust. At the same time, darting hands grabbed and slammed Freeman's wrist against the plank bar edge so hard the blade skittered across the boards, knocking an empty glass to the floor. Freeman howled in pain and rage.

Jethro pumped two short rights and a left into the other's kidneys. Freeman staggered back on broken glass, gasping, but still groping for his adversary. Jethro easily knocked his hands away, then slammed a long straight right into the already flattened nose.

Jethro waited as Freeman wiped blood and tears, then

glided in. A moccasin toe slammed into the big man's crotch. Freeman splashed blood as he doubled over; a dark left hand grabbed his mane and pummeled the mangled face with savage uppercuts and another looping fist to the belly. It ended when a knee slammed against Freeman's jaw, driving his head against a barrel support with a resounding "thunk."

"The road to the Rio Feliz?" Jethro asked.

The bartender rattled in Spanish for several seconds before realizing Jethro did not understand.

"Down the Rio Hondo, Senor. Take the road following the Rio Hondo toward the Rio Pecos. Ten miles. Another road leaves the road you are on. It will go south to the Rio Feliz. To the right. Will the Senor care for something to drink before he begins his dusty journey? Juan Baptiste Morales Gonzales—which is myself— will be honored to give such a gift to an honest gentleman on a difficult journey."

Jethro sucked on a split knuckle during the bartender's directions, then flipped a two-bit piece on the bar planks and jerked a thumb at Freeman. "Buy him a drink when he comes to, Juan. Tell him I'm getting annoyed."

The country to the east changed: no pinon or juniper, and its hills were lower and more rolling. Cholla cactus grew abundantly, along with scattered yucca and low-spreading mesquite brush. Thick grama grass swaddled the gentle slopes.

Occasional farms dotted the banks of the Rio Hondo, and corn reached thick and tall beyond fields of oats, wheat, and barley. Cattle were scattered throughout surrounding hills, and small flocks of sheep, goats, chickens, and pigs appeared part of each farm. Horses were here, too; most were of poor quality to Jethro's practiced eye. A few men wearing white cotton blouses and pantaloons and topped with big straw hats, and women in bonnets and faded print dresses labored in fields or garden plots. Children chased each other through the dust of barnlots and corrals.

After the fork to the Rio Feliz, Jethro made camp, hobbled the mare and stretched atop his woolen blanket with his head propped against the saddle. His mind wandered to the Musselshell, and the wanton butchery of a Blackfeet Indian village by a U.S. Cavalry detachment commanded by a glory-mad officer. The vision of bloody squaws and children limping and screaming atop packed snow, plunging into the ice-filled river, dying amid artillery blasts and a hail of bullets brought a snarl from him, and he leaped to his feet to prowl aimlessly about camp.

After exacting vengeance upon the officer responsible, young Jethro Spring fled an aroused United States Army post. For nearly seven years as a wanted murderer, and under a series of aliases that now included Jack Winter, he continued to drift, always peering behind.

The lone man sighed and stirred the embers beneath the coffee pot.

He slept fitfully and was up and feeding twigs to coals before first light kissed the barren knob above his camp. Soon the odor of fried sidemeat and black coffee wafted. And the sun was barely up when Jethro trotted the mare up the road to the Rio Feliz.

A crude sign told of a trail to Pajarito Spring—the high trail to the Ruidoso. A fresh set of horse tracks on the trail caught his eye. He reined his mare twenty feet back, ground-hitched her, then returned to crouch over the new tracks.

His mountain man father—one of the best of the breed—taught his son well. And a fugitive's life had honed those skills and senses to fine polish. What Jethro saw as he squatted in the dust were prints of a large horse carrying a heavy load. A big man?

Jethro scratched his chin. The rider had pulled up at the junction, so he, too, could study tracks in the road? He'd even ridden a few steps toward the Rio Hondo, as if to satisfy himself others had not recently traveled there. Then the heavy horse had trotted off toward the Rio Feliz.

Why had the horseman studied the Rio Hondo road so carefully? No dew had fallen on them, so the tracks he left were but a few hours old. That meant the rider was here around daylight—an unlikely time to be at this out-of-the-way place.

He swung back into the saddle and clucked to his mare. As she again swung into a singlefoot, her rider slid the Winchester from beneath his leg and levered a cartridge into its chamber. Then he checked his Colt, cocking it to each chamber, spinning the cylinder.

As he traveled, Jethro studied the roadside in detail, gazing at every mesquite bush, every rock, every hump of ground. A hot August sun burned mercilessly down and sweat trickled from beneath the man's dusty hat to course along his neck and between his shoulder blades. He cursed at the human animals of the world, about the pride that made some crankier than a wounded grizzly. He knew Freeman lurked somewhere between him and the Rio Feliz. He knew also that this time there'd be no gunbarrel along the ear, nor fists to the finish. This time, a rifle would crack from behind a rock and a body would spin from a saddle.

At least that's the way it would be if Frank Freeman had his way.

Jethro considered his options. He could swing wide and ride crosscountry to the Feliz, probably reaching Tunstall's before dark. That would merely postpone the inevitable. A man like Freeman wasn't likely to give up. A bullet might come tomorrow, or the next day, or the next. Now at least, Jethro knew Freeman lay ahead, waiting in some hidden place, cheek pressed against a rifle stock.

Two could play that game, however. Jethro Spring had long ago learned patience and cunning and was acutely observant. This country and its rolling, grassy, cactus-studded hills hardly favored an ambush. With a little care, a little patience, and a little luck....

The road topped a low rise. Jethro ground-hitched the mare several hundred feet shy of the top. He pulled his Winchester and cradling it, trotted up the slope, crawling the last few feet on his belly, worming to the crest. At the top, he studied the road and the land beyond the hill. Satisfied at last, he returned and rode over the rise to the rolling hills ahead.

So they progressed, mare and man. Twice, Jethro studied boulder patches that could easily hide a rifleman. In both cases, he concluded a bushwhacker would be too far from his horse to escape if anything went wrong.

Jethro judged from the sun that two hours of light remained when he found Freeman's lair. He spotted it right away—a jumble of boulders thrusting from a rolling hill. The rockpile was only fifty yards from the ribbon of road and within just a few feet of a low hilltop. Freeman's horse would be beyond the hill, hitched for quick escape—if Freeman was there.

He was there. Jethro could feel it. The gray-eyed man lay behind his screen of cholla like a sunning lizard for fifteen additional minutes, studying every inch of ground within sight. Then he backed carefully away and ran to his horse.

Another half-hour passed as Jethro picked his way around Freeman's hiding place. At last, he tied the mare to a low-growing mesquite and ran the last half-mile up a dry arroyo. Cautiously poking his head above the arroyo bank, the man spotted a big dapple-gray gelding standing with a hoof tilted in repose, just fifty feet away.

The man whistled softly. When the sleeping gray lifted his head and stared, Jethro crawled from the arroyo, eyes on the hilltop beyond. Coming to his feet, rifle at the ready, he cooed in a low voice to calm the big horse at his approach.

The gray blew through his nostrils and smelled first the man's hand, then his arm and shoulder. Jethro rubbed the neck, pulled the slip knot from its mesquite bush tether and eased the horse away, taking care to keep the big animal between him and the hilltop.

With the gray safely hidden in the coulee, Jethro was heading for the hilltop at a crouching run when Freeman came for his horse. Of a sudden, the black-bearded head poked above the crest; Jethro shot from the hip and Freeman's head disappeared. Cursing, Jethro dove back into his arroyo just as Freeman's rifle barked.

"You bastard!" Freeman cried. "Coyotes will pick yore bones afore dark, y'hear?"

Jethro leaned against the arroyo bank, puffing. "You want your horse, Freeman—come get him!"

The giant's rifle barked twice in rapid succession and bullets whined and ricocheted over Jethro's head.

The younger man glanced up and down the winding arroyo. Freeman had the advantage of elevation, but his cover couldn't be as good. Nor did he have the mobility the arroyo afforded. Jethro crept to a mesquite bush undercut by erosion and wind, yet clinging to the bank's rim. The man dug at the mesquite's tenuous roots until the thorny plant was about to shudder into the coulee. Then he picked up a bone-dry stick brought down the arroyo by some long-ago mountain freshet.

Jethro chanced a quick glance through the mesquite, then at the sinking sun. Only a few minutes left. He drew his Colt, reversed it and pounded the stick into the clay bank, about a foot below the mesquite. A bullet whined overhead, then another.

Jethro left six inches of the stick protruding. Working quickly, he holstered the Colt, took two .45 cartridges from their loops and with strong white teeth, pulled the slugs, poured the powder from each on the stick's base and rubbed it into the wood. Removing his gunbelt, he rebuckled it around the mesquite's roots. Careful not to let revolver or belt swing its weight on the shaky bush, he ran the end of the stick through the weapon's trigger guard and left the gun and belt balanced precariously on the stick. Taking a deep breath, he popped his head up and down behind the bush, drawing another Freeman bullet. It was then when he struck a match and touched off the gunpowder.

There was a flash, then the stick was burning. Jethro snatched his rifle and sprinted back down the arroyo in a crouch. Fifty yards away, he pushed his rifle through a clump of sacaton grass and watched the spot where he thought Freeman might be.

The stick burned through faster than Jethro expected; when the heavy Colt and cartridge belt fell free, it jerked the undercut mesquite into the arroyo amid a cloud of dust.

Freeman fired into the puff of dust, then levered another round and fired again. The levering movement caused the outlaw's head to bob, its outline showing clearly behind a clump of cholla.

Jethro squeezed the trigger, then fired twice more before dropping down to lean against the coulee wall.

"Freeman! Had enough?" Only silence returned.

Two hours after the evening star began its bright passage, Jethro Spring crawled to the cholla and saw the inert form sprawled in the moonlight like a rag rug blown from a clothesline. He thumped a rock against Freeman's head. Finally fingering his cocked Winchester, Jethro glided forward until he could nudge Freeman with a moccasin-toed boot. The only thing alive on the bearded giant was his pocket watch.

The moon was setting by the time Jethro led the dapple-gray up the dry streambed. The well-trained horse trembled and snorted, yet stood quietly enough for Jethro to tug the limp body from the arroyo bank onto the saddle.

With the dead man's hands and feet swinging below the gray's stirrup levels, the dark man and his mare led the other animal back to the Pajarito Spring trail junction. At the sign-post, Jethro chucked a couple of rocks at the outlaw's horse and the gray trotted toward Pajarito Spring and the Ruidoso.

CHAPTER SIX

The sorrel mare halted before a rambling plank building Jethro Spring took to be the bunkhouse. There was just enough light so he could make out a jackrabbit squatting beside a corral post. Dust and dirt were ground into his clothes and he fingered a tear in his new shirt. The way he hunched in the saddle, along with the pinched lines of his face, was clear evidence of exhaustion.

A door opened and a young, clean-shaven man stepped onto the porch, the hint of a grin on his angular face. "You're a blinkin' mess, lad. You must have had a deuced time last night."

Jethro used the saddlehorn to push himself upright and said, "You must be Tunstall."

"And you need coffee," John Tunstall replied, "perhaps with a tot of rum, what?"

"Best offer I've had today."

Tunstall's smile spread across his face. "We'll be having

breakfast in a minute. Let's take that mare to the corral. Give her a bit of feed and water. She's had it tough, too, eh?"

The rider swung down. "No need to trouble yourself, Mr. Tunstall. Just point me, and I'll take care of her."

"No, no. No trouble. If I stay inside, I'll have to help with the bloody cooking. And that, my dear chap, is a fate...." He rolled his pale blue eyes skyward and shuddered.

Jethro threw his saddle over a corral rail while Tunstall poured a half-bucket of oats for the horse. "I bring a message for you, Mr. Tunstall. From Antanasio Salazar."

"A message? Pray tell, what is it?"

"Well, I don't really know. Antanasio just said to tell you I bring word of him."

"Yes. Go on." When the dark-faced stranger only shook his head, Tunstall said, "Is that all?"

"That's all. He said you'd know what it meant. But you don't?"

My word, no. I wouldn't have any idea. Are you sure there's not more?"

Jethro shrugged. "That's all. I thought it was some sort of code."

"I shouldn't think so. Not one I understand, at any rate." Tunstall laughed. "But that Antanasio is a sly old fox. There may be more to this."

They walked to the bunkhouse in companionable silence. At the porch, Tunstall said, "See here, I shall need your name in order to make introductions."

"Jack Winter." Jethro watched to see if there was any reaction. None. Apparently word of recent happenings in Lincoln hadn't yet reached the Rio Feliz.

"And I'm John Tunstall. Any friend of Antanasio Salazar who would ride forty miles out of his way to deliver an incomprehensible message from that old coyote, well, he's a friend of mine, what?"

Jethro took the extended hand and smiled, easy in

another's company for the first time in months.

Three other men were busy inside the sprawling all-purpose ranch building. Around them were saddles, bridles, leather straps, horse collars, hames, tugs—some hanging from the north wall, others scattered upon the floor. Rows of bunks took up the south end, the center was devoted to kitchen and dining table.

"The curly-haired one doing the cooking—if you can call it that—is Dick Brewer, Mr. Winter. When he's not sweating over a hot stove or tending his own ranch on the Ruidoso, Dick is my foreman, such as he is."

Brewer wiped a greasy palm on a faded shirtfront then held it out while eyeing Jethro's tied-down revolver. "Winter, did the lobsterback say? Pleasure to meet you."

"The villainous one scurrying for the coffee pot just now is John Middleton. When he's not sacking cities and burning Christians, Mid is a better than average cowman with a pleasant disposition—which belies his appearance."

A jagged pink knife scar ran from the left eyebrow to the man's chin, causing the eyelid to droop. Coupling that with a low forehead, heavy eyebrows, a scrubby beard, and unusually long arms, John Middleton did indeed look fierce. He came forward now with a rolling gait, extending a full coffee cup with one of the long arms.

"And the other—the narrow-eyed, shifty one trying uselessly to hide behind his coffee cup—is Bob Widenmann. Basically lazy and consistently confused about his place in an orderly scheme of things, young Bob has some redeeming characteristics that are, at best, difficult to discern without a practiced eye."

Widenmann grinned and waved from the table.

"Flapjacks and ham all right, Winter?" Brewer called from the stove. "I'm not saying they're good, but they are filling."

"Great. Best offer I've had all day."

"Bless me," Tunstall said, slapping his forehead, "that's what you said about my rum offer and I dearly overlooked it."

The Englishman hurried to a bunk and rummaged beneath, returning with a bottle half-filled with a thick dark liquid. He tipped a generous portion into Jethro's cup, then sank to a chair as Brewer commanded, "Sit."

The foreman set out a plate filled with flapjacks and a second laden with fried ham. Middleton refilled coffee cups and thumped a jar of blackstrap molasses on the table.

"Dig in, boys," Brewer said.

Jethro eyed the plentiful food and each of the four men in turn. He lifted his cup and said, "Here's to what looks like a cheerful camp."

"Hear, hear," Tunstall said.

The men ate ravenously. After the ragged edges of their hunger dulled, Tunstall asked, "Are you seeking employment, Mr. Winter?"

Jethro shrugged. "I'm not exactly a cowhand, Mr. Tunstall. I carry a rope on my saddle, but I'm not much good with it."

"Most men aren't," Brewer observed. "But few will admit it."

"Took me a while to learn," Widenmann said.

Tunstall laughed. "That it has, Bob. And it will undoubtedly take you twice longer."

"You worked any on a ranch?" Brewer asked.

"I was raised on a poor one, of sorts. All we had was horses. No cows. Knocked around some after that. I'm not afraid of work, though. Any kind. From sloppin' hogs to building fence. But I've never worked around cattle."

"Horses, though?"

"Uh-huh. We understand each other—me'n horses."

"Did you know this is also a horse ranch, Mr. Winter?" Tunstall asked.

"No, I didn't see any coming in. But it only got daylight about the time I reached your headquarters. I did notice a few head in the corral, but I figured they were working stock."

"Yes, they are. But we have some good mares out on pasture. Eventually we hope to raise blooded horses as well as top-grade beef."

Jethro nodded, returning to his food.

"Well, boys," Brewer said, rising, "we'd better get at it. Mid, you bring in the team and hitch the wagon. I'll round up the grub. Bob, check on them steers on the Penasco divide. Chouse 'em back if you need to. Do that today. Tomorrow you probably should ride down the Feliz. John, it's still your week for the dishes." Tunstall groaned.

"After that you can look in on the mares."

"And tomorrow?"

"Well, there's still a few posts left to set for that corral wing. You get those in and Mid and me'll be back with more tomorrow night."

Jethro said, "Let me clean the kitchen. It's the least I can do for putting me up for breakfast."

"Fine," Brewer replied. "Of course, you're welcome to stay as long as you want, Winter."

"The name is ..." Jethro hesitated a moment before adding,

"... Jack."

Brewer said, "And mine is Dick. We call Middleton 'Mid' 'cause we assigned 'John' to the lobsterback. Widenmann's is Bob."

Jethro set about cleaning off the table. Before he'd finished the dishes, a heavy freight wagon rolled out of the yard carrying Middleton and Brewer. Minutes later, both Widenmann and Tunstall loped off on two fine-cut, 15-hand horses. Jethro heated more water, took a bath, washed his clothes and mended his ripped shirt. Then he laid out his bedroll on an empty bunk. The rest of the morning he spent tidying up the long room, sweeping, and finally mopping, the floor.

Tunstall came back shortly after noon and halted at the door. "I say, you'll make someone a splendid wife."

"Least I could do, Mr. Tunstall."

"The name is John, sir. I thought we'd settled that."

"We did and I'm sorry. There's a pot of stew on the stove, John. It's a tad fresh to really be at its best, but likely it'll be filling."

"Stew! So that's the delicious smell. My word, you're a handy bloke."

The two dished up heaping plates of mulligan. As they ate, Tunstall said, "Tell me, what's been going on at Lincoln town, Jack."

"I wasn't there but a day or two."

"My store was still intact, I trust."

"Still in one piece when I left. I even done a little trading there."

"Bully! May I ask why you selected Tunstall and Company?"

Jethro chuckled. "Matter of fact, I went to the big store first. But their prices was a little steep. Caught your place on the backlash."

"We try to be fair." Tunstall fell silent, then pounded the table. "I don't know what you know about Lincoln County, Jack, but that other store has kept this country in economic servitude for years. They've been conscienceless—exorbitant prices and underhanded dealings. Why, they've reduced the people to virtual penury. Shameful!"

Jethro stared at his plate.

"And bless me, they've cheated their own government. You'll not believe this, but there are manipulations at high government levels by that shameless company."

Jethro chanced it: "And you aim to take their place, John?"

Tunstall snorted. "I plan to either drive them from business or force them to mend their bloody ways. If I do that, then I will have earned the right to the measure of respect fellow citizens already accord me simply because of my money."

Jethro was struck by the man's apparent sincerity. "Isn't that an, uh, unusual approach, Mr. Tunstall?"

"*John*," Tunstall said, frowning. "There are certain obligations to wealth. Obligations to mankind, to society in general, to self."

"A pity others don't recognize it. A pity Dolan ..."

"Obligations, unfortunately, are not always discharged by those to whom they accrue. Instead, those with the greatest obligations are often those least inclined to discharge them."

"You are an unusual man, John."

"I hope so," Tunstall chuckled. "I'd like that as my epitaph."

Jethro began cleaning the table. "Oh bother the dishes, Jack. Have you been outside?"

"No."

"Then come with me. I'll show you around."

The two men walked out into a mid-afternoon heat so intense it drove the flies to shade. The Englishman seemed unaffected by it. He showed Jethro the outbuildings and corrals, pointed where other buildings were planned, talked freely of hopes and dreams. The two perched on a corral rail, Jethro listening as the Englishman discussed his idea of southwestern New Mexico's future.

"Look at the land, Jack. Snow is a seldom-seen phenomenon, yet constant winter snows in the surrounding mountains waters it well. Nourishing grass for cattle eliminates the chore of winter feeding. How can it fail?"

"Is that where you're building a new wing?" Jethro pointed to a half-finished corral and some scattered posts and rails.

Tunstall sighed. "Yes. I should set the remainder of those posts. And I shall in the morning. But now, frankly, I'm enjoying the opportunity to once again bore someone with my dreams."

"Is that where Brewer and Middleton went—to bring in more posts and rails?"

The Englishman nodded. "Up in the Sacramentos. Dick is a practiced dreamer. Like me. Extensive corrals and all that. He's a superior individual, you know."

"Seems like it. Has he been in the country long?"

"Several years. He has a nice little place on the Ruidoso—there's an example of Dolan-Riley perfidy. They supposedly sold that place to Dick and the poor soul paid them considerable money before discovering it wasn't theirs to sell. They also forced him to sell his corn and hay to them at below-market prices, while buying supplies at inflated rates. Fortunately my friend—the Lincoln attorney, Alexander McSween—apprised poor Dick and the young man broke their shackles before they bankrupted him."

The Englishman and his visitor gazed at the distant mountains in companionable silence until Tunstall asked, "I don't suppose you had a chance to meet Alex during your short stay in Lincoln?"

"As a matter of fact, I did."

"Prince of a man, isn't he?"

"I suppose."

"I've offered him a chance to buy a small percentage of my store—I respect him so much. An absolute prince, believe me. I've given him a year to come up with ten thousand dollars for a quarter interest, but I doubt he'll be able to raise the money. A pity. One would endeavor to help a truly good man like Alexander McSween in any way possible. Don't you agree?"

"Taking care," Jethro muttered, "not to misplace one's faith."

"I assure you, that would be impossible with a man such as he."

Changing the subject, Jethro said, "Tell me about the rest of your crew, Middleton and Widenmann."

"Mr. Middleton certainly belies his appearance, doesn't he? Terribly fierce in countenance, but actually a sheep in wolves' clothing. A quiet fellow. Excellent cowman. I was lucky to obtain his services. I really don't know much more about him, other than I think he came here from Kansas. Or perhaps Nebraska."

"He wears a long-barreled Colt. Can he use it?"

"Oh yes. I've seen him shoot rattlesnakes. I doubt he's fast—if that's what you mean. But he's deucedly accurate."

"And Widenmann?"

"Bob? Harmless enough. Teutonic, you know. His father was a German consul in Michigan. Bob grew up there. He came west, I believe, two years ago."

Jethro shifted position on the rail.

"Poor Bob," Tunstall continued. "He'd desperately like to be a feared western gunman and practices by the hour. Unfortunately, clumsy German stolidness simply isn't structured for speed."

"And what does he do for you?"

"Anything we find for him. Dick has serious doubts he'll ever be a decent ranch hand, but I've not given up on him as yet. Perhaps I'll try him as a clerk in my store."

Jethro said, "Speak of the devil." Dust from Widenmann's approaching horse curled up behind the distant rider.

"My word, you have sharp eyes."

As both men studied the oncoming horseman, Tunstall mused, "It's a peculiar thing about Robert Widenmann, however."

"Oh? What's that?"

"He's well-connected, so to speak. His father is a personal friend of Carl Schurz."

"Carl Schurz?"

"Secretary of the Interior in the present administration."
Jethro leaped from the fence. "I'll go start supper."

------·•·------

The following day, Jethro helped Tunstall set their
remaining corral posts and rails. Finally the Englishman said,
"If you are to work like a regular hand, you may as well go
on the payroll. Thirty a month and found. What?"

Brewer and Middleton rolled in with a wagonload of
posts and rails an hour after dark. Later, as the crew sat down
to eat, Tunstall said, "Looks as though your work went well,
Dick."

"Tolerable. Seems like yours did, too." The curly-haired
man appeared pensive.

"Yes. Bully, isn't it? Jack did most of the corral and barn
work. Perhaps I should tell all of you, I've hired him. Mr.
Winter is now one of us."

Brewer jerked visibly.

"What is it, Dick?"

"We ran into Jose Salazar up in the Sacramentos."

"Oh?"

"He brought news of Lincoln; news concerning Mr.
Winter, here."

Tunstall looked from Brewer to Jethro. "Yes? Jack told
me he'd been in Lincoln."

Dick Brewer locked on their newest member's penetrating gray eyes. "Did he tell you everything?"

"Everything? See here, Dick," Tunstall said, "what are
you trying to say?"

"What he's trying to say, Mr. Tunstall," Jethro cut in, "is
there was a little excitement the night I got to Lincoln. A
couple of drunks shooting up the town. I calmed 'em
down."

Brewer's voice was soft, "Ask him who the drunks were, John."

"Who?"

"A man named Freeman," Jethro replied, "and another named Bowdre."

"My heavens!"

"Good God!" exclaimed Widenmann.

"He not only stopped 'em," Brewer continued, "but went into McSween's house to do it. Chisum was at McSween's and Freeman went there to call him out. Him and Bowdre pumped over thirty rounds into the house while McSween's wife and their servant women were there. Then they broke in and threatened to gun down everybody in it. Before that, they tore up Montano's store and triggered up more of the town. And Freeman gunned down a black trooper that he left for dead."

"Then?" Tunstall asked, shifting forward in his chair.

"Seems like nobody knows. It turned quiet in the house and when somebody got guts enough to peek in the front room; Winter here was settin' on top of Freeman, cleaning his nails and Bowdre was off in the corner blubberin' like a baby."

Tunstall turned to Jethro with his eyebrows raised.

"That's not all, John," Brewer murmured.

"No?"

"Dolan and Riley offered him a job."

Tunstall's pale blue eyes narrowed.

"So did Chisum. So did McSween."

"Really?"

"Word has it the offers went to a hundred a month."

"Oh my word!"

"Eighty," Jethro said.

"Eighty?" Tunstall repeated wonderingly.

"But he didn't take any of the offers," Brewer continued. "Instead, he faced Dolan and Riley down at Wortley's over a slur on Mrs. McSween, then rode out."

"Well, Jack," Tunstall said, "a real bonkers of a time, what?"

"Let me finish, John. Winter stopped at San Patricio to ask directions. Freeman was there—did I tell you a squad of soldiers from Fort Stanton picked him up the next day after the shooting spree and he 'escaped' before he was hardly out of sight of Lincoln?"

"No, I don't believe you did."

"Well, that's what happened. And he was in Gonzales' Cantina when Winter walked in."

Both Tunstall and Widenmann leaned forward.

Brewer shook his head in apparent wonder. "Freeman figured to wipe up the floor with Winter, but got used as a mop himself."

Widenmann's breathing sounded like a braying mule.

"Gonzales told Jose he'd never seen anything like it. Freeman never laid a hand on Winter, and Winter tossed him around like a baby. Said first time Freeman hit the floor he went for his gun. Winter kicked it into a corner. Second time Freeman hit the floor he came up with a knife."

"Good Lord!" Tunstall exclaimed.

"Winter took away Freeman's knife, knocked him cold, then left."

"Astounding."

"Gonzales said Freeman woke up, grabbed him and shook him until he told where Winter was headed."

"Oh, my heavens! We must put out an immediate guard. Freeman might be lurking just outside."

Brewer shook his head. "Not likely."

"No? Why?"

"We ran into young Beckwith from over at Three Rivers. He caught up with us on the wagon road on his way to Buck Powell's. He said Freeman's dapple gray wandered into San Patricio yesterday morning...."

All eyes were on Brewer.

"... packin' Freeman's dead body."

It was so quiet it might have been a church rectory at midnight. Then Tunstall said, "Is any of this true, Jack?"

"Better eat up, boys," Jethro Spring said. "Otherwise it'll get cold."

CHAPTER SEVEN

Though Jethro Spring settled easily into his duties at Tunstall's ranch, there was a barrier between him and his companions. To Bob Widenmann, he was nine feet tall and the easterner who aspired to gunfighter fame lost no chance to be close to the taciturn newcomer, keeping a running monologue about adventures discovered in dime novels. John Middleton, that fierce-visaged cowpuncher, avoided contact when possible, seemingly fearful of Jethro's mere presence. The Englishman appeared bemused by the turn of events that made one of his common ranchhands larger than life to those in Lincoln County. But it was the foreman who held especially aloof.

One early-September day, Dick rode in as Jethro bent to repair a corral where an unruly bronc had earlier crashed through. Aware that Brewer sat his saddlehorse nearby, Jethro straightened and said, "There's something about me you don't quite have a handle on, ain't there, Dick?"

Brewer jerked off his hat and trailed dusty fingers through a curly mop. "Yeah. You could say that."

"Well, it's not a rattlesnake. We don't have to fight shy of it."

"You're trouble, Winter. People in Roswell say Freeman's friends are going to even things up." When Jethro made no reply, Brewer added, "Don't that bother you?"

"Should it? Do they know who to even things up with?"

"They want the man who did in Freeman."

"And somebody thinks it was me?"

"Wasn't it?"

"Did I say so?"

"He tried to ambush you, didn't he?"

The gray eyes flashed. "Brewer, are you trying to say I killed Freeman? Well, you'll never know. Nobody will. If Freeman set out to bushwhack me, he got what he deserved."

Brewer toyed with his hat before saying, "If anybody deserved killing, Freeman did—I'll give you that. But Tunstall's got enough troubles buckin' Dolan and Riley without you bringing the Jesse Evans outfit down on us."

"Who's Jesse Evans?"

"Freeman's friend. He runs a damned well-organized gang of rustlers with powerful connections. Mostly they're Texas drifters with a long rope, a running iron, and a mean gun. They've been hoorahing Lincoln and Dona Ana counties for a couple of years. Generally the law's looked the other way."

"They're tough?"

Brewer nodded.

"How are they organized?"

"Likely they got some ties with Dolan-Riley. They been hitting Chisum's herds pretty hard and got into ours a couple of times. Me and Tunstall think them cows went to the reservation as part of Dolan-Riley contracts."

Jethro lifted a moccasin heel to a corral pole and rested his elbows on an upper rail. His eyes left Brewer, scanning across posts, poles, and restless horses to the mountains beyond. A cloud shadow passed over the corral and its occupants. When the shadow was gone, Brewer discovered the disconcerting gray eyes fixed on him again. "You don't make too much sense, Brewer. You say Tunstall's got enough trouble with Dolan-Riley without me bringing the Jesse Evans gang in because they want to even a score with me over Frank Freeman. Next, you say the gang is part of Dolan-Riley anyway, and they've hit Tunstall already. Know what I think?"

Brewer tapped his hat in place, then leaned forward, forearms resting across the saddlehorn. "Why don't you tell me."

"There's something about me that sticks in your craw—something you find hard to trust. Right?"

Brewer nodded. "You're working here for thirty a month. You was offered eighty by Dolan and the same from McSween. Why you working here for thirty?"

Jethro shifted his gaze back to a distant peak. The reply came slow-paced and soft—so soft Brewer had to strain to catch it:

"This may be a little hard for you to understand, Brewer, but I came into Lincoln County minding my own business. I dropped into the first town I'd hit in two months, wanting only a haircut, a bath, and a soft bed. Trouble came along and it headed right for some women. Nobody else took a hand, so I stuck my nose in.

"Next thing I know, both sides in a local feud offers me jobs at triple the going rate—gunfighter's wages—and I'm wanting nothing to do with it.

"So, I'm shaking the dust of this godforsaken country from my boots. First, though, a kindly old man who sits all day in the sun and probably drinks mescal all night wants me to deliver a gibberish message to some rancher on the Rio Feliz.

"Only thing is, the rancher don't understand the message either. It turns out, though, that he's a decent fellow with what looks like some pretty straight-shooters working for him. We hit it off, me and the rancher. He offers me a job, not because he's looking for somebody to fight battles for him, but because he thought I might do a day's work.

"And I took the job for the same reasons Tunstall offered it. I took it because I finally figured out why Antanasio Salazar sent me here with a damned message nobody understood: Tunstall needed me and he knew Tunstall was the kind of man I'd work for.

"Now that's a God's fact, Brewer. And it may not suit you. But I'm here, and this is where I'm going to stay whether it suits you or not."

Dick Brewer continued to lean across his saddlehorn, gazing fixedly at Jethro Spring. At last, he shook his head and grinned, swung from the saddle, took off his gloves and dusted his clothes with them, then held out his hand. "I'm three kinds of fool, Jack. And I'm telling you I'm sorry."

"The Evans bunch hit the agency horse herd a few weeks ago," Brewer announced at the supper table the next evening. Probably about the same time Mid and me was up cuttin' posts and rails."

"Good. Perchance they'll put the cavalry after the blighters?"

"Already did, I guess," Brewer replied to his boss. "Cavalry lost 'em though, somewhere over on the Tulerosa."

"Headed for the Shedd place," Widenmann ventured.

Brewer shrugged. "Probably. Then on down to the Rio Grande, and maybe Texas."

The men lapsed into thoughtful silence until Jethro asked, "Where's this Shedd place?"

"Across the Tulerosa Valley and the white desert beyond," Brewer replied. "Stopover for rustlers. It's up along the east side of the Organ Mountains, along a road to the Mesilla Valley and the Rio Grande."

"Tough place?"

"Good place to stay away from. Hard to do, though, if you're goin' to Mesilla from here."

"Perhaps good will come of the theft," Tunstall said. "If Evans and his bunch of ne'er-do-wells know the Army pursues them, they'll stay away from this part of the country."

With Evans' rustlers checked by the Army, Brewer decided to move the best of Tunstall's blooded mares, along with a couple of line-backed mules the Englishman was particularly fond of, to his own fenced pasture on the Ruidoso. The plan was for Charlie Bowdre to keep an eye on them while the Tunstall outfit proceeded with roundup.

The Englishman chose to help Brewer and Widenmann with the drive, planning to go on to Lincoln and look in on his store. After the others left, Jethro helped Middleton trim and shoe most of the remaining horses in preparation for their coming hard use. Finally, with the sun sinking to the west and the last horse shod, Middleton "sanded" the fire while Jethro groaned like one tree sawing against another in a windstorm. "Back's killing me," he said. "How about you?"

Middleton grunted and started for the well pump.

Jethro followed and after they'd washed their faces and hands, then doused their heads and chests and arms, he said, "I'm not as bad a fellow as you might think, Mid."

The fierce-visaged hulk laughed hollowly and mumbled, "Course not."

"Then why you act like I bite off snake heads?"

"Aw, Jack, I don't."

"Yeah you do. Look, I try to do my share of the work. Right?"

"Shore," Middleton said, glancing fearfully at Jethro.

"I worked right alongside you out there today."

"Shore you did. Nobody said ..."

"Look, Mid, I want to learn something about cattle, and I'd like to learn to rope. You're the best man to teach me, too. But you avoid me like the plague."

Brewer rode in at sundown the next day and found them practicing with lariats. He was still laughing at Jethro's clumsy efforts when he entered the bunkhouse.

Tunstall and Widenmann returned three days later and reported Brady had finally been prodded into action by Indian Agent Godfroy and was investigating a report the Evans gang was nearby, at the mouth of the Rio Penasco.

The next evening, a lone rider galloped to the ranch on the Rio Feliz. Charlie Bowdre reined his sweat-streaked horse to a sliding stop as the Tunstall crew crowded out of the bunkhouse. The dust-covered rider slumped in the saddle. His lips pinched and the dark eyes were only narrow slits. "They got the blooded mares from your place, Dick."

CHAPTER EIGHT

The news hit Tunstall hard, but not nearly so hard as it did Brewer. After the initial shock, the foreman asked, "Which way'd they go, Charlie? You know?"

"They headed up the Ruidoso. I even know who they was. Ab Sanders seen 'em. He named Evans, Baker, and Hill. He thinks Provencia and Hindman was there, too. And a couple others. They came by his place just at daylight, while he was out to pee."

"What day?"

"Why, today! This mornin'! Jesus Christ, you don't think I'd leave it stew any longer'n it took me to get here, do you?"

"They're headed for the Shedd Ranch again, dammit!" Brewer wheeled to Tunstall. "We've got to go after 'em."

"What about roundup?" Tunstall asked.

"It can wait."

"Oh Dick, you know better than that."

"I'll take Winter. He'd be the most useless at roundup, anyway. You other three can start and we'll help wind it up when we get back."

"I don't like it, Dick! Sanders saw seven men. Just you and Jack? Surely you can see the odds are ridiculous."

Brewer turned to Bowdre. "How about you, Charlie? Will you go with us?"

"I ain't no coward, but the odds ain't good enough to suit me. 'Sides, I ain't exactly up to leavin' just yet, since I rode all day to get here."

"Okay. I'll ride to the Ruidoso tonight and see if I can't pick up Sanders and Scurlock and the Coe boys. Charlie, you and Jack come tomorrow. We'll borrow a change of horses for you two, and we'll all get on the trail as soon as you get there."

Tunstall said, "Dick, is it necessary for you to ride all night?"

"I think it is."

"Then let me set out some guidelines. No violence. The horses are not worth one of you getting killed. Do you hear?"

Brewer ducked inside and grabbed a bedroll. Tunstall followed. "Dick, I must ask you again if you understand. The only way I will accept return of those horses is if they're returned legally."

Brewer sighed. "All right, John."

—————•◦•—————

Charlie Bowdre and Jethro Spring rode out before daylight the following morning. The smaller man set the pace on one of Tunstall's best horses. They watered at Pajarito Spring and while resting their mounts, Bowdre pointed at the sorrel with his chin and said, "That's a good animal."

"Uh huh." Jethro picked a dead grass stem and thrust it

between his teeth.

"How'd you get Freeman?"

The grass stem stopped wriggling. "Who said I did?"

"Me. And ever'body else."

"I'm somebody. And I never said I did."

"You did, though. But you had help. Ain't no way you could load anybody as big as him all by yourself."

Jethro made no reply, so Bowdre said, "Let's get going."

As they swung into the saddle, Bowdre's eyes found Jethro's. "You know I owe you, don't you?"

"That right?"

"I don't want you to forget it, 'cause I ain't. And I'm smarter'n Freeman."

Brewer and Doc Scurlock waited with fresh saddlehorses. "Doc's the only one could get away, but we got enough," Brewer said. "Change horses and let's ride."

Minutes later, four grim-faced riders set out up the Ruidoso. They traveled through the black of night, topping the divide between the Rio Ruidoso and Rio Tulerosa sometime around midnight. They passed Blazer's Mill in the small hours. Weary, dusty and hungry, they trod the streets of Tulerosa just as a rising sun brushed its whitewashed walls.

Brewer swung from the saddle, steadied himself against his horse for a time, then said, "Find a place to eat and order me something. I'll be along soon 's I find out if our horses passed through."

The Tunstall foreman joined his men a few minutes later. "I got fresh horses lined up."

Jethro asked about the missing livestock.

"Nobody'll say nothin'," Brewer growled. "And that's a hell of a good sign them mares came through here." He dug hungrily into his food and with mouth still full, said, "Odds're good they'll rest at Shedd's. We'll catch 'em there."

"Then what?" Scurlock asked.

"Be tough to blow 'em out of there," Bowdre muttered.

"Are we still in Lincoln County?" Jethro asked.

"No. Dona Ana," Scurlock said.

"Where's the county seat?"

"Mesilla. That's across the Organs. Down along the Rio Grande."

Brewer sighed. "Jack's saying we gotta go to Mesilla to swear out warrants against the bastards."

They made camp that evening at a shallow spring near the base of the Organs, resting the horses they'd rented at Tulerosa. Brewer left for Mesilla at daylight. Around noon, the others rode to the Shedd Ranch, a scattering of unpainted buildings and poorly mended corrals.

Several fine-lined horses milled in one of them.

"I see the mules," Jethro whispered. "Those are our mares, too."

"Now all's we gotta do is get 'em back," Bowdre muttered.

They tied their horses to a hitchrail, then walked toward the main house, Bowdre in the middle. A sandy-haired man who Jethro could find forgettable under ordinary circumstances stepped out on the porch, followed by three others. All wore tied-down guns. Sandy hair in the middle and the one to the left—a Mexican—sported two.

Stopping twenty feet short of the porch, Bowdre said, "Howdy Jesse. We came for our horses."

Evans grinned. His right hand shifted back a bit from his belt buckle. "The hell. Which ones are yours?"

"You know which ones, Jesse. We'd be obliged if you stood aside. You done caused enough trouble, as is."

"Well now Charlie, them ponies caused me'n these boys trouble, too. Ain't seemly, then, that we'd just turn 'em over to you, now is it?"

"What ain't seemly, Evans," Scurlock broke in, "is for us all to be standin' out in the hot sun talkin' about matters o' life and death. Why don't we all go in and set some and talk it out?"

"All right, Doc," Evans said, stepping aside and waving them in. "You always was one to cut through to the heart of a matter."

As he strode in, Jethro took note of two riflemen at the windows. A wizened, scraggly-haired old man slouched at a long kitchen table. Jethro assumed him to be Shedd.

Shedd left the room as Evans told the Mexican to bring coffee. The two-gun man brought a big pot and several cups.

"Now, what's this about you three boys wantin' to steal our ponies?" Evans asked.

"Jesse," Bowdre said, clearing his throat, "you oughta know better'n to hit Brewer. You know he won't take it."

"We didn't hit Brewer. We hit Tunstall. Ain't the same."

"It is to Dick. You stoled 'em off his place."

"By the way," Evans said, "why ain't Brewer here?"

"He's bringin' a posse from Mesilla," Scurlock said. "Give us our hosses and we'll meet 'em and tell 'em no need."

"Do tell?" a blocky, scar-faced man laughed. "It'd have to be a big posse to get these horses."

"Seems like a lot of trouble to go to, just to hold onto sixteen head of stolen horses," Jethro murmured.

Evans turned pale blue eyes to him. "Who's this?" he asked. "You and Doc I know, Charlie. But this bastard I ain't seen."

"Him?" A faint smile parted Bowdre's lips. "His name is Winter. Jack Winter. Works for Tunstall."

A deathly quiet fell on the room. It was finally broken by Evans' harsh cackle. "Well, well," he said. "*The* Jack Winter. I never figgered to run into you this easy."

The riflemen at the windows shifted. All eyes locked on Jethro and the hair at the base of his neck prickled. Only

Shedd was out of sight. His gaze returned to Evans. "Was there something you wanted to talk to me about?"

The blue eyes narrowed. "Yeah. I guess you could say that. Freeman was a friend of mine. Of Hill and Baker, too."

"What's that got to do with me?"

"Me and the boys grieve over poor old Frank."

The unexpected kla-klatch of Jethro's Colt being eared back beneath the tabletop caused Evans' eyebrows to dart upward, while a muted ripple swept the room.

"On the other hand," Evans continued, "Old Frank did get a mite ornery now and again. Maybe what happened to him couldn't be helped."

Bowdre let out an audible sigh.

"Let's talk about the horses," Jethro pressed.

"Gawdamighty, Winter!" Bowdre exploded, "he's offerin' to let you walk outta here—no more questions asked."

"The horses," Jethro said.

"The horses," Evans repeated, leaning back in his chair. "The horses are ours by right of possession. You ain't getting 'em without a fight. And you got as much chance of winning that as a one-legged man in a footrace, even starting with a gun in your hand."

The gray eyes swept the room, returned to Evans.

"Far as Freeman goes," Evans continued, "Frank never was worth dyin' over. I'll even forget you pulled iron on me—provided you lay it on the table. Then you boys can drink your coffee and get the hell out. If you don't...." Evans raised his coffee cup, his meaning abundantly clear.

Jethro hesitated while grudgingly admiring Evans' guts. Then he lifted the Colt free and laid it on the table.

Evans sighed. "Nick, you and Bill trot on out and give these boys' ponies a gallon of oats apiece. We don't want nobody saying we don't show hospitality when pilgrims show up unexpected."

CHAPTER NINE

Brewer arrived at midnight on a lathered horse. "No posse," the foreman said, bleak face shining in the firelight. "Not even warrants. They said we've got to get 'em from the county where the theft took place. That means we got to ride clear to hell back to Lincoln, get warrants, then ride clear to hell back to Mesilla and see if they'll put a posse together. Then we got to come clear to hell back to Shedd's and see if our horses are still there. Are they?"

Jethro nodded.

"Damn!"

"Doc and Bowdre are watching to see they don't take 'em out."

"Evans?" Before Jethro could reply, Brewer said, "Of course it's him. Nobody but Evans would have the gall to stop with a damn bunch of high-priced horses this close to where he stole 'em."

"It'll be tough for us to get the horses, Dick. I counted

seven hardcases up there. Could be there's more."

Brewer kicked at the fire, scattering coals and sparks in the hot night air. "You heard Tunstall—he said no violence. The only way he'd accept the horses was if they came back legally."

"That's what he said," Jethro agreed. "But I'm not sure I heard it too well. I'm willing to make a try if you are."

Brewer collapsed on a rock, physically beaten. "You said yourself there's too many. We can't wait 'em out. Hell, we got a roundup goin' on and we ain't there. It'd take too long—a week—to get Lincoln County warrants and get back here."

Jethro left at daybreak to recall Bowdre and Scurlock while Brewer broke camp. At Tulerosa, the dejected band traded for their own horses, then headed over the mountains to the Ruidoso. The coolness and fresh scent of Ponderosa pines in the Sacramentos' high country was lost on the somber riders. Scurlock dropped off at his farm and Bowdre at his. Brewer offered each a simple clap on the shoulder and a mere thanks. It was enough.

Jethro Spring and the morose Brewer slept that night in Dick's tiny cabin. The next morning, Brewer started for the Rio Feliz to tell Tunstall of their failure and to pitch into roundup. Meanwhile, Jethro crossed the Rio Bonito divide to Lincoln to report the theft to McSween and ask his help in swearing out warrants.

———— · ————

McSween answered his knock. Surprised, the attorney invited Jethro in and listened to his story.

"Certainly I'll help, Jack. We'll just walk over to Judge Wilson right now and swear the warrants. Then we'll look in on the sheriff, though frankly, I doubt that will do much good."

"Alex, are you out here? I though I heard ..." Her wind chimes voice trailed off as Susan McSween burst radiantly into the foyer, laughing and clapping with excitement. "Why Mr. Winter! How delightful!"

Jethro snatched off his misshapen hat and mumbled, "How do, Mrs. McSween."

"Oh," she said in mock severity, "is that the best greeting I get from my one-time savior?" She came forward boldly, holding out both hands. When Jethro took one to shake it, she stood on tiptoe to kiss him lightly on the cheek and say, "How wonderful to see you again, Jack. You've been missing from our lives too long."

Jethro's dark face turned deeper and he wondered if she could feel the perspiration on his palms. She smiled and let her hand fall as he defensively glanced at her husband. McSween's smile was cordial.

"How long will you be here?" she asked. "John said you were working for him. I'm so glad. That was a terrible thing that happened to that dreadful Mr. Freeman. No one blames you, of course. Such a horrible man. I've never quite forgiven you for riding away without saying goodbye. You will stay for supper won't you? Alex, it would be all right if Jack used a room in the wing, wouldn't it?"

"Of course."

"There, you see? Now you must stay at least one night."

Jethro shook his head. "I've got to get back, I reckon. There's a roundup going on and they'll need me."

"Nonsense," McSween said. "It's a good forty miles by trail to the Rio Feliz. It's mid-morning now and will be at least high noon by the time you could get back on the trail. Of course you must stay over."

"You heard him," Susan said, mock-pouting. "You are to stay over. Alex, you must make him."

"All right, dear. I'm sure Jack will see the light of reason. Now, however, we must go about our business. If you'll excuse us, I'm afraid Jack's visit is not merely social."

"Is something wrong?"

"I'm afraid so. It seems the Evans gang got away with a big share of John's valuable horses. Unfortunately they included the filly he promised you."

Antanasio Salazar tilted in the same way, in the same chair, against the same wall, with the same sombrero resting in the same place. The old Mexican's eyes followed the two men as they walked across the dusty street to Judge Wilson's home. The warrants took only a few minutes to swear, then they walked to the sheriff's office. The lawman failed to take the warrants seriously.

"Look, Winter, I'm not empowered to go into Dona Ana County. They got a sheriff. Go talk to him."

"We did. But he said we had to come here for warrants."

"Don't rightly understand that. They got justices, don't they?"

"They do. But they wouldn't issue warrants against Dona Ana men to Lincoln County men."

"Why?"

Jethro's gorge was rising. "I don't know why. All I know is they wouldn't."

"Well by God, they come cryin' to get warrants or help in servin' 'em over here, I'll send the bastards packing."

"Aren't we missing the point?" McSween broke in. "What is going to be done to recover the horses and apprehend the thieves?"

"Not much I can do, McSween," Brady said. "Not if they're in another county."

"You mean they have to come back to Lincoln County before you can go after them?" Jethro demanded.

"That's the size of it."

"They won't have the horses when they do!"

"Look Winter, I do what I'm empowered to do. I don't do what I'm not empowered to do. You want this job done different, you run for it."

"Thank you, sheriff," McSween said, taking Jethro by the arm. "We'll keep you informed if anything develops."

———•—•———

Alexander McSween finished his noon meal, leaned back in his chair, patted his lips with a napkin, and asked to be excused. "I must get back to work. It just keeps piling up. Never enough time. You will excuse me for the afternoon won't you, Susan? Jack?"

Jethro pushed from his chair and said, "I suppose it would be foolish for me to start back to the Feliz today. I'd like to do a little visiting and maybe buy a couple of things at Tunstall's store."

"Excellent! Our home is your home. You will have supper with us, too?"

Susan McSween and her taciturn guest were each locked in private thoughts after McSween retired to his office. At last, she said, "I must thank you for defending my honor, Jack."

Jethro shifted in his chair. "I'm not sure what you mean."

"I mean defending my honor against that horrid Mr. Dolan, while all his henchmen and cronies were gathered around. That took great courage. Alex said you quite cleverly turned them defensive. That, of course, is another example of your courage and common sense coming to the fore in a crucial predicament. Very commendable."

"Ma'am ..."

"Susan."

"Where I was raised," he said, "a decent body never talked about any woman that way. Dolan needed to be told, that's all."

"Susan," she said, smiling.

Jethro sighed and his gaze returned to her, flowed over her, fixed on the rich tawny hair and slender white throat. She touched his arm and he jumped.

"Say it. Say *Susan*."

A boyish smile flashed upon the dark face. "Susan."

She clapped her hands. "Excellent. That completes today's lesson. See that you don't forget, or I may have to punish you."

The boyish smile faded as he stared at her. He thought of a beautiful Fort Worth church organist and ... he shook his head to clear it and jumped to his feet.

"Jack, is something wrong?"

"No, Mrs. McSween. It's ... just that I must go talk to someone. Stable my horse. That kind of stuff."

"Our stable is in the rear."

"Thank you, ma'am."

"*Susan*."

"Susan."

As Jethro started away, she arose from her chair and asked softly, "Having to leave is really not what sobered you, was it, Jack? I reminded you of another woman, didn't I?"

He was startled by her intuition and turned to face her. "No it's not, Susan. And yes, you did." He grinned and nodded at her beehive mass of fawn hair. "I liked your hair better first time I saw you—when it wasn't piled on top."

She curtsied. "I'll see if I can do something with it. Supper will be promptly at six."

When Jethro walked into the kitchen, old Wortley pulled a pie from the oven and glared at him. "Never figgered to see you back here again. You ain't got a lick o' sense."

"I want a room, old man. My horse is in your stable eating your hay and your oats. I left a dollar on your desk. I need bathwater, too. All you've got to do is get that and my change and tell me what room is mine. I'll do the rest."

"Jesus Kee-rist. You got a bunch of demands. Water's

hot now, you want it. Won't do you much good, though, to take a bath, then stick back on clothes you been rootin' in a pig sty with. Take the same room as you had. And, dammit, I don't want no ruckus in my dinin' room this time, hear? You cain't get along with the reg'lars, get your ass out."

"Don't figure on me for supper, old man. That way I'll get along for sure. Don't know about breakfast, but by then, it won't make no difference. I'll soon enough be gone."

Jethro nodded to Antanasio Salazar as he entered Tunstall's store. He nodded again on his way out. An hour later, freshly shaved, bathed, and dressed in new shirt and trousers, he halted in front of the old Mexican's chair."

"What a change, Senor! You are transformed from the wolf to one in swaddling clothes."

Jethro grinned. Antanasio waved away an offered cigar. The younger man lit one, then squatted with his back to a porch post. "Antanasio, your nose is as good as your eyes, but you're a pious old fraud."

The weathered face crackled into its familiar cavernous grin, but Salazar's voice feigned sadness. "It saddens me, Senor Jock, to hear you say this thing about me. I have done nothing to cause such a thing."

"Your message. You sent me with it hoping me'n Tunstall would hit it off and I'd go to work for him."

Antanasio squinted from beneath white brows. "You did not get the horses back from the ranch of the *bandido* Shedd, eh?"

Jethro murmured, "Word travels fast."

"Senor Coe—the one called George—he tells me of the stolen horses, two, three days before. He also tells me Senor Brewer goes after them. Then you return without the horses. This I know for you go to the judge, Senor Wilson. Then, with papers in hand, you go to Senor Brady. You still have papers in hand when you come away. The sheriff, he will not help you, no?"

Jethro shook his head in wonder. "How'd you know we were at the Shedd Ranch?"

"Is stopping place for *Bandidos*. Also, five, perhaps six days from here if one goes and returns, as you have."

Both stared thoughtfully at the other. Jethro said, "Antanasio, Dolan and Riley, they got the *bandidos* in this country workin' for them?"

"Perhaps the *soldados*, too, Senor."

"The soldiers! My God, the deck is stacked against you, isn't it?"

"Against us, Senor Jock. You are now one of *us*."

"Which is why you are a pious old fraud...."

Alexander McSween gazed fondly across the table at his wife. "Susan, I must say I like your hair much better. Don't you, Jack?"

Jethro, who'd noted little else since arriving for supper, pretended to study Susan McSween. Her luxuriant light-brown hair, parted in the middle, hung in fluffy ringlets to the shoulders. With fetching waves above the hazel eyes, the effect was indeed stunning.

"I've suggested she let her hair down before, Jack. It's much more fetching for her than wearing it high. I'm pleased she's taken my suggestion at last."

"Do you really think it looks better, Jack?" Susan asked.

Jethro toyed with his steak. "Uh huh."

"Such fervent praise is calculated to make any woman giddy." Then she changed subjects. "I simply cannot understand why you chose to stay at the Wortley Hotel when we offered you a room."

"Well, I've got to leave early in the morning."

"Susan is right, of course," McSween said. "You needn't have born the expense. But beyond that lies another reason—Wortley's is a gathering place for that Murphy faction. Perhaps you didn't know that."

"Maybe I did. Maybe that's why I decided to stay there."

"I don't understand."

"I'm not afraid and I want them to know that."

"For what purpose?"

"We had a little row, Dolan and me. It ended in a Mexican stand-off. If I don't go back, he might make a mistake about my courage that could be fatal for one of us."

McSween opened his mouth to say something, but Jethro waved a hand and continued. "You see, Mr. McSween ..."

"Alex."

"... Alex. If there's trouble now, or trouble brewing, I want to face it head-on and know when it's coming. You may know about the legal and administrative end of things, but I've learned the hard way about trying to side-step trouble not of my own making. And side-stepping's not the way. Leastways, it hasn't worked for me."

"But to expose yourself to unnecessary risks!"

"Better to be exposed expecting it than to be exposed and have no idea it's coming."

Susan murmured, "I do hope you'll be careful tonight, Jack."

After a pause, McSween said, "You spoke of a confrontation with Dolan when you were last here—I believe it appropriate to say I appreciate your able defense of my wife's honor."

Jethro studied McSween. He wondered if the lawyer had sent his wife, unescorted, to Wortley's stable. He murmured, "There's no reason for your wife to need a defense, sir."

McSween dismissed the subject with a wave, then said, "How fortuitous that you ran into John Tunstall."

Jethro's brows wrinkled. He took out a small notepad

and pencil stub from his shirtpocket.

Both McSweens stopped eating. "What are you doing?"

"I just heard a new word, Mrs.—Susan. When I hear one, I try to write it down. Then I try to look the new ones up when there's time. Let's see … F-O-R-T-I-S …"

"F-O-R-T-U-I-T-O-U-S." spelled McSween. "It means fortunate. It's fortunate you stumbled onto John's ranch."

Jethro nodded, staring at the new word, burning it into his mind.

Susan craned to see a page covered with many such words. "Alex, don't you think it wonderful how Jack methodically improves his mind and vocabulary?"

Jethro wrote M-E-T-H-O-D-I-K-A-L-Y, took a last look at both words, then stuck the pencil and pad back into his shirt.

"Again, Jack, how was it you happened to turn up on the Rio Feliz?"

An image of the old man crossed Jethro's mind, but he wondered what could be gained by telling McSween. He shook his head. "Like you said, just lucky I guess."

After supper, McSween said, "Jack, I really must talk seriously with you."

"Okay." Jethro swiveled in his chair to throw an arm over its back.

"The Rio Feliz is far from the center of action, and you're an action man—a natural leader." He paused while his gray-eyed guest remained impassive. "We need you here in Lincoln."

"I'm happy at the Rio Feliz and I don't think Tunstall wants me in his store."

"I'm not talking about working for John Tunstall."

The dark forehead creased. "You're asking me to quit Tunstall?"

"Jack, this is the crucial spot. You could be a tremendous asset if you were in Lincoln." His right hand idly waved to the southeast. "John's ranch is forty hard miles from here—forty miles from where you will most likely be needed."

"Does Tunstall know you feel this way?"

"I wanted to point it out to you first." McSween's soft hands played with the edge of his empty plate. "My interests and John's are so intertwined you might better protect him if you were here."

"I told you before, I'm not interested in hiring out my gun."

"Of course not. I know that. Susan and I would not expect it. All we'd expect would be for you to follow the dictates of your conscience and...." The clipped voice trailed off.

The inclusion of Susan's name surprised Jethro. Gray eyes flicked to those of hazel and back again. "Just what are your interests, Mr. McSween?"

"Alex," McSween muttered.

When Jethro failed to respond, McSween took a deep breath, shifted in his chair and said, "I want to see Murphy's dynasty broken. I want to see Dolan and Riley in jail. I want to see the people of Lincoln County treated fairly and honestly. I want to see this territory grow."

"Is that any different from Tunstall's dream?"

"I'm a realist. John tends to be romantic."

"Meaning?"

"McSween rubbed his chin and pulled on his moustache, the smile became engaging. "Please understand, Jack, I would not care to say one single disparaging word about young John Tunstall. He is well-intentioned in every possible way. But he is unfortunately naive about the lessons of history. He is sailing his own blissful sea, neither fully aware of present danger, nor of future opportunity."

Jethro settled more comfortably into his chair, lacing fingers across his chest. "And you are?"

"I believe so. Listen, Jack ..." McSween earnestly leaned

over the table, "there are tremendous economic possibilities for an honest but aggressive trading firm in Lincoln County, especially after Dolan and Riley are eliminated. It may well be one developed by a local person. One who can see clearly into the future. Perhaps by me."

"And Tunstall?"

"John is a personable young man who happens to have a wealthy father. I cannot see his long-term interests satisfied in Lincoln County."

Jethro's chin sank to his chest, then he lifted his head and stared squarely at Susan McSween. He wondered how deeply this woman was involved in her husband's plans?

"We could make it monetarily attractive, Jack."

Jethro swung toward the woman's husband.

"Let's say one hundred per month, with an opportunity to purchase up to twenty percent of whatever trading company I wind up owning."

Jethro found a blank spot on a far wall. "Does Dolan and Riley have any idea what you have in mind for them?"

McSween smiled. "They no doubt know they have competition. Fortunately—fortuitously—it's unlikely that they know my long-range plans."

"And does Tunstall know of your plans?"

"Nothing could be gained by telling him I'm standing by in case he tires of it all."

Jethro's chin again dipped to his chest. He thought of Tunstall's allies: Chisum and McSween. He shook his head, fully aware now of the pitfalls lying ahead of the young Englishman. Then he recalled Brewer and Bowdre and Scurlock and Salazar, and of the countless other little people, both Mexican and "gringo," that Tunstall was trying to help.

Susan McSween's bosom lifted and fell disconcertingly. "I'll get more coffee." As she left the room, her image remained: a white waist with fitted collar, a skirt with a deep circular flounce flowing smoothly over slender hips....

"What do you think Dolan and Riley will do when they realize you're dealing the hand so as to ease them out?" Jethro asked. "They're playing rough now and so far, it's only for matches."

Susan returned carrying a silver urn. Jethro grinned, remembering her terrible coffee. After she'd poured, McSween said, his voice reflective, "They'll react. Probably violently. I'm willing to take the risk, but I'd much rather do it with someone like you at my side. I have my adherents, but they need an able fighting man to lead them." He quickly added, "Not to fight, please understand, but to galvanize them."

Jethro took his pencil and pad and wrote A-D-H-A-R-A-N-T. Upon finishing, he asked, "How do you expect to fight their government ties?"

"That's my role, not yours. Though there undoubtedly is collusion in high places, I'm not without my resources." McSween glanced at his wife. "However, you'll just have to accept my word on that."

McSween waited patiently while Jethro wrote C-O-L-U-S-H-O-N, then said, "Well, Jack?"

Jethro considered the proposal he had no intention of accepting. McSween was right, Lincoln would be the centerpoint for future trouble. He finally sensed the real depth of the young Englishman's problems and his lack of real support. But to further risk already shaky alliances by an abrupt refusal would benefit neither Tunstall nor the small farmers and ranchers. At last, he said, "I believe for the time being I should continue with Mr. Tunstall. Like you say, you're not in any real danger, while they probably have Tunstall in their sights as somebody to step on and squash now. Stealing his horses shows that."

McSween sighed.

"I'll promise to keep an eye on Lincoln, however. And if

you need me, I'll see what I can do."

"You may be too late."

Susan McSween leaned forward to lay a hand on Jethro's. "Please reconsider, Jack," she said in a husky voice. "I'm afraid Alex may come into danger."

The gray eyes flickered to her. Impatience crept into his voice. "Perhaps John Tunstall already is in danger."

She squeezed ever so slightly, then withdrew her hand.

CHAPTER TEN

The ranch on the Rio Feliz stood deserted when Jethro Spring arrived in mid-afternoon. With no idea where the roundup was taking place, the tired rider corralled the mare and threw her a couple pitchfork loads of hay. Then he warmed some beans and crawled into bed.

He found the roundup by the following noon. From that point, his days ran together, full of bawling calves and bellowing cows, dust in his nostrils and sand in his food.

Finally, their gather complete and the herd divided, Tunstall and Jethro were assigned by Brewer to shove the holdover cattle—breeding-age cows and young stuff—slowly back to the Feliz ranch. Meanwhile, Middleton and Widenmann would help move the market herd to Chisum's place at Bosque Grande where they would join a Chisum herd destined for the nearest railhead at Trinidad, Colorado.

The aroma of fresh-boiled coffee filled his nostrils as Jethro poured himself a cup, then squatted away from the tiny blaze to stare into the blackness. A coyote howled from a distant hilltop and their two saddlehorses shuffled at their picketline.

A bone-weary John Tunstall sprawled nearby, gazing into the fire. "Bless me, Jack, but I'm glad this is over. Oh, it's exciting to begin, but bloody drudgery after a few days."

The crouching man nodded, sipping at his scalding coffee.

"Really, I must get back to the ranch and into Lincoln," Tunstall continued. "The new contracts are to be let soon for Fort Stanton and the Mescalero reservation. Alex should have the bid returns by the time I arrive." The Englishman sighed. "No rest for the wicked, is there, old man?"

Jethro cocked his head to the darkness, then set his cup on the ground and glided into the night. The Englishman talked on for several minutes before discovering his companion missing. Just as he rolled to his knees to search for his hired hand, Jethro returned carrying an armload of dry willow branches for their fire.

"I didn't even know you were gone," Tunstall said. "My, but you are the silent one."

"Sorry, John. Thought I heard something." Jethro threw his wood alongside a few sticks already collected.

"You seem a bit rabbity lately, Jack. Is there a reason?"

Jethro shrugged.

The two arrived at the headquarters ranch near dark the following day, their scatter complete. They were surprised to find Dick Brewer unsaddling his horse. "Evans and his bunch are at Seven Rivers, John," Brewer said. "This time I'm going to get the bastards."

"Where are our other men, Dick?"

"They're bringing the roundup ponies back a little slower. Should be here tomorrow night. Chisum's taking the herd in for us. I came on ahead because I'm riding on up to the Ruidoso tomorrow to get some help."

Tunstall threw his saddle on a rail. "Is this information reliable?" he asked.

"I think so."

"We should talk about this, Dick."

Jethro said, "I'll take care of the horses. Why don't you two go on to the house and start a fire."

Tunstall's and Brewer's exchange appeared heated on their way to the bunkhouse. When Jethro opened the door a few minutes later, there was no fire and Tunstall was saying in a condescending tone, "But, Dick, we don't know Brady won't cooperate. You must admit our position would be much stronger if we could induce the bloody damned sheriff to lead the posse."

Brewer wheeled from a window, obviously seething. Dark curly hair stood out in disarray, one lock across his forehead. "John, if we let them bastards get away with this, you may as well pack it in—go on back to the north wing in some goddamn English castle and stay there! They won't figure there's any limit on what they can steal from you!"

"I'm not talking about letting Evans and his bunch off, Dick. I'm talking about persuading the legally constituted sheriff of this county to apprehend the villains."

"And I'm saying there's fat damned chance in him doin' just that!"

"At least let's give it a blinkin' try, don't you think?"

"Hell no, I don't think!" Brewer shouted. "No, goddammit! All he'd do is give a warning to that bunch at Seven Rivers."

"They were my horses," Tunstall said stubbornly.

"And it was my fault," Brewer shot back. "You can only turn the other cheek so long before they eat you alive. If you intend to do it any longer, forget me. I ain't workin' here no more!"

"Whoa, boys," Jethro broke in. "Sounds to me like the fat's about to fall in the fire. John, why don't we tap one of them bottles you got stashed under your bed? Maybe that'll help find an answer that'd suit everybody."

Tunstall hurried to his bed to rummage under it for a bottle of Jamaica rum. Meanwhile, Brewer brought three tin cups.

"Let's all take a chair," Jethro said. After Tunstall poured and each sat, he said, "Okay, way I see it, you both want the same thing—to see the Evans bunch in jail. Right?"

His companions nodded.

"The only difference, then, is how to go about it."

"We must use legally constituted means, Dick." Jethro sighed—Tunstall was begging.

"I could care less about that!" Brewer snarled. "I'm sick and go-to-hell tired of the law protecting them bastards. I just want to get 'em so they stay got."

"But you're no gunman."

"To hell ..."

Jethro pounded the table so hard their cups bounced. "Why don't we do it both ways?"

Tunstall's eyebrows lifted. Brewer asked, "How?"

"Okay, try this on for size. The warrants have already been issued. Right? To me."

Tunstall nodded.

"Dick, you want to hit the Ruidoso and round up some help?"

"I know I can get half a dozen good men to ride to Seven Rivers," Brewer replied. "They're fed up, too."

"Will six be enough?"

"It will be with me and Widenmann and Mid. You'll go, too, won't you Jack?"

"I'll go."

"Now see here ..." Tunstall began.

"Please let me finish, John. Dick is probably right. Brady

would scotch the whole thing if we leave it to him. Whether he'd do it on purpose or not, isn't really important. The point is, he'd foul it up one way or another, so the Evans outfit would get away."

Tunstall's mouth opened, but Jethro held up a palm.

"What if we organized things first, then asked him in at the last minute?"

"But what if he refused to go?"

"He won't. He's still got to know he's the sheriff. He's too much of a blowhard not to realize what people'd think if he didn't go along. Our big problem is not to give him enough time to get advice from Dolan and Riley. If we don't let them get to him, he'll come."

"But what if he doesn't?" Tunstall insisted.

"We can cover that, too," Jethro replied. "I'll go into Lincoln with you while Dick rounds up the Ruidoso people and assembles the posse here at the ranch. The warrants are in my name. McSween can get Judge Wilson to swear me in as a deputy. That's when Brady will be sure to go—when he sees we'll win with or without him."

A broad smile lit Tunstall's face. "*Fait accompli*," he breathed.

Jethro looked curiously at him, reaching for his notepad. "What does that mean, John?"

Stars were yet out when the posse surrounded the Beckwith home at Seven Rivers. The house itself was a "choza"—a dwelling with as much of the house underground as above. Sheriff Brady, a reluctant participant from the outset, issued orders that were uniformly ignored; it was Dick Brewer who, for all practical purposes, was in command. Brady sought sympathy from the man he knew as Jack Winter:

"Dammit, Winter, I'm the sheriff here. Where does Brewer think he's got the right to give orders?" When Jethro didn't answer, the sheriff growled, "And you. You're a deputy. You goin' to let him get away with it?"

Gradually the men identified details in the growing light. Jethro squinted through a crack in the stick and mud sidewall of a tiny lean-to stable. First, a saddle thrown over a corral rail came into focus, then a bulky posse member prone behind a pile of posts, then the choza door, and at last the latch on that door. Just then the latch wriggled and a man opened the door and stepped out.

"Beckwith!" Brewer called. "This is a posse! We got you surrounded! We want Evans and his bunch!"

The elder Beckwith froze when Brewer first called, one foot poised in mid-step. Carefully, he set it down. "Ain't nobody here named Evans!" he cried.

"Goddammit, Beckwith," Brewer shouted, "there's at least three horses in the corral we know Evans stole. Now send 'em out or we'll drag 'em out over your body."

Beckwith hesitated. "I can go back in?"

"Get the hell out of my sight, Beckwith! You have two minutes to save you and everybody in that goddammed building!"

Beckwith jumped for the door. An eerie silence descended on the scene until a high-pitched voice broke it: "Who are you?"

"Brewer! We got a lot to talk about, Evans! Now come on out."

A burst of rifle and pistol shots from the choza shattered the stillness of the squalid ranch. It was drowned in a concentrated roar erupting from the fourteen rifles surrounding Beckwith's. Dirt and dust flew from the choza's adobe walls; passing bullets constantly picked and plucked window curtains and splinters flew from door jambs.

Another hush fell. It was broken when a quavering voice

called from the choza, "Who the hell else is out there, for Gawd's sake?"

"I'm here, Jesse! Charlie Bowdre. I'm here to tell you to come out willing, or you'll come out dead."

"This is Doc Scurlock, Evans. We ain't play-actin'."

"George Coe here, Evans. We're bringin' you out—dead or alive!"

"The sheriff is here, too, Jesse," Jethro called.

"Brady?" a voice shouted from the choza. "You there, Brady?"

"I'm here, Evans!" Brady shouted. "Give yourself up and you'll get a fair trial."

"Okay. We'll think on it."

"Take as long as you want, Evans," Brewer called. Meanwhile, he fired systematically into the house. Others followed his lead and only seconds later, a white flag waved at one of the windows. All shooting stopped and the choza door opened. Jesse Evans came out first, his hands over his head. He was followed in order by Frank Baker, Tom Hill and George Davis.

Brewer told the four to move to one side, then he ordered Beckwith, his wife, and two grown sons to come out. Evans, Baker, Hill, and Davis were taken to Lincoln.

Less than a month later, they escaped jail. The Las Vegas Gazette editorialized about the escape. The editorial's last two sentences were most telling:

> … Evans, Baker, Hill and Davis and others held for horse stealing, were rescued by an armed force of 32 men. The doors of the jail were not even found locked.

The Evans gang stopped off at Dick Brewer's farm, stole seven horses, burned the house, and generally wrecked the other buildings.

Brewer and Jethro Spring were setting posts for a corral

extension at Tunstall's when George Coe rode in to report the escape and its aftermath. But for a tightening jaw, Dick Brewer received the news of his home's destruction stoically. He shrugged and grinned ruefully at Jethro, saying, "Well, that takes one load off my mind. Leastways, I'm not a farmer any more if I ain't got no farm."

CHAPTER ELEVEN

Tunstall raged at news of the Evans gang's escape and pillage and insisted on personally investigating. Brewer begged the rancher not to go to the Ruidoso and Lincoln. "Hell, the place I had wasn't worth much anyhow—wouldn't even raise a row—and the horses was all just scrub stock."

"They shan't get away with it, Dick. By all that's holy, I'll see them rot in hell first!"

"I tell you it's not worth it," Brewer repeated.

"Oh bosh the money. It's the principle, Dick, the principle. I'll see that you are reimbursed your losses, but I'll be damned if I will sit idly by and let them make such a mockery of justice."

"John, listen to me," Brewer pleaded. "They'll be expecting us to come with blood in our eye. What the hell do you figure to do, anyway?"

"I'm going and that's that!"

"Then I'm going with you."

Jethro pushed from the corral rail where he perched listening to the exchange. "No you're not, Dick. I'm going. It's you and John they're after. So let's keep both of you away from Lincoln at the same time."

———— •—•—• ————

The only thing stirring in Lincoln when John Tunstall and Jethro Spring tied off at the jail's hitchrail was two children scratching hopscotch squares in the road dust. Jethro took comfort from Antanasio Salazar's presence in his accustomed spot.

Brady met them at the jail's door, eyes darting about. "What the hell do you want?"

"We want an explanation for your behavior, Sheriff," Tunstall said immediately. "We want to know how it happened the jail doors were unlocked the day Evans and Baker and the rest escaped? How it happened their shackles were already filed to loosen them? Why it was you were not vigilant?"

"I resent that." Brady's voice broke as he said it. "I resent your questions. I'm doin' my job. What right you think you got to ask me that, anyway? You ain't even American."

"I am," Jethro said. "I'm American and I want to know what you were doing when they broke out."

"You'd be better off, half-breed, if you kept out of this."

"Half-breeds are Americans, though, Sheriff," Jethro replied, his voice edged. "What *were* you doing?"

Brady's darting eyes quickened. "I was out to the fort askin' the Colonel for help to guard the jail."

"Convenient," Tunstall murmured.

The sheriff's voice turned to a whine. "What's that s'posed to mean?" He licked his lips and looked up and down the street.

"What about their shackles, Sheriff?" Tunstall asked. "And the unlocked doors?"

"I'm investigating that."

"Umm. Has this investigation disclosed anything?"

"When I'm ready, I'll file a report."

"Then there is nothing?"

"Not to you, there ain't."

The friends exchanged glances. Jethro pointed up the street with his chin and Tunstall shrugged. "What can we do?" Tunstall asked as they led their horses toward the Englishman's store.

"One of us could ride to the fort and check Brady's story. I'm pretty sure the Colonel will back him, but he should be a little nervous about tying himself too close to outlaws and a useless sheriff. Anyway, it'll make 'em sweat."

"That sounds reasonable."

"I think you ought to be the one to do that. You have more standing with the Colonel. Maybe see him first thing in the morning? Meanwhile, I'll try to get a feel for what other folks around town think about our trusty sheriff."

Tunstall nodded and strode on into his store. Jethro looked up and down the empty street, then crouched in front of Antanasio Salazar....

Alexander McSween projected bonhomie to his two sudden guests, but his pasted smile was only partly in place and Jethro saw him eyeing Tunstall hesitantly. *He's wondering if I told the Englishman he tried to hire me,* the gray-eyed man thought. But when Tunstall warmly shook his friend's hand, their host visibly relaxed.

"Bloody nuisance why we came, what?"

McSween nodded, smile creeping back into place. "Have you talked to Brady yet? I can get nothing from him."

"A wretched man, Alex. Can he be defeated for re-election?"

"After this? A virtual certainty. Unfortunately his term isn't up for three more years."

McSween hung their coats and hats on hooks in the foyer and ushered them into a sitting room. Susan McSween perched on a stool by a large upright piano, her hair in a style much the same as when Jethro last saw her, with ringlets to her shoulders. She spun on her stool, jumping up at their entrance.

"John! Jack! So good to see you both."

The Englishman took her hand and bowed gallantly. "Ah, Sue. Bless me if you don't make life in this godforsaken country worthwhile."

She curtsied, then hurried to Jethro, hands outstretched. He took a hand and shook it vigorously, murmuring self-consciously, "How do, Mrs. McSween."

She stretched to her tiptoes to kiss him on the cheek. He thought he heard her whisper "Susan" and reddened all the more.

"Well, Sue, are you going to play for us?" Tunstall asked.

"I will if you wish," she said, sweeping back to her stool.

"I couldn't possibly wish for more than just that. Have you heard her play, Jack? She is magnificent."

Jethro shook his head. Despite the fact Tunstall was dressed but little better, he felt out of place in trail clothes.

"What would you like to hear?" Susan called.

"Well, my dear," Tunstall said, "I still favor your Stephen Foster, you know."

She immediately began playing a soothing Negro spiritual. Though Jethro could not name the tune, he recognized it. Then, when John Tunstall picked up and repeated the line, "*Way Down Upon the Swanee River*," he had it. Susan followed with a rendition of *Old Black Joe*; then upon Tunstall's demand for a livelier piece, swept into *Oh!*

Susanna, switched to *Camptown Races* and ended with *Jeannie with the Light Brown Hair*.

Throughout, Jethro was entranced. She used no music and seemed to be playing for him alone. He wondered if McSween and Tunstall felt the same? His mind swept back to the church organist in Fort Worth and how the specter of a "JETHRO SPRING - DEAD or ALIVE" poster tacked to the Post Office wall ruptured their future. The reverie of Nell Tucker snapped when Tunstall and McSween began clapping. He joined feebly.

"Did you enjoy the music, Jack?" she asked, coming toward him.

"Yes, oh yes. It was beautiful, Miss Tucker."

She tilted her head and stared up at him as if she'd never before seen him. For his part, he seemed to be looking through her … beyond. "My name is Susan."

"I … I'm sorry."

"Is dinner ready, Susan?" McSween asked.

"Yes, I think so. Give me a moment, though, and I'll check with Maria."

"What are we to do, Alex?" Tunstall asked as Susan left the room.

McSween shook his head. "The bare effrontery of it all! I cannot see how they would dare outrage the entire community so, John. It will return to haunt them."

"Has the governor been advised?"

"He has. But we can expect little there."

"What is our recourse, then?"

"Well," McSween said in his best courtroom voice, "aside from a little surprise I have for you later this evening, it still seems as though our newspaper campaign is it. That and continuing to bombard Congress and the administration with informative letters."

Susan announced supper.

Table talk was light, little of it addressed to Jethro. He

let his mind return to the beautiful music and, to Nell Tucker, realizing for the first time how really similar she and Susan McSween were in hair, eyes, and size. From there, though, all resemblance ended. Nell, shy and reserved, had suffered much personal tragedy. Susan, on the other hand, seems a bold and vital woman, well-educated and obviously moves easily among the upper crust. In addition, Susan McSween is probably wealthy beyond Nell's dreams.

And she's married.

"I asked if you will not stay with us tonight, Jack?"

Startled from his reverie, Jethro found all eyes upon him.

"I've already checked into Wortley's."

"I'm blessed if I can understand it, Susan," Tunstall said. "I told him he was welcome to sleep in the store, but he declined. Even took his horse to that place."

"Why do you persist in this nonsense?" she asked. "Surely you must realize your danger there increases with each stay."

"Could be," Jethro said, "my danger actually decreases each time."

"Fool's talk, Jack," McSween boomed. "You keep crawling into a den of vipers, sooner or later, you'll be bitten."

Jethro shrugged.

McSween patted his mouth with a linen serviette and said, "Now for my surprise, John."

Tunstall leaned back, legs crossed, one hand resting on the table. "Lately I've come to distrust surprises."

"This one you'll like, I guarantee it. Robert Widenmann has been appointed a deputy United States marshal for southeastern New Mexico."

"What!" Tunstall lunged to his feet. "You're joking!"

"No I'm not, John. His appointment came through yesterday. Chief Marshal Sherman in Santa Fe just informed me."

"How, for heaven's sake?"

McSween drummed the table with his fingers, enjoying the Englishman's reaction immensely. "You know of Widenmann's father's friendship with Secretary of Interior Carl Schurz?"

"Certainly I know of it. My heavens, for a while Bob talked of little else. What I should like to know is how did the appointment come about? Surely you cannot expect me to believe such things are done on a whimsy of a busy administrator."

McSween chuckled. "Actually, John, it was Widenmann's idea. I helped him apply for the appointment some time ago. Its arrival yesterday is mere coincidence. But it is timely, isn't it?"

Tunstall settled into his chair. "I don't know, Alex," he said after reflecting a moment. "Somehow I can't imagine Bob Widenmann as a U.S. marshal. What does it mean?"

McSween tapped his fingertips together, staring at them as if fascinated. "Well, John, for one thing, it means we have the more powerful peace officer in our camp."

"In what way?"

"He can arrest people on U.S. warrants. They're much more formidable than mere territorial warrants. He can even initiate them. And he has the power to demand federal help in serving them, and in making arrests. John, Widenmann can ask help from Fort Stanton and *they must give it to him!*"

"Bob Widenmann now possesses these powers?"

"Indeed he does."

Tunstall shook his head in disbelief. As if on cue, both men turned to Jethro. It was Tunstall who asked, "What do you think of this, Jack?"

Jethro pursed his lips and eyed a dark spot on the heavy oak table. "I would not care to be Robert Widenmann," he said at last.

"Why?" demanded McSween.

"Is it possible for too much power to be placed in the

hands of one who has little idea how to use it? Nor the tools to apply it."

"The entire weight of federal government provides an array of tools for application," replied McSween. "As far as Robert knowing how to use the power, I am certainly available—and eager—to advise him."

The gray eyes lifted to McSween, transfixing the attorney for several seconds until the barrister averted his eyes.

Tunstall said, "Then I must release Bob as soon as we return?"

"Oh, no, John. That's the beautiful part. Widenmann's position as deputy marshal has but little salary. It is merely a part-time position requiring other employment for the holder. He will still work for you, though it does strike me that it would be all for the better if he were to work here for Tunstall and Company."

"That's bully," Tunstall agreed. "I was considering moving him to the store at any rate."

McSween pushed back his chair. "And now, ladies and gentlemen, would you care for a glass of sherry to celebrate this first in our long string of victories!"

Jethro raised his glass with the others, then sipped it thoughtfully.

The toast complete, Tunstall said, "To business, Alex. Might we go over those procurement bids? You say it appears 'the house' had access to ours before they submitted theirs?"

"Only five cents per hundredweight less on the flour. Corn, the same. Ten cents per hundred on beans. They were exactly the same on each line item of pork. I could go on and on—it's consistent. You should see what they did with Chisum's beef bid."

"May we go over to the store and look at the papers?"

"Certainly. Would you excuse us, Susan? Jack? We shouldn't be long."

"Of course, dear. Take as long as you must."

When the door closed behind Tunstall and Susan's husband, Jethro thrust his hands into trouser pockets and shifted from one foot to the other. Susan watched from beneath lowered lashes. At last, she said, "Please sit down, Jack."

His eyes fled before her bold appraisal. He looked at (but did not see) an ornate cabinet clock, the brocaded drapes, a heavy oak-and-glass China closet.

"She must have been beautiful."

His eyes flicked to her. "I beg your pardon?"

"The woman you were thinking about."

"Woman?"

"Earlier this evening. While I was playing for you. And again during supper. You were thinking of a very special woman. I believe her name was—or is—Miss Tucker?"

As if his head was pulled by puppet strings, Jethro nodded. "She's lovely."

"And you loved her deeply?"

Jethro nodded again.

"I'm jealous," she said throatily.

A shiver ran through the man.

"I never really realized it before this evening, but you are an unusually appealing man, Mr. Winter."

He shook his head and a faint smile crinkled the eye corners. "Jack," he said.

She laughed gaily, then sobered. "Tell me of her."

"You look very much alike. Same size. Same color hair, eyes...." His voice trailed off.

"You knew her ... well?"

"Well enough."

Silence fell between them. Then Susan asked, "Where?"

"That's an unfair question."

"I'm sorry. Though I'd like very much to know, I shan't ask what happened."

Again a pall of silence descended. Then Jethro murmured, "She played the organ. Beautifully."

"Oh Jack! Then she was a pianist, also."

"I don't know. But she played the organ as well as you play the piano."

"Did you know that tonight I played for you alone?"

His sigh was enormous. "I felt as much."

After another period of silence, he said, "What I don't know is why?"

Her voice was again husky. "You are a strange, strong man, Jack Winter. You have high moral values, loyalty, honesty to a fault. You are kind and considerate and compassionate. You are thoughtful and careful, yet bold and decisive. You are fearless, capable, generous, and not at all ugly. Those are characteristics any woman would see as desirable. Throw in your inherent shyness and you, sir, are nearly irresistible."

His eyes had fallen to the tabletop as she spoke. And it was to the tabletop that he asked, "Even to a married woman?"

Her throaty reply was to the same tabletop: "To any woman."

"Perhaps this conversation has gone far enough." He stood.

"Yes, I suppose it has." She, too, stood to lead him to the foyer.

As he shrugged into his coat, she moved around him to lean against the door. "I'd not wish for you to infer too much from tonight's conversation, Jack. I'm no hussy, and there can be nothing between us."

He regarded her at length. "I know that."

She stepped toward him, tiptoed and brushed her lips lightly against his. At the same time, her hands gripped his shoulders. "Be careful, Jack. I worry about you."

Then he was gone.

CHAPTER TWELVE

It was a subdued hotel dining room. Jethro hunched over his breakfast in silence, avoided by Sam Wortley's other patrons. He'd entered the dining room early and dallied over his meal, his presence deliberate.

Brady took a chair at the table's far end—an act not unnoticed by others. Riley nodded stiffly when he entered and took a chair only a few feet away, a knowing smile working his mouth corners. It was left to Jimmy Dolan to show the greatest reaction. Riley's partner stopped abruptly at the dining room's door. The man's face twisted and he unbuttoned his coat to reveal the pearl handle of a small revolver.

Jethro yawned, unfolded a clasp knife and began picking his teeth, staring blankly at Dolan.

Dolan took a seat by Riley, saying loudly enough to carry to the room's far corners, "Something stinks in here."

Grinning, still picking his teeth, Jethro slid from his chair and ambled out, back squarely to Dolan and the rest of Wortley's remaining breakfast patrons. In his room, he sprawled on the bed and waited for Lincoln to come to life. After a few minutes, he flicked the thong from the Colt's hammer, re-set the gun in its holster, picked up his coat and left his room.

As the chill morning air of late November bit through his coat, he thought of south-bound geese in far-off Montana. He glanced at a lowering sky, wondering if an early snow was in the air of these southern mountains. Then his thoughts angled elsewhere—whether to visit Jose Montano or Judge Wilson. True, Antanasio Salazar had told him the Evans gang's escape outraged the entire community, but he still wished to get a feel from other Lincoln residents.

A rider straddling a big bay trotted from the corral behind Tunstall's store. Jethro pushed his hatbrim up and watched the bay turn up the street. John Tunstall, as if on cue, headed for Fort Stanton and a confrontation with Brevet Colonel Purington.

Just then, the front door of Dolan and Company's store flew open and a ragged scarecrow staggered out to sprawl upon the porch. The surly clerk Jethro remembered as Bill Burns rushed after, trailed by a bearded man in a leather apron. Burns savagely kicked the fallen man, grabbed him by his coat's lapels and jerked what Jethro could now see was merely a youth to his feet. The clerk slapped the youth several times, whirled him around and kicked him into the street. "You little sonofabitch! Don't let me never again see your shittin' buck-toothed face in this store. Hear?"

The youth lay sprawled headlong in the dust in front of Jethro. "What'd he do, Burns?" asked the man the clerk knew as Jack Winter. "Finger the merchandise?"

"This ain't none o' yore business, mestizo!"

There was a shuffle at Jethro's feet; the youth slipped a Navy Colt from beneath his ragged coat. The gray-eyed man stepped on the skinny wrist, then kicked the fallen gun away.

"Why you little bastard!" Burns shouted as he and the leather-aproned clerk lunged forward. "Ain't nobody pulls a gun on Bill Burns and gets away with it!"

Burns got in one solid kick before Jethro knocked him sprawling. Leather apron plowed in from the side, carrying Jethro back and down in a heap. A blow to Jethro's temple elicited a roar of rage; doubling his legs beneath the leather aproned clerk, he hurled him away. He'd just made it to his knees when a kick from Burns exploded against the back of his head and again he plowed dust. Burns threw himself forward, but a dazed Jethro twisted free, rolling away as leather apron stumbled over Burns.

Jethro met leather apron's delayed rush, gave with the momentum, fell to his back, again levered his feet into leather apron's belly. This time Jethro's thrust and the man's rush propelled the bearded man six feet over and beyond. Jethro leaped up, head clearing. A straight left whacked into the charging Bill Burn's throat, gagging him. Then a boot slammed into the clerk's crotch, doubling him over. A clubbed fist slammed behind the ear ended Burns' day, driving him nose-first into the dust.

Jethro whirled to meet leather apron. Giving ground, he flicked deadly lefts to the blocky man's pug nose.

"Come here, you bastard," leather apron snarled.

So Jethro came with the grace of a dancer. As he closed, he buried a right hook deep into the outsized belly, then brought up a crashing head-butt to the jaw. He grabbed the big man's shoulder, jerked him around, planted a foot in the small of his back and gave a mighty shove. Leather apron piled up just short of Dolan and Company's steps.

John Riley stood spraddle-legged on the porch, a pipe hanging from his teeth. He gave Jethro a mock salute.

Jethro gripped the inert Burns's collar and dragged him across the street to drop alongside the moaning leather apron. Riley blew out a cloud of smoke and said,

"Impressive, Mr. Winter. Very impressive. It confirms my initial opinion of you."

"Say bully, Jack!" Tunstall cried from his dancing bay. "That was worth viewing!" The Englishman packed a grin that must have been visible from the far end of town.

Jethro paused to gaze down at the frail youth who sat dejectedly in the dust, tears of rage streaking his dirty face.

"You stayed out of this, mister, I'da got even on my own." Then he muttered, "I still will, too."

Jethro appraised the youth: what he saw was torn wool pants, run-over boots, a worn sheepskin vest over grimy long underwear. No shirt. A red cotton handkerchief knotted around his throat and a ragged wool coat completed the ensemble. Jethro shook his head. "Your way ain't the right way," he said simply. He retrieved the Navy Colt and handed it back.

The youth thrust it beneath the frayed coat. He held up a hand and Jethro pulled him to his feet. The youth laughed. "I do believe you're gonna have a mouse under that eye, mister. Might make you purty. You sure ain't no great shakes now."

Jethro gestured toward the store. "What was that all about?"

"Aw, they said I was trying to steal something."

"Was you?"

"Hell, yes. When a body's plumb down and out, he can steal or starve. While I'll admit neither appeals to me, ain't much question which I'd choose."

"Likely there's another choice. You could try working."

"Now that," the youth grinned his odd, buck-toothed smile, "would be best of all. Only thing is, roundups are over, and places to work are damned few and far between."

"Perhaps we could use him, Jack," Tunstall said from his horse. "After all, with Bob moving to the store, we should replace him with someone. What do you think?"

"Who's he?" the youth asked, gesturing at the Englishman.

"John Tunstall," Jethro replied. "I work for him. He owns a store down the street and a couple of ranches to the southeast."

"The hell!" The youth stalked over to Tunstall and stuck out a scrawny hand. "I'm your man, mister. Name's William Bonney."

Tunstall leaned down to take the hand. "William Bonney? I don't believe I know the name. However, we'll give you a chance, young man. That's as fair as we can be."

"More'n fair enough to me, Mr. Tunstall."

Tunstall nodded and spurred his horse toward the fort.

Bonney returned to the gray-eyed man. "Queer duck, ain't he? Called me 'young man'. Hell, he ain't much older'n me."

Jethro held out his hand. "Jack Winter."

Bonney took it and pumped it, studying Jethro as if it was the last chance he'd have. "You ain't much older'n me, neither."

Jethro grinned. "Well, if you're working for Tunstall now, I guess it's up to me to figure out what to do with you."

"You the foreman?" Bonney asked.

"For now, you can figure it that way. I'll do 'til we get back to the ranch. Right now I think we ought to put you into a new outfit. I don't know if John would approve, but maybe it'll keep you from stealing what you need."

Bonney locked his arm in Jethro's and began whistling as they walked down the street.

Jethro said, "William Bonney. Do they call you Will or Bill?"

"Mostly they call me Billy. Some of my best friends call me 'kid', or 'the kid'. Don't make no difference to me."

"Okay, I'll call you 'Billy the Kid'. How's that?"

⇒ Chapter Thirteen ⇐

By the time Jethro shut him off, Billy Bonney was into the Englishman for almost three month's wages—all credit purchases of shirts, trousers, underwear, coat, scarf, hat; even new boots. The end neared when Billy ordered two cases of cartridges for his Navy Colt. "What the hell are you figuring to do with a thousand rounds of .45s, kid?"

"Practice," Billy replied, peering at Jethro from the corners of his blue eyes. "You know what practice makes, don't you?"

Jethro recalled his own days and weeks of practice when, many years before, a Texas Ranger had taught another ragged youth to use a six-gun. He wondered if he'd looked as useless then as this kid does now?

"What do you say?" Billy asked.

"You can have the shells. But nothing else, hear? You got everything you need, then some."

"Just a couple boxes of .44-40, Jack. I'm low for my rifle. C'mon."

Much to everyone's surprise, Billy Bonney proved an excellent cowman. He roped better than Middleton and straddled an unruly bronc as well as Brewer. He was open and cheerful, turning the lopsided, buck-toothed grin on in all kinds of weather and during all kinds of work. And though the youth appeared frail, he turned out to be as tough and resilient as bullhide leather.

Every free moment, the kid spent with his Navy Colt. The bark of the old revolver from behind a nearby hill became a common sound to the Tunstall men. One day, Jethro Spring ambled out to watch the young man practice shooting across a dry wash at some rocks and cans he'd set up. Billy jerked the gun from its holster and blazed away, scoring on two of five.

"Reckon you can do better?" he asked, punching out the spent brass. To Billy's surprise, his dark friend slipped out his walnut-handled Colt and fired deliberately. A can spun into the air. Four continuous roars spun the can twenty yards away with the impact of four additional bullets.

Frank admiration was mirrored on Billy's face as he whistled. "Not bad! You'd be damned dangerous, could you get it in your hand as fast as the next man."

Jethro smiled and punched out the empties.

"I can beat you," Billy said. "I know I can."

Jethro glanced up to see Billy's blue eyes dancing. "You got any live ones in that gun?"

"Not yet, but I will in a second."

"Leave it be and let's see," Jethro said, settling his empty revolver into its holster.

Billy grinned and holstered the Navy. "Anytime you're ready, old man."

Jethro nodded imperceptibly.

Bonney moved. The muzzle of Jethro's Colt rammed into his belly, then tilted up. Billy looked down. The other's pistol barrel appeared the size of a smokestack on a locomotive. His buck-teeth gleamed. "You can't do that again."

But three times more, Billy's draw was met with the speed of a striking snake. The kid flashed his grin. "What am I doing wrong?"

Bonney proved a quick student. Already surprisingly proficient with his Winchester, he quickly acquired similar skills with the Colt.

Every bit as surprising as Billy's quick mastery of the handgun was his growing, dogged devotion to John Tunstall. The Englishman's generosity, easy good humor, and obvious concern for his employees struck a responsive chord with the one-time homeless waif, and Billy made it a point to be around him as much as possible, hanging on Tunstall's every action, every word.

Christmas came to the Rio Feliz and with it, news that Dolan-Riley had taken the offensive. Widenmann sent word that McSween and Chisum were both in jail at Las Vegas.

"Las Vegas? What are they doing at Las Vegas?" Dick Brewer asked.

The stunned Tunstall stared down at the deputy marshal's letter. "Alex and Susan were accompanying Chisum on a business trip east," he said. "Alex told me about it when last we were together. Apparently it had something to do with Chisum's latest cattle transfer. Alex was along as legal advisor. It was to be a St. Louis vacation for Susan. They were arrested in Las Vegas."

"What's the charge?"

Tunstall's choked-off laugh seemed out-of-place.

"According to Widenmann, they're holding Chisum for unpaid Arkansas notes from years ago."

"And McSween?"

"Apparently they're claiming embezzlement of ten thousand dollars from the estate of Emil Fritz." Tunstall peered around the room. "That's absurd, isn't it?"

"Of course it is," Brewer snapped. "They won't get away with it, either. McSween and Chisum are probably out of it now and planning how to get even."

"What about Susan?" Jethro murmured. "Where is she?"

"Robert doesn't mention Sue," replied the rancher.

Jethro stared out a window. "How can we find out?"

"One could ride there, I suppose."

Jethro slammed the door on his way out. He was saddling the sorrel when the Englishman appeared. "Jack, be reasonable. It must be two hundred miles."

Jethro paused as he hooked the left-side stirrup over the horn. "Did McSween pay you ten thousand dollars for a twenty-five percent interest in your store?"

Tunstall's mouth fell open. At last, he asked, "How could you know that?"

Fog from their breaths hung in the chill January air; each appeared lost in his own thoughts. At last, Tunstall said, "I'm sure there's a plausible explanation for the coincidence. We must give him the benefit of the doubt."

Jethro stared at the toes of Tunstall's boots. "Who was Emil Fritz?"

"I never knew him," Tunstall replied. "But as I understand it, Emil Fritz was the original partner of L.G. Murphy and thus, one of the founders of the store."

"And McSween? How did he get involved in the estate?"

"Alex once did legal work for the store, back when it belonged to Murphy. Murphy himself commissioned Alex to collect a supposedly uncollectible insurance policy of Emil Fritz."

When Jethro said nothing, Tunstall added, "As far as I know, the money has not been collected, but Alex told me several months ago that prospects looked good for a settlement."

Jethro sighed. "Well, as you say, there's a logical explanation. But right now, I'm worried about Susan."

It was three o'clock on the afternoon of December 28, 1877, when a sweat-streaked, mud-encrusted roan plodded into the substantial Pecos Valley community of Las Vegas, New Mexico Territory. The roan was the third horse its rider straddled since leaving the ranch on the Rio Feliz.

As weary as the gelding seemed, its rider was worse. Dust, the thick and constant companion for Pecos Valley travelers, had turned to mud from the melting of the previous night's seldom-seen snow. As a result, the rider's trail-stained, wide-brimmed hat drooped at the brim; his red-plaid wool coat dripped dye-stained crimson droplets. A three-day beard added deeper shadows to the drawn face. Jethro Spring lifted bleary, sunken eyes to stare at adobe false-fronted buildings.

A sign across the street caused him to check the roan. "Must be it," he muttered.

The man dismounted and clung to the saddlehorn while his legs steadied, then fumbled for the buckles to his chaps. He gave up in disgust, stumbled into the courthouse and said, "Jail?" to the first person he met.

A heavy, horse-faced man leaned indolently in a swivel chair, spurred boots gouging deep scratches in a worn desktop that had suffered many such indignities. A tin star glittered from the front of the man's left shirt pocket. He looked inquisitively up at the newcomer's approach.

"McSween and Chisum. Are they here?"

"They are."

"I'd like to see them."

The deputy eyed Jethro. "Why?"

"Friend. Rode from Lincoln. Like to talk to 'em."

The deputy sighed and swung boots to the floor. He reached for a soiled ledger and picked up a pencil. "Name?"

"Winter. Jack Winter."

"All right, Winter. I'll give you five minutes. Leave your gun here."

Jethro fumbled beneath his batwings, then laid the Colt on the desk.

The deputy pulled a set of keys from a drawer. "Any more?"

"No."

"Knives?"

"A couple of little ones."

The deputy laughed. "I should get 'em from you. But you look near 'bout as helpless as I ever seen. So I'll just stand and watch you instead."

Jethro shrugged.

They passed through two locked doors, halting before an open-barred cell.

"Well, I'll be go to hell!" Chisum said, smiling broadly. "McSween, looky here what the cat drug in."

"Jack!" McSween shouted, extending his hand through the bars. "My word, you're the last person I expected."

"What can I do to help?"

Chisum's cackle held its own irony. "Fat chance. If you're as bad off as you look, you couldn't help a sick whore off a piss-pot."

"You might look in on Susan," McSween said. "She's at the Wagoner Hotel, Jack. She's fared badly through this sordid ordeal."

Jethro nodded. "What's this all about, Alex?"

McSween grimaced. "About the price of opposing

Dolan and Riley. It'll be all right. You'll soon see."

Jethro rubbed his red-rimmed eyes.

Chisum sobered. "My problem runs some higher'n that, boy. Mine runs plumb up to the governor and his attorney gen'ral. There's a mighty big ring. And I know we pinched 'em purty tight when we near beat the bastards out on beef and supply contracts."

"Well, what are ..."

"Time's up, boys," the deputy broke in. "You want to finish it, you'll have to do it later."

"C'mon back tomorrow, boy," Chisum said. "Me and Alex'll get together on some telegrams and feed 'em to you."

Back in the muddy street, Jethro gathered up his reins and headed for a livery stable. A half-hour later, he stumbled to the desk at the Wagoner Hotel and asked for Susan McSween's room number.

The clerk sniffed. "I'm afraid that's impossible."

Jethro peered down at his soggy, mud-splattered clothes and felt the stubble on his chin. "Look, I'm a friend."

"I don't care if you're God Almighty, mister. We don't give out room numbers of our guests."

Even though he knew the clerk was only doing his job, Jethro was too weary for formalities. The gray eyes turned to flint.

The clerk swallowed, then swallowed again before the newcomer said, "Tell you what let's do. You take me to the lady's room. You stand there while I knock on the door. You take this ..." Jethro fumbled again for his Colt, reversed it and handed it butt-first to the clerk. "... then when she opens the door, you shoot me if she don't want to see me."

The clerk took the revolver, fumbled for a key and said, "Follow me, Mr. ..."

"Winter."

Susan opened the door at the first knock. She fell back a

step as her hand flew to her mouth. "Jack!" Then she hurtled into his arms.

Jethro held her tightly with one arm, while he reached for his Colt with the other.

Sobbing and laughing, she pulled him into the room. "How ... why ... I don't understand."

Jethro kicked the door closed and threw his saddlebags into a corner. "I came as soon as I heard."

"Oh darling ..." A blush crept to her cheeks, but she hardly paused before going on: "That's perfectly apparent." She began giggling. Then peals of laughter burst out. Between gasps, she pointed and laughed almost uncontrollably. "Your chaps. And—and that hat! My God, it's—it's worse than the first time I saw it! And the mud. Have you bathed in it?"

He laughed too, infected by her hysteria, until both were helpless. Then they fell silent. The hazel eyes sobered, her face seemed to age. Susan gasped, then threw herself sobbing into his arms. Her full lips sought his, her body arching against him. She pulled his head down and pressed her face upward so their teeth grated and their lips were crushed.

"Oh, Jack!" she cried. Twisting away, gasping and sobbing. "Oh, Jack! I'm so glad you came. It's terrible what they're doing to Alex and Mr. Chisum. I prayed. Oh God, please let Jack come and everything will be all right. That's all I ..."

Jethro held her at arm's length. Tears coursed freely, ruining her facial powder. "It's all right, Susan. Everything will be all right." He pulled her gently to him and patted the small of her back until the heaving subsided.

She stirred, pushed back, flushed of face and red of eye. "How could I?" she said, a coquettish smile flashing. "Carrying on like an idiotic schoolgirl. You must think terrible of me."

"Susan, I understand." He'd never seen her look more

helpless and vulnerable.

"You must think terribly of me." Then a fist pressed against her mouth as she leaned back to better see him. "Oh my God, it's you we must think of. You look positively worn." Taking his hand, she led him to an upholstered chair. "Come sit down. I can't make you a cup of coffee, but I can offer you a glass of Alex's whiskey." Then in mock anger, she shook her finger at him. "Don't you know it's impolite to call on a lady while wearing those ugly leather chaps?"

He again fumbled for the buckles.

When she returned from the next room with a tumbler of whiskey, she found the man she knew as Jack Winter, sprawled in the chair, fast asleep. The stubborn chaps still wrapped his legs, but the soggy wool coat lay by his boots. After a bit, her vexed face softened and her expression turned to amusement as she stared down at the slumbering man. Occasionally she sipped from his whiskey. Soon she began to hum.

Jethro's eyes flicked open. He glanced to the window, then turned his face from the bright winter sun to stare puzzled at the ceiling. His hands dangled below the armrests of a large overstuffed chair. One arm tingled—asleep from hours of hanging inactivity—and he rubbed it as his eyes wandered about the room. At sight of the chaps still shrouding his legs, his mouth curled into a laconic grin.

It appeared to be a sitting room in which he'd slept. The room had two doors. One, the door through which he'd entered the previous afternoon, was closed. The other stood ajar.

Jethro pushed stiffly to his feet, moved to the mirror of a huge chest of drawers, and peered curiously at his reflection. He glanced beyond the door at an untidy bed. To all appearances the room was empty. "Hello," he called tentatively.

The floor squeaked as Jethro strode to the window and looked out on Las Vegas' main street. He fumbled behind for the waist buckle to his batwings, then flipped loose the leg snaps and hung the heavy chaps on one of the wooden ladderback chairs. Striding back across the squeaky floor, he rubbed his chin and again stared into the mirror.

The hallway door swung open. "Well, well," Susan said, "The dead hath risen."

Jethro smiled, staring frankly at her loveliness in the mirror. She saw the chaps and said, "Now, that is an improvement, Jack."

"Not much."

"True," she replied. "I must say, if you move no faster than one garment every twelve hours, you'll not be really presentable for at least a week."

"Don't forget the coat. Wherever it is."

"I hung it on a clothestree in the bedroom."

"First thing I should do is get a room. Then buy some new clothes and order up a bath, shave, and generally try to make a rose out of this weed."

She giggled. "There's little use in your rushing out to obtain a room, sir. My reputation is already thoroughly compromised."

His face clouded. "Oh hell. I didn't mean to ..."

"Oh don't be a ninny," she said. "I could care less what tongues may wag here in Las Vegas."

"But I did stay in your room all night."

"Yes, I know. And I dare say no woman ever was compromised with less excitement."

Jethro mumbled, "I'll get my coat."

"You'll do no such thing. I've ordered breakfast. You just have time to wash. You'll find a pitcher of water and a wash basin on the nightstand by my bed."

Jethro closed the bedroom door, unknotted the silk neckerchief, then unbuttoned his shirt and slipped it off. Turning to the nightstand, he poured water and lathered his chest and arms. He'd just plucked a towel from its peg when the bedroom door opened. "Breakfast is here, Jack."

He turned, towel in hand.

She smiled. "I'm sorry. I ..." She came toward him as if entranced. Her fingers traced the ugly scar where a bullet from a pursuing dragoon's carbine ripped through his right shoulder. She moistened her lips with her tongue and stared in fascination, fingers trailing down his arm until they fell from it and brushed the walnut grips of his Colt. Her eyes fell to the gun and she caressed it. Hazel eyes met his, the hand dropped. She spun and left the room.

Mechanically, Jethro toweled himself. Then he donned his soiled shirt and neckerchief and stepped into the adjoining room where he pulled out a chair, avoiding her eyes.

"I trust ham and eggs are suitable, sir," she said with hollow-sounding light-heartedness. "I also ordered biscuits."

"Fine." He helped himself while she poured coffee from a pewter service.

"Additionally, I ordered double portions for you, Jack, assuming you've not eaten properly for days."

For some reason, her nearness seemed precarious to him and he glanced nervously about as he ate ravenously. She sensed his distraction and sought to quell it. "Thank you for coming, Jack."

"It's nothing," he said, continuing to avoid eye contact.

"It is *everything!* No man can understand the feeling of helplessness that overcomes a woman in a situation such as this. Least of all, a man with your strength and vitality."

When he said nothing, she asked, "What can we do?"

His eyes briefly met hers, then returned to his plate. "I don't know. Chisum asked me to come back for some telegrams."

"It's all so unfair."

The sheriff leaned back with his spurred boots atop the desk in a mirror image of his deputy the night before. "You the advance scout for Pitzer?" he asked.

"Say that again?" Jethro said.

"I asked if you're Pitzer's advance scout?"

"Pitzer who?"

The sheriff snorted in Disgust. "Pitzer Chisum, dammit! That's 'Pitzer who'."

Jethro had heard John Chisum had a brother, but they'd never met. However, it was a Chisum horse he'd traded for on his wild dash to Las Vegas and he assumed the sheriff had checked the brand. "And you're asking if I'm a scout for Pitzer Chisum?"

The face above the star scowled. "We hear Pitzer's headed this way with a hundred cowhands to bust his brother out. That right?"

"Sheriff, I wouldn't know. I don't work for Chisum. All I want to do is see him."

"Why you in Las Vegas, then?"

"I'm a friend of Alexander McSween," Jethro patiently replied. "And of Chisum's, too. I'm here because I want to help them. Now, may I see them?"

"Yeah. If Pitzer and his cowhands come thundering in, a whole bunch of 'em will stay permanent. You tell Pitzer that for me."

"By Gawd, Alex," boomed John Chisum when Jethro halted in front of their cell, "he ain't clean, but he looks some better."

"Did you see Susan?" McSween asked.

Jethro nodded. "She's fine, Alex. Just waiting for you."

"Tell her it won't be long. For me, at least. Tell her I

must go immediately back to Lincoln to demand a trial, then an accounting."

"I'll tell her."

"We got telegrams for you, boy." Chisum thrust a sheaf of notes through the bars."

The sheriff reached past Jethro. "Here, I'll take those."

"Hold on, Sheriff ..."

"You want to send telegrams, you hand 'em to me. I'll pass 'em on when I see there's nothing slipping between you."

McSween gestured disgustedly to Chisum and the old cattleman passed the pages to the sheriff, who nodded at Jethro. "Your time is up, Winter."

"Five minutes?" Jethro protested.

"You want to talk some more, tomorrow will do."

As Jethro turned, McSween said softly, "An attorney, Jack. Get us Burton."

Back at his desk, the sheriff shuffled through McSween's and Chisum's notes, clucking to himself like a nosy spinster leafing through a schoolgirl's diary. Jethro waited, anger mounting. Finally the sheriff finished reading and passed the sheaf to Jethro.

"Chisum's tellin' his brother he's gonna set it out until we get tired of feedin' him," the sheriff said. "Must be some kind of code."

Jethro took the notes, then his gun. He sent the telegrams, then stopped at Burton's office. After a short discussion with the barrister, he dropped into a mercantile for new clothes, went to a barbershop for a shave, haircut, and bath, then left his muddy clothing at a Chinese laundry. By mid-afternoon he'd taken a room at the Wagoner from the same clerk who'd been so hostile the day before. This time, butter wouldn't melt in the young man's mouth. "Yes sir, Mr. Winter. Room 211. Only three doors down and across the hall from Mrs. McSween."

At last, Jethro Spring kicked off his moccasin boots and dropped fully clothed on his bed and slept.

A knock awakened him. He glided to the door in his stocking feet and cracked it. Susan smiled through the crack. "The room clerk was kind enough to tell me your room number, Jack. Since I hadn't heard from you I thought I would ..." She trailed off.

He swung the door wider, but filled the opening, sleep still hanging heavily upon him. "You're not inviting me in, I see," she said coyly. "You would compromise a lady in her room, but not invite her into your own. Why is that?"

"I'm sorry. What time is it?"

"It's after six and I'm starved."

"Let me splash a little water on my face and we'll go down to the dining room."

They ate in comfortable silence, each lost in private thoughts. Finally Susan asked, "Aren't you going to tell me of Alex and John."

"Huh—oh yeah," he said a little too quickly. "Your husband said to tell you it won't be much longer. But he said he'll want to return to Lincoln as soon as possible for a trial and an accounting."

She sighed. "I did so wish to visit in the East."

"From the tone of a couple of telegrams I sent for him, Chisum sounds as though he's figuring on calling their bluff. He says the debts are false, that they've been dredged up by his enemies to discredit him. Claims he'll rot in jail before he'll pay a penny he doesn't owe."

Susan's gay laugh startled him, filling the dining room. "That sounds like John. It's the end of December. Fall roundup and shipments are complete. Spring roundup is four months away. His business trip can easily be postponed. I do believe he will sit right where he is and try to embarrass his enemies by the preposterousness of their deeds."

Jethro's hand strayed to his shirt pocket and its notepad.

He wrote P-E-R-P-O-S-T-E-R-U-S-N-E-S-S while asking, "You think he'll do it, then?"

Yes. It sounds like him."

He appeared to study his notepad, then said, "I don't like it."

Susan's eyebrows arched. "Why? It sounds perfectly all right to me if he wants to sit in jail over an unjust charge."

"Yeah, but it leaves him two hundred miles from where the battles may be fought. I'd feel better if Chisum ramrodded his own outfit right now."

Susan considered this. He interrupted her thoughts to ask, "Do you know Pitzer Chisum?"

"I've met him."

"Does he think for himself? Can he take over?"

"I really can't say. John has always been so forceful."

"If it really comes down to it, Susan, do you think we can depend on John Chisum?"

Susan's eyebrows again arched. "You're asking if he can be trusted?"

"No. Can he be depended upon?"

"Alex always thought so."

Jethro laid down his knife and fork and leaned back in his chair. "I know Alex thinks so. I also know John Tunstall thinks so. What I asked, Susan, is do *you* think so?"

Her hands fluttered. "What would a woman know of such matters?"

"Just any woman, perhaps nothing. You are, however, a shrewd observer. You've also been involved right from the beginning. I suspect you are aware of more than most folks'd believe."

"Oh, pshaw. To date I've been merely a silly woman who sometimes lapses into childish displays—such as last night. Were you nearly as embarrassed about my foolishness *then* as I am *now?*"

"To tell the truth, ma'am, I was so tired I didn't have

time to be anything." The thought that she'd avoided the question flitted through his mind.

Susan giggled. "You were so bedraggled." When he only smiled, she sobered and said, "You really shouldn't have come, you know."

"I wanted to."

Her eyes moistened. "I'm glad."

They paused at her room and she handed him the key. He opened the door, stepped back. "Good night, Susan," he said, handing her the key.

"Always the gallant, aren't you, Jack?" She lifted her chin to kiss him on the cheek, whispering, "Eight o'clock."

The winter sun had already burned frost from the windows when Jethro Spring knocked softly and said, "Would you care for breakfast?"

She opened the door in a moment. Her hair was down and natural curls framed the exquisitely oval face. She wore a fine dimity dressing saque that ended at her hips. A blue silk nightgown flowed beneath—daringly, only to her calves. His face darkened, but she smiled and conspiratorially said, "I'm a little late this morning. Please come in while I ..."

"I'll stay here," he interrupted. "No, I'll come back later."

She stamped her bare foot. "Jack Winter! You'll come in here this minute!"

He glanced up and down the hall, then, like a thief in the night, slipped in.

Susan leaned against the closed door, watching as his progress to the window was marked by the creaking floor. "You're so frustrating."

"Why?" he asked, pulling a curtain aside to peer down at the street.

"I laid awake most of the night thinking of you."

"Breakfast," he said. "Breakfast is what we're talking about."

"*You're* talking about breakfast! I'm talking about us."

He focused those hypnotic gray eyes upon her. "And your husband? Let's not leave him out of this."

"Damn you! You didn't ride two hundred miles to talk to me about my husband!"

"I came because I thought I might help."

She stomped across the room, her bare feet slapping unusually loud on the oak floor. "Jack, what in the world is wrong with you? I'm a woman. You're a man. You're like a moth dancing around a candle flame. You won't let yourself go. Why?"

He sensed real danger and a calm washed over him. "You're another man's wife."

She tried to wriggle close, but he gripped her shoulders and held her at arm's length, his grip like iron. "Let me go!" she said through clenched teeth. He shook his head. She began to cry.

Suddenly he scooped her into his arms and strode to the bedroom. Tears turned to a radiant smile and hunger built until she writhed with it. He threw her upon the bed and stared icily down. "Tell me, Susan," he said, biting the words, "where did your husband get the ten thousand dollars he paid John Tunstall for twenty-five percent of the Englishman's store?"

The hungry fire in her hazel eyes dimmed and died, and she averted her face to sob. He wanted desperately to reach out, but instead ordered, "Get dressed. I'll wait."

And the bedroom door slammed as he left.

❧ CHAPTER FOURTEEN ❧

Alexander McSween was released from the Las Vegas jail on January 4, 1878. On a warrant of New Mexico Attorney General Thomas B. Catron, he was bound over to the Third Judicial District Court of New Mexico Territory, Judge Warren H. Bristol presiding. The Third Judicial District was comprised of Lincoln, Dona Ana, and Grant counties, and headquartered in Mesilla. McSween was given leave to return to Lincoln to await scheduling for his Mesilla trial. He returned under custody of two San Miguel County deputies, A.P. Barrier and Antonio Campos.

The party also included Alexander McSween's friend, Jack Winter. Meanwhile, at her own request, Susan McSween continued on her delayed visit to St. Louis.

The five days from Las Vegas to Lincoln was much more leisurely than Jethro's previous forced march to aid his friends. McSween drove the private carriage he and his wife had used on their interrupted journey to the railhead. Both deputies and Jethro rode their own horses. From time to time, one man or another would accompany McSween in the carriage, saddlehorse trailing behind.

At the first opportunity, McSween said, "I, ah, understand you asked about the Fritz estate, Jack."

Jethro nodded. "I asked Mrs. McSween if there was any relationship between the estate money and the money you paid to buy into Tunstall's."

McSween chuckled, eyes only on the road. "A natural mistake. Actually, Jack, I tried several times to dispense that money to the estate heirs, Charles Fritz and Emile Fritz Scholand. For a variety of reason, the exchange was never consummated. Then, some two months ago, those greedy Dolan and Company curs filed a claim against the money. They said Emil Fritz owed it to the original L.G. Murphy Company. Naturally, I refused to turn it over. Dolan took advantage of my absence to convince Mrs. Scholand—who lives in Las Cruces—that I embezzled it."

Jethro considered the lawyer's explanation. "Why don't you just give the money to the heirs and be shut of the affair."

"And have Dolan and Riley get their hands on it?"

"Seems to me like the Fritz people caused a lot of your trouble, especially this Emile Scholand. Serve 'em right, seems to me, if they lost the money."

McSween's laugh boomed. "I agree, Jack. I agree. But I don't agree that the Dolan Company should benefit thereby."

Hours later, Jethro recalled Alex McSween had not told where he'd obtained the ten thousand dollars paid to Tunstall. Nor, if he agreed the Fritz heirs deserved to lose their money, who he thought they should lose it to.

Jethro Spring returned to the Feliz to find John Tunstall agitated. "Here, Jack, read this." Tunstall thrust a copy of the January 3, 1878 *Santa Fe New Mexican* in his hands. An article reporting Governor Samuel Axtell's message to the territorial Legislature was marked with an "X." A paragraph dealing with delinquent county taxes was circled and a sub-paragraph underlined:

> … the present sheriff of Lincoln County has paid nothing during his present term of office.

Jethro handed the paper back to Tunstall. "Interesting. What does it mean?"

"Mean?" Tunstall thundered. "It means Brady collected over twenty-five hundred dollars and forwarded none of it to Santa Fe."

Jethro yawned. "What did he do with it?"

"Hmph," Tunstall said, miffed. "Obviously he pocketed it. Or else he turned it over to Dolan and Riley. But no one except people around Lincoln know how blatantly dishonest these people really are. Jack, this matter of the tax money has the entire territory's attention. If we could only prove our county officials connived to divert public funds to their own use—can't you see? That then makes a mockery of their claim of embezzlement against Alex."

"Does two wrongs make a right, John?" Jethro asked. "What if McSween is guilty?"

"Preposterous, Jack. You must know that's simply not true."

Jethro gazed at a distant ridgeline without comment.

"Enough," Tunstall said. "Let's hear about your trip."

When he'd finished telling his story, Jethro asked, "Any excitement going on around here?"

Tunstall busied himself with his fingernails; Middleton dug out his Bull Durham pouch and rolled a cigarette. In the silence, Jethro glanced at the open, almost questioning stare of Billy Bonney, then at Brewer, who waited, coffee pot in hand.

"Billy had it out with Burns, that clerk at Dolan's," Brewer said.

Tunstall said, "It was quite right, Jack. Billy and Burns merely met in the street by accident. Words were exchanged. When they rolled Burns over, he still had his gun in his hand. It was ruled self-defense."

There was a mocking smile behind the Kid's blue eyes.

Tunstall mailed a letter to the *Mesilla Independent.* The letter was published January 26, 1878. It accused Lincoln County Sheriff William Brady of gross malfeasance and tied missing funds to canceled check affidavits in the J.J. Dolan Company.

During the same period Tunstall's explosive letter was published, Alexander McSween, accompanied by his guard, Las Vegas Deputy A.P. Barrier, and a large group of supporters and well-wishers, traveled to Mesilla from Lincoln. The actual trial results were inconclusive despite obvious badgering of McSween and his witnesses by District Attorney Rynerson and hostility from District Judge Bristol. Twice, Judge Bristol ordered the courtroom cleared because of vocal partisanship by McSween supporters. Finally Judge Bristol agreed to a continuance until the early April meeting of the grand jury at Lincoln.

Bail for McSween was set at eight thousand dollars and Deputy Barrier was ordered to take McSween back to Lincoln.

Accompanied by John Tunstall and Judge John B. Wilson, McSween began his return trip to Lincoln February 5. Nightfall caught their carriage near San Augustin Pass, on the east side of the Organ Mountains. As customary for travelers, the party camped at the Shedd Ranch, near a small spring.

With horses tended and supper cooking, the four lounged near the carriage tailgate. Tunstall cocked his head at a sound in the night.

"Howdy," Jesse Evans said as he stepped into the fire's feeble light. Frank Baker and John Long followed. Tunstall glanced at McSween and Judge Wilson. Barrier, his badge flickering in the firelight, took a step forward.

"Howdy yourself," he said. "What can we do for you fellows?"

Evans' eyes glinted as they swept the group. "Well, well, now this is some little party, ain't it?"

Barrier was puzzled. Though he didn't understand the undercurrent in the exchange, he was steadfast. "Is this a friendly visit, mister, or are you out hunting for something?"

Evans' attention flicked to the deputy, then to the his badge. "Do I know you?" he asked.

"A lot of questions flyin' around," Barrier observed, "but damned few answers. Tell you what you do, mister," he said, "you state your reason for being in this camp, or get the hell out."

Evans continued to stare at Barrier, taking the man's measure. Finally he said, "Just wonderin' if you boys passed Jimmy Dolan on the road. We heard he was gonna spend the night here."

Barrier shook his head. "We didn't pass nobody."

Tunstall said, "We have it on good authority that Mr. Dolan is planning to leave Mesilla in the morning."

Baker guffawed. "We got it different, English. And Jimmy always showed prompt when he was s'posed to." Evans, Baker, and Long melted into the darkness.

Barrier said, "What was that all about?"

"Outlaws, Sheriff," McSween replied. "Jesse Evans, Frank Baker, and a man named Long. Evans and Baker are horse thieves. Judge Wilson issued the warrants for their arrest. They escaped—were 'released' is more accurate—from our noble sheriff. We three, I'm afraid, have the dubious honor of being targeted for revenge by the gang."

Barrier nodded. "I remember reading about that bunch and their escape. Jail doors unlocked, wasn't it?"

"And the guard miles away," added Tunstall.

"Can we hitch up the horses and beat it out of here?" Judge Wilson asked.

Barrier shook his head just as McSween said, "The horses are tired. Even if we could get away, they'd catch us before we hit the white sands."

"Perhaps back across the pass?"

"No! By the Gods, I'm not going!"

The others turned as Tunstall smacked a fist into an open palm. "Why should we bloody run? We've done nothing wrong! Are we like sheep to be stampeded by blood-sucking coyotes? I'm not moving one step until I'm ready. Show fear before these blighters and they'll be nipping at our heels."

"Mr. Tunstall's right," Barrier said. "Maybe for the wrong reasons, but he's right. Our horses need the rest—it's too far to the next stop from here."

"But John, if Evans is right and Dolan shows up," McSween asked, "what then?"

"What of it?"

"After your letter to the newspapers, he's not just after me, you know."

The judge stared into the night and shivered. "This must be the loneliest place on the face of the earth."

Dolan's party arrived at Shedd's in the middle of the night and went into camp some distance from McSween's. The sun's first rays kissed the carriage as Barrier and Tunstall busied themselves hitching horses. McSween murmured a warning just as Dolan and Evans stepped from a corral, thirty-five yards away. Dolan carried a rifle pointed at Tunstall.

"Are you ready to fight, you slimy English bastard?"

Tunstall looked blank. "Do you wish me to fight a duel?"

"Goddamn you, you cowardly sonofabitch, I want to settle up with you once and for all!"

Barrier moved quickly between the two. Just then a voice floated in from the surrounding creosote brush:

"Dolan! This is Jack Winter. You make one more move with that rifle and you're dead."

"Evans!" came a different voice from another point in the scattered brush. "This is Bonney. 'Member me? I don't miss with a Winchester, if you recollect!"

McSween audibly expelled the breath he'd been holding and Wilson muttered, "Thank the blessed Lord for all favors."

"You two just stand firm while that wagon is hitched!" Jethro's voice had an unmistakable ring of authority to it and Dolan and Evans obeyed. "John, get to it, double-time!"

Tunstall and Barrier swung to the horses and McSween and Wilson threw their remaining gear in the carriage. Jethro's voice floated in once more:

"Anybody at the house who wants a hand in this had best think again. We got seven rifles out here."

McSween whipped his team to a fast trot. Dolan and Evans waited for five minutes after the carriage disappeared. Finally Evans cried:

"Winter! Bonney! We're moving now."

There was no answer.

⇒ CHAPTER FIFTEEN ⇐

John Tunstall rode into his ranch four days later. Jethro Spring sat in the bunkhouse drinking coffee with a newcomer. The Englishman strode directly to the table where he held out a hand and said, "I'm John Tunstall. You must be our cook."

The man nodded, taking the outstretched hand. "Yessir, Mr. Tunstall. I'm Gauss. Brewer hired me."

Without looking at Jethro, the Englishman said, "Winter, you get around."

Jethro stared into his coffee. "Have a good trip?"

A smile cracked Tunstall's face. "I don't suppose there's a chance in the world for me to find out how you happened to be at the Shedd Ranch on the evening of February 5?"

Jethro ignored him.

"Or how long you've been gone from the ranch? If you and Billy were in Mesilla throughout the trial? Where you were while our carriage labored up through the White Mountains and down to the Ruidoso?"

"Which question do you want answered first?"

Tunstall chuckled. "I must confess I've never heard a sweeter voice than yours at that outlaw haven. Thank you, Jack."

Jethro waved a dismissive hand.

"There is one thing I'd dearly love to know, however—who were the other five men?"

Again, Jethro waved a hand.

The news Bob Widenmann brought three days later was disastrous. "John, they've attached the store."

"What? What are you talking about?"

"Brady. He's got a warrant of attachment from Mesilla. The warrant says for him to attach enough of McSween's property to guarantee payment in his court case."

"But that case has been continued! There hasn't been a decision rendered. Alex hasn't been found guilty, for heaven's sake."

Widenmann nodded, his face drawn. "That's what I told 'em, too. I also told 'em the store wasn't McSween's."

"How could they ..."

"Brady just said they know the store is McSween's, too. They took my keys, John."

"But you're a United States marshal."

"They're working on a New Mexico warrant, John. I can't do a thing."

Tunstall shuffled to the window, wringing his hands. After a moment he returned. "There are surely laws governing this kind of conduct. We shall start for Lincoln in the morning."

The following afternoon, four somber riders reined to a halt in front of Tunstall's store. The Englishman and Widenmann dismounted and strode inside. Billy glanced at Jethro. "I ain't all that much in favor of this deal, Jack. The cards are stacked."

Antanasio Salazar's chair lay overturned on the porch, empty for the first time since Jethro first saw it. He stared toward the house with the white picket fence, knowing Susan was still in the East. Everything is empty, he thought.

Bonney reached down, pulled his Winchester from its scabbard and laid it across his saddle, blue eyes scanning the street. The two could hear an argument raging within the store:

"What right do you men have, may I ask, to take property of mine for a McSween debt?"

There was some garbled conversation, then Tunstall's voice rang loud and clear. "Let one thing be perfectly clear, gentlemen—all who are involved in this damned high-handed business will be made to suffer. That much I assure you."

"Careful, John," Jethro murmured.

"Look, Tunstall," came a voice, "you think you're getting a raw deal, you can take it to court, you know."

"I've just recently had occasion to see how much justice one can presume in a district court presided over by Judge Bristol and argued by Colonel Rynerson."

"Well," the other voice said, "if you can't get justice in the district court, you can try the United States Court."

"Ye gods, man, you can't get justice there, either. It's the worst outfit of all and is completely in the hands of that damned Santa Fe ring."

The voices moved to the store's rear and Jethro could no longer hear individual words. Soon, Tunstall and Widenmann came out. Tunstall, still hot with anger, paused before Jethro. "They've even impounded my horses in the corral."

The Englishman stomped along the dusty street to see Brady. The other three followed wordlessly, Widenmann leading the rancher's horse. Their employer plunged into the building and a muffled but heated exchange between Tunstall and Sheriff William Brady ensued. Tunstall emerged a few minutes later, handing Bonney a slip of paper.

"Billy, this is a note from Brady exempting my horses from the writ of attachment. Please take the note to Mr. Longwell, up at the store, then take the horses back to the ranch."

Bonney took the paper as Tunstall bit his lip. "I suppose you'll need some help." The Englishman looked at Widenmann and the man he knew as Jack Winter, then shook his head.

Widenmann said, "McCloskey's up at the store. Want me to see if he'll help?"

Tunstall sighed and nodded. Bonney and Widenmann turned toward the store and Jethro made to go with them.

"A moment please, Jack."

Tunstall glanced at the nearby jail and said, "Let's walk across the street." On their way, the Englishman leaned conspiratorially close. "I'm afraid they have things their own way, Jack. Yet not entirely. Apparently, Alex is not incarcerated, as yet. Brady says Barrier will not release him to Lincoln County jurisdiction, despite the court's instructions. It seems Barrier fears for Alex's life, so he has him confined in the McSween home. Bless him. Brady is wild with rage. Alex is trying to raise bond. Jack, we must stay here to assist the poor man."

Jethro nodded, then asked, "What if they move against your ranch?"

"Move against my ranch? How do you mean?"

"Impound it. Or your cattle."

"None of that belongs to Alex."

"They seem to be doing a lot of things not exactly legal, John."

Tunstall considered that for a moment, then said, "All right. I shall send Widenmann back, too. As a U.S. marshall, surely he'll be able to forestall such an attempt."

Jethro muttered, "If anyone takes Bob seriously."

Two hours later, Widenmann, Bonney, and McCloskey drove eight Tunstall horses out of Lincoln. John Tunstall and Jethro Spring called at the McSween home shortly thereafter. A.P. Barrier opened the door. The San Miguel deputy smiled and shook hands with Tunstall. "A pleasure to see you again, John. Wish it was under better circumstances."

"Me, too, Adolph. Meet our savior: Jack Winter."

The deputy held out his hand. "We already met, on the way down from Las Vegas—although I wondered if you was the same young fellow these two bragged up. You are."

Jethro took the firm hand. "Mr. Barrier, moving in front of Dolan's rifle was a brave thing."

The deputy dismissed the compliment with a wave.

"And it's a brave thing keeping Alex in your custody," Tunstall said, turning the conversation to a present note.

"Some folks down here in your county have strange notions of justice, Mr. Tunstall," Barrier said, his lined face becoming grave. "Now I ain't a-saying who's right or wrong in this matter, but if I turned McSween over, I wouldn't take a dollar against a dog turd he'd live to see a sunrise."

"Where is he?"

"Back in the kitchen, talkin' to a man. Go right on back. I know he'll want to see you."

A wan McSween looked up from the table, his pasted smile askew. He made no attempt to rise. "It's good to see you again, John. I'm terribly sorry about the store. I had no idea." McSween appeared to have aged years in the last few weeks.

Jethro moved to lean unobtrusively against the far wall.

"John, do you know Dr. Blazer?" McSween gestured at

the other seated man whose shirt buttons appeared ready to pop from a too-tight vest.

"Yes, of course. Dr. Blazer and I met once. At the Fourth of July picnic, I believe."

Blazer nodded, jowls flapping. They shook hands.

McSween pointed to Jethro. "Jack Winter—you may have heard of him. Oddly, he is the only man among us who has the respect of Dolan and Company."

Blazer extended his hand. "Yes, I believe I've heard of you, young man."

An awkward silence filled the room until McSween said tiredly, "The good doctor, whom I've asked to help on my bond, has some disturbing news. It might interest you, John."

"Yes?"

"It would seem 'The Ring' is turning the thumbscrews. Did you know Rynerson is here in Lincoln?"

"The district attorney?" Tunstall asked.

"I presume he came in with Dolan yesterday.

"Why?"

"We can only suppose ..." Then McSween said, "Well, never mind. Apparently they—Dolan and Riley, and perhaps Rynerson—have already threatened Dr. Blazer."

"Threatened him? Do you mean if he goes your bond, they've promised him bodily harm?" Tunstall asked.

Blazer shook his head. "Colonel Rynerson told me they were thinking of indicting me on an old charge of cutting sawtimber on federal land."

"But that's blackmail!"

"Dr. Blazer is not the only one either, John," McSween said in a monotone. "Hindman and Peppin both told Jose Montana his business would be ruined if he went bond."

Tunstall pulled out a chair and sat abruptly. "This is unbelievable! And the United States district attorney is directly involved?"

"We must have pinched them harder than we thought, John."

The Englishman clinched his teeth. "Put me down for twenty thousand, Alex. I'll go that much on your bond. We'll show them, what?" Tunstall then turned to Blazer. "Surely you'll not let them frighten you, Doctor. Surely you'll make a bond portion, won't you?"

Dr. Joseph Blazer, one-time military dentist, hung his head.

———•+•———

Jethro Spring laid his saddlebags on the floor of the Wortley Hotel dining room and pulled out a chair across from Dolan and a tall, trim, muttonchopped man in a black clay worsted suit. "Howdy, gents. You don't mind if I sit here, do you?"

The effrontery caught everyone in the dining room by surprise. All babble died. Amid the silence, Jethro leaned to extend his hand across the table. "I'm Jack Winter. You must be Colonel Rynerson? Pleased to make your acquaintance."

Surprised, Rynerson took Jethro's hand.

Dolan choked, jumped up and shouted, "Damn you, Winter. I've had all your goddamned brass I'll take!"

Jethro took his chair, ignored Dolan and turned to Brady. "Please pass the spuds, will you, Sheriff?"

Dolan jerked at a gun beneath his coat. Rynerson gripped his wrist, face flushing. "Jimmy, what's gotten into you?"

Lanky John Riley handed Jethro a plate of sliced beef, an amused smile on his face. Dolan subsided into an angry silence.

Rynerson studied the newcomer through piercing black eyes. "Tell me about yourself, Mr. Winter. Are you a local rancher?"

"Nope. I work for one, though."

"Who, might I ask?"

"The Englishman. Tunstall."

"I see. And what is it you do for Mr. Tunstall?"

"Set posts, replace rails, drive nails, shoe horses, fetch water, clean saddles, oil leather, check cows, split wood, fork broncs, make shakes, patch roofs, pitch hay, tote oats, salt stock, carry ..."

"I think I get the picture," Rynerson cut in dryly. "Have you worked for Tunstall long?"

"Six months, give or take."

"As a matter of fact," Riley said, "we offered Mr. Winter a position when he first appeared in Lincoln. As it turned out, so did McSween and so did John Chisum. The lad was in demand."

"I'm curious, Mr. Winter," Rynerson said, "why did you choose Mr. Tunstall over the others? Did he pay that much more?"

"No. I like him and admire him. But more important, he didn't hire me because I pack a gun where other men could see it."

"Oh? Can you use a gun?" Rynerson asked.

"Tolerable."

The Tunstall cowhand's audacity amused the politician. He leaned back in his chair. "What, precisely, does 'tolerable' mean, Mr. Winter?"

Jethro grinned and helped himself to a slice of pie. "It means I can snip off a horsefly's wings at fifty yards, and him in full flight."

"My, my, that's impressive," Rynerson said. "Let me ask you—do you intend to use that gun, Mr. Winter?"

"Right now?" Jethro asked in wide-eyed innocence. "Here?"

"Anywhere. Any time."

Jethro studied Rynerson. Then his gaze shifted to Dolan

and swung to Riley, then Brady—an implied statement. The gray eyes came back to rest on the District Attorney. "The pie is good, isn't it, Mr. Rynerson? Must be tinned peaches, huh?"

Rynerson slid back his chair. "You have the kind of nerve I admire, young man. But unfortunately, it's misplaced. I feel compelled to tell you your little stage performance is in support of a losing cause."

"Short run, or long run, Colonel?"

"There isn't but one 'run', Mr. Winter. And that's for the benefit of the people of New Mexico Territory."

"For all the people in the territory? Or just for a few people, Colonel?"

Annoyance flushed the District Attorney's face. "I refuse to be baited, Mr. Winter. Therefore I shall leave. But before I do, a word of advice? Put more faith in the law than in the speed of your trigger finger."

Rynerson smiled down as Jethro pondered. At last, the younger man said, "Two things form my creed, sir. Survival is one and justice the other. Law without justice is of little value to me."

It was Rynerson's turn to consider. "A point, Mr. Winter," he conceded. "Now, where do you place survival in relation to justice? Is it more important?"

"I don't know, Colonel. I've never been faced with an either/or choice. Survival might someday be my own choice, alone. Justice, on the other hand, can't be a lonesome thing. Others have a hand in that. It's got to be out there for everyone, this I know—Mexicans, gringos, cowboys, and judges." His gray eyes were penetrating. "Where do you stand on that one?"

Rynerson chuckled. "Who can be against God and motherhood? Right now, though, I stand for a belt of good whiskey. Lacking that, I will stand for a big belt of bad whiskey. What do you say, John and Jimmy? Shall we ask this young gentleman to join us?"

Dolan angrily tossed off the suggestion, but Riley said, "It's up to you, Colonel. If you find him amusing."

Rynerson raised an eyebrow at Jethro, but the dark man shook his head. "Not me, boys. Tomorrow, I've got a tough day ahead of me. I need my rest."

Rynerson, Dolan, and Riley moved to the single table in Wortley's dim bar. "Tell me about the young chap back there—this Jack Winter."

"He's the one who threw down on me at Shedd's."

"Oh, I know that, Jimmy," snapped the District Attorney. "I also know I told you that was fool's play in the first place. Where did he come from? What's he doing here?"

"Nobody knows," Riley said. "All of a sudden, he was here."

"He seems confident, perhaps capable."

Riley nodded. "He's the one who got Freeman."

"He's just a drifter," Dolan said. "Nothing to worry about. It's McSween and Tunstall we want. Then Chisum. Don't lose sight of the real problem and chase after a nobody."

"You may be right, Jimmy, Rynerson mused. "On the other hand, perhaps we shouldn't underestimate that young man."

CHAPTER SIXTEEN

The day following Jethro Spring's exchange with District Attorney William Rynerson, Alexander McSween presented a bond of thirty-five thousand dollars in the form of sureties with the following names attached: John Tunstall, $20,000; James West, $4,000; John Copeland, $3,000; Isaac Ellis, $4,000; Refugio Valencia, $2,500; and Jose Montano, $1,500. Rynerson promptly rejected it on the pretext the sureties were not worth what the bond indicated.

"You're joking," McSween said. "Judge Bristol set bail at eight thousand. There's far more than enough value here to cover that!"

"Sorry, McSween," Rynerson replied. "That's my decision. You don't like it, you can appeal."

"I find it odd you chose this moment to make one of your rare appearances in Lincoln, Colonel. Was it solely to reject my bond?"

On Wednesday, February 13, Robert Widenmann galloped into Lincoln with the news that a sheriff's posse attempted to attach Tunstall's cattle:

"Billy Matthews and six others showed up along towards sundown. We seen their dust and scattered out to wait. Dick hollered for them to hold up fifty yards from the house. Then he told Matthews to come on in alone and state his business.

"It was a war party, sure enough. George Hindman, Johnny Hurley, Buckshot Roberts, Manuel Segovia, Jesse Evans, Frank Baker, and Tom Hill—all loaded for bear."

But that's impossible," Tunstall exclaimed. "Evans, Baker, and Hill have outstanding warrants against them. You carry copies. How could they be deputized members of a sheriff's posse?"

"All I'm telling you is who was there, John," Widenmann said. "Matthews, he came in and told Dick he was coming to attach your cows in the McSween case. Dick, God bless him, told Matthews he could look the cattle over; if he found any McSween cows and he could prove they weren't yours, he could take them. Otherwise the cows would stay on the ranch. He said they could leave a man to watch things 'til the courts settled it all."

Jethro Spring leaned against a kitchen wall. Tunstall, McSween, and Barrier sat at McSween's table, stricken by Widenmann's tale.

"Well, Matthews said he'd think on it. Then Dick said it was near supper and why didn't they shove their legs under our table. I was against it from the start and I told Dick so. But he said things were too close to blowing loose and he figured maybe eating together would soothe things down. As soon as they got in, I told Matthews I had some warrants for Evans, Baker, and Hill."

Jethro's eyes flicked to Tunstall and his mouth pinched.

"Things came close to popping then," Widenmann said.

"Hell, we was outnumbered with seven of them and six of us, counting a worthless cook and McCloskey, whose side we don't know he's on.

"Well, Matthews finally said he'd have to go back for an okay from Brady and they rode away. I'll tell you it was close, though."

Widenmann waved at Jethro. "Boy, Winter, we missed you. If you'd been there, we'd have cut 'em down."

Jethro stared blankly at Widenmann while Tunstall's head sagged into his hands. "What are we to do?" the Englishman asked.

It was later that afternoon when the dejected party learned more about what to expect when McSween answered a timid knock at the kitchen door.

McSween opened the door to a towering black man. "This is George Washington, gentlemen. He's an ex-cavalry trooper and he keeps his ears open." McSween glanced up at Washington. "Do you know all these people, George?"

"Him I know," Washington said, pointing at Tunstall. "And him," pointing at Widenmann. "But the others I ain't knowin'."

That's Deputy Sheriff Barrier, in whose custody I find myself. And the man leaning against the wall is Jack Winter, an employee of ..."

The black man ignored Barrier to smile broadly and hold out his hand to Jethro. "So you are the one what done in Freeman!" White teeth flashed amid a toothy smile. "Well, suh, you are worth knowin' and I'm fair proud to be in the same room with you."

Jethro took the ham-hock hand, murmuring "Pleased to meet you," up at the towering ex-soldier.

"What kind of news do you have, George?" McSween prompted.

"They say they gonna settle up with you and Mr. Tunstall, suh. They say they got fo'ty-three men ready to ride on Mr. Tunstall's place. They say they can't lose 'cause they got the district attorney and the judge and even the whole Santy Fe gov'ment behind them, suh. It doan look too good fo' you, and I says to myself, George, you better go down there an' tell Mr. McSween."

A death-bed silence stole over the room. Like a sleep-walker, McSween pulled out a few bills. He pressed two in the black hand, then led Washington to the door.

When McSween returned, Jethro was speaking earnestly to Deputy Barrier. "I know he's in your custody and I know you can't take sides. But I'm telling you the only way for these people to survive is to cut and run. You've got to take McSween to a safer place; the rest of us will take for the hills."

"But the law!" Widenmann interrupted.

"Is on the side of Dolan and Riley for now," snapped Jethro. "Dammit, I'm talking survival!"

"What of our people at the ranch?" Tunstall asked.

"I'll carry the word to them to clear out." Jethro saw their hesitation. "I'm not talking about running away. I'm talking about staying alive to fight another day."

"And the cattle?"

"John, you may lose your cattle and your life."

An awkward silence descended. At last, the Englishman said, "I've been taught to believe in justice, and that laws achieve that end. Now, however, I'm beginning to believe something else. Perhaps we must fight fire with fire."

"Yes!" Widenmann exclaimed.

"No, John," McSween said. "Our methods have been legitimate. Our only hope is to continue that."

"How much longer must we endure this, Alex?" Tunstall asked. "I see no redress except from the barrel of a gun."

"Hear, hear!" shouted Widenmann.

"How do you off-set forty guns?" Jethro murmured.

Widenmann answered, "Patron, Salazar, all the Mexicans; the farmers and ranchers along the Ruidoso; all the little people. There's enough. Chisum, too. He's got fifty, sixty men, at least."

Jethro slammed the wall with his fist. "If you got all the Mexicans and Anglos in Lincoln County who've been ground under Dolan-Riley's heel—all the folks along the Ruidoso—you might come close to pulling it off. But what if half of them decide they'll sit this one out? The rest wouldn't stand a chance and that's a damned good reason for them not to go either. Right now, if we got into a shooting war, we're certain to lose because they've got the law behind them, clear up through the territorial government."

"You never struck me as a coward," Widenmann muttered.

After darkness fell, Jethro left McSween's home. He passed the jail, passed Brady's house, passed the home of Isaac Ellis. At last, he turned toward a small adobe bungalow where he started to rap on the door.

"*Buenas noches*, Senor Jock," came a greeting from Jethro's rear. "You do not have the eyes of a cat. Do you have ears to hear all that is being said?"

"This I do not know, Antanasio," Jethro said without turning. "Perhaps that is why I came to see my friend."

"Alas, even Antanasio Salazar is blind and without ears, now that he can no longer sit in the sun below the roof of Senor Tunstall's store."

Jethro pivoted. The gnome squatted beneath a spreading lilac. "I doubt that my friend. Antanasio Salazar is much too important to be cast into darkness merely by the loss of his throne."

The old man chuckled. "Did you hear Senor Dolan's horse leave our humble village an hour ago?"

"No."

"It is said Senor Dolan goes to the Rio Penasco to join

men from his ranch and to obtain others from the bandidos of Seven Rivers. It is said he will take personal command of this great army when it goes into battle, which, it is said, will be soon."

Jethro sighed. "Where do your people stand, Antanasio?"

"We will fight, of course. But only if we have a chance for victory. Senor Jock, such is not the case now."

"I fear you are right, my friend."

"And your people? What do they do in this time of great trouble?"

"They want to fight, but they do not know how and they do not have the strength," Jethro said. "If your people do not fight, the people of the Rio Ruidoso would be fools to try."

"Unless Senor Chisum would join in such a fight."

"Do you think that possible, Antanasio?"

"No, Senor Jock. Such a thing would not be like the grandee of the great ranchero."

"And your people will not join at this time?"

"Please, Senor Jock," the old man said. "Without the law, it would be foolish."

Jethro nodded. "Thanks, Antanasio. I'll see if I can stop a disaster in the making."

Tunstall and McSween were in animated discussion, while Barrier and Widenmann watched. Jethro waited for a lull, then said, "Salazar said his people will not fight."

"What's that?" McSween asked. "Who said that?"

"Antanasio Salazar. I just came from a talk with him. He says the Mexicans will not fight at this time."

"What the hell does he know?" Widenmann burst out.

Jethro ignored him. "He said the law is stacked against us right now. The law and Dolan-Riley firepower. He says they'll fight when they have a chance to win, but that time isn't now."

"Bullshit!" Widenmann said. "Where does he think he can speak for the rest of the Mexes? They'll fight. I know they will. We'll all fight."

Jethro sighed. "Bob, you're beginning to get on my nerves.

"Just a minute," McSween broke in. "The point Bob raised is a valid one. Did you say Antanasio Salazar? Is he the old man who sits on the porch of our store every day?"

Jethro's eyebrows raised at McSween's use of "our store," but he only nodded.

"Are you implying that he is a spokesman for the Mexican element?"

"No. I'm telling you he's the one they're most likely to listen to."

"Why that's preposterous. Patron is their leader."

Jethro shrugged.

Tunstall said, "Jack may be right."

"About that old man being their leader?" McSween cried. "Think, John. Juan Patron is young and courageous. He's already carrying bullet holes from Riley. He's a school-master and a clerk of the County Court."

"And at the present time he's at the territorial Legislature in Santa Fe," Tunstall said.

"Even if Patron was here, I'd still believe Salazar," Jethro said.

"I would agree," Tunstall added.

McSween capitulated. "Well, John, if you and Jack both believe this fellow, that just about precludes confrontation from being an option, doesn't it?"

Tunstall looked at Jethro. "And you don't think the Ruidoso people will come in?"

Jethro shook his head. "Not without the Mexicans. It'd be suicide for them to try."

"Perhaps this is all a bluff," Tunstall mused. "What if they are merely trying to frighten us into quitting?"

"Dolan left town an hour and a half ago," Jethro said, "riding for the Pajarito Spring cut-off. Antanasio said word is out he plans to take charge."

Tunstall shook his head, as if to clear it. He mused, "That only leaves Chisum, doesn't it?"

"I'd say that's right, John ... if you're determined to fight. But with John Chisum still in jail up in Las Vegas there's even less chance of help from that quarter. Pitzer? You tell me."

"I hate to just turn my ranch over to the blighters...." Tunstall's voice trailed off.

Jethro took a deep breath, then said, "If fight it's going to be, then we can't waste another minute. You and I must see if Chisum will help. I'd go alone, but they'll never listen to me. You could go alone, but your life isn't worth much to some folks who might be riding the same road."

Tunstall nodded. "All right. What else?"

"I want Widenmann to ride back to tell Dick what is happening. But tell him not to try to hold the ranch if the posse gets there before we do."

Tunstall nodded. "Yes, yes. That's right. When should we leave?"

"Right away. I'll get my horse."

"What about me?" McSween asked. "What can I do?"

"Well," Jethro said after thinking a moment, "if all your personal devils are on the Feliz, you should be safe here with Barrier. Maybe you ought to stick with what you do best, Alex: figure out from your books how we can get some justice from the legal system."

"He ain't here," Jim Highsaw said. "Pitzer's up at Bosque Grande and won't be back 'til next week."

Tunstall sighed. "That bloody well cuts it, doesn't it, Jack?"

The Jinglebob foreman was a man Jethro took to instantly. Tanned by wind and burned by sun, the whip-lean Highsaw was a stern, no-nonsense foreman with a passion for just one thing in life: the ranch for which he was responsible. His fearlessness, along with his relentless hatred for rustlers and thieves, were legendary throughout southeastern New Mexico.

"Go ahead and tell Mr. Highsaw why we came," Jethro said to his employer.

Highsaw listened intently to Tunstall's tale. At its conclusion, the foreman shook his head and said, "I'd turn out every man on the place to help you in a minute, Mr. Tunstall. But I don't know as John would, and I sure can't tell you what Pitzer would do. You can ride on up and check with him, though."

Tunstall raised an eyebrow at his companion. Jethro murmured, "There's no time."

"We don't know how long it will take Dolan to round up his crew for an attack," Tunstall said.

"It's forty miles up to Bosque Grande, John. Then seventy-five or eighty back to the Feliz. That's two days of damned hard flogging, and we're wore out already."

"You go on to the Feliz. Tell Dick and the boys there's still hope. I'll ride up and beg Pitzer."

"No, John," Jethro said. "The Feliz is where some hard decisions will have to be made. That's where you should be. I'll go talk to Chisum." He returned to Highsaw. "Can you get us fresh horses?"

The Jinglebob foreman nodded. "Sure. I can do better than that. I can send a note with you telling Pitzer I'm gathering the crew here in case he tells us to move."

"One other thing. Can you send a couple of good hands to be sure John makes it to his ranch?"

"Yep. But I got to tell 'em to come on back after he gets there—unless I hear otherwise from Pitzer, that is."

"Fair enough."

The two switched their saddles to fresh horses. Jethro said, "I don't hold out a lot of hope for the go-ahead, John."

"I know," Tunstall murmured. "But that bloody Scot, Robert Bruce, tried and tried again. Can we do less?"

"I'll be back by tomorrow night. Dolan might get there first. If he does, promise me you and the boys will get out ahead of 'em, and not try to fight."

Tunstall nodded after only a brief hesitation. "You're right, Jack. Anything else at this point would be foolhardy."

A gusting wind blew dust devils about the buildings on the evening of Sunday, February 17, as Tunstall and two Chisum men arrived at the ranch on the Rio Feliz. The bunkhouse and barn stood war-ready, with portholes cut in adobe walls and sandbags stacked against doors.

Brewer eyed the two Jinglebob cowhands with a gleam of hope. But when Tunstall told him the men were to return the following morning, that gleam died.

"Don't give up yet, Dick," Tunstall said. "Jack is at Bosque Grande to see Pitzer. There's still a chance."

Brewer shook his head. "They're over at the Paul Ranch on the Penasco—at least thirty, maybe forty of 'em. I figure they'll come tomorrow."

Bonney lounged against a nearby corral rail, chewing absently on a blade of dry grass. Widenmann stood just to one side.

"What do you think, Dick?" Tunstall asked.

"Well, John, me and the boys been talking. We think we'd like to give a try at holding the place."

"I tried to talk them out of it, John," Widenmann broke

in. "Hell, they got an *army* over there."

Tunstall glared at the U.S. marshal, then turned again to Brewer. "How long could we last?"

Brewer shrugged. "A while. I know that. Maybe a week. Who knows?"

"But eventually, any success would be contingent on receiving help?"

Brewer nodded. "But we don't think the whole damned country would let us down, John."

Tunstall distanced himself from the other men, for several minutes, standing hands in pockets, at the corral's far end. At last, he returned. "We're pulling out tomorrow at daylight. We'll wait in Lincoln."

In the bunkhouse, Tunstall told Gauss to stay on the ranch. To the new man, McCloskey, he said, "Bill, I'd like for you to leave quite awhile before daylight and take a note to Martin Martz. I intend to ask Martin to be our representative. No one can construe that irascible old Dutchman as partisan."

Bonney asked, "What about the horses me'n Bob and McCloskey brought in the other day? Do we leave them?"

"I should think our title to them is clear. After all, Sheriff Brady specifically exempted them. We'll take the horses with us."

Tunstall and his four men left shortly after the stars winked out in the east.

Around mid-morning, a large body of armed men surrounded the buildings. Only Dutch Martz and Godfrey Gauss, the crippled cook, answered the posse's hail to come out.

"Where the hell did they go?" Dolan demanded of the frightened cook.

"They left for Lincoln near two hours ago. Maybe a little longer, Mr. Dolan. They just left me here to watch the cookhouse."

"Why are you here, Martz?" Matthews demanded.

"I have a note. Mr. Tunstall, he asks that I come see you take only cow what belongs to McSween. So I do this thing."

"What do we do now, Jimmy?" Matthews asked. "We ain't got no grounds to chase after 'em."

Dolan's eyes narrowed to slits as he peered about. "Where's the horses?" he muttered. He leaned from his saddle to point an accusing finger at Gauss. "I don't see but one horse in the corral. Where's the rest of them, damn you?"

Gauss backed from the man's fury. "On the range, I reckon, Mr. Dolan. 'Ceptin' for the ones come in from Lincoln t'other day. Them, they took back with 'em."

"Which ones is that?"

Matthews broke in. "That's the ones Brady released, Jimmy."

"How many, I said!"

"Eight, I think," Gauss whispered. "'Ceptin' for the ones they rode."

"How many men?"

"Five."

"Billy," Dolan said, spinning back to Matthews, "your orders are to impound the livestock on this place."

"Yeah," Matthews said. "McSween livestock."

"Yet there is conclusive evidence here that Tunstall has violated your agreement by deliberately removing some of that livestock."

"But Brady exempted ..."

"Damn it, Billy!" Dolan exploded. "that is not for you to decide. Let the courts do that. Your job is to enforce the law."

"Well, okay I guess. But I still don't ..."

"Now, I want you to select a dozen good men to bring back those horses if they can catch up to 'em before they get to Lincoln."

"Who do you want I should pick, Jimmy?"

———— • • ————

The hours crawled with Tunstall's band. They'd taken the Pajarito Springs shortcut and neared the Rio Ruidoso late in the afternoon. Here, the trail wound through a narrow wooded canyon. Tunstall, Brewer, and Widenmann led the loose horse band, which in turn was trailed by Bonney and Middleton. The lead riders rounded a bend and startled a flock of wild turkeys. Widenmann whooped and shouted, "C'mon boys. Roast turkey tonight."

Brewer said, "You go, John. I'll stay on point. Go get yourself a turkey."

Tunstall shook his head. "No, Dick. My spirit isn't quite up to a turkey hunt today. You go on."

Brewer pointed his horse after Widenmann, spurring hard through scattered juniper and pinon pines.

Meanwhile, the drag riders let their horses amble and graze, dropping behind the plodding loose horses. Bonney's sixth sense made him whirl in the saddle as a body of riders streamed over a low rise behind. "Run for it, Mid!" he screamed. Bullets began whizzing about them.

Bonney, driving spurs and slashing with rein-ends, dashed into a thick stand of juniper, Middleton at his heels. They paused only a moment, but it was enough to watch the posse race through the scattering horse band and disappear around a bend in the trail. Then Bonney and Middleton pointed their own horses through the trees, up the ridge, heading for a jumble of rocks that offered a place to "fort up." Widenmann and Brewer were already at the rocks when they arrived.

"Where's Tunstall?" Bonney cried, leaping from the saddle.

A volley of shots rang out below. Middleton murmured, "They just killed him."

CHAPTER SEVENTEEN

When the first shots rang out, driving Bonney and Middleton up the hill, John Tunstall checked his horse and reined him around to face an oncoming drum of hoofbeats. Buck Morton, the sub-posse leader, was first in a group of gunwaving riders to spur around the bend. Morton was followed by Jesse Evans, Frank Baker, and Tom Hill. Spotting the motionless Englishman, the four posse members slowed their horses to a walk.

He must have known their intentions. Despite such certainty, a great calm settled over John Tunstall as he folded hands across the saddlehorn, looked fondly at the late afternoon sky, and breathed deeply of the fresh February air.

The posse surrounded the Englishman....

The sorrel mare sucked greedily from the stream while her rider slumped in the saddle, their journey nearing an end. Jethro Spring considered again what he must say to his friend: There will be no help from Pitzer. He won't make a move without his brother's approval and John's still hiding out in a Las Vegas jail.

The sorrel lifted her head, water dripping from her muzzle. She stared upstream, also sensing home range.

Jethro had returned to South Spring Ranch early that morning to trade a hard-used Chisum horse for the mare. While switching saddles, he told a disappointed Jinglebob foreman the results of his useless ride. Jim Highsaw shook his head and said, "I got a feeling, Winter, that we're gonna fight them bastards sooner or later."

"Maybe, Jim. I don't know. Maybe on the other hand, there won't be enough of us left to fight."

When he topped the last rise before the ranch, he reined in and studied the place. There was little doubt he was too late. Then he clucked to the horse, guiding her toward the buildings.

It was a raucous camp with some thirty posse members milling about the house and yard while their three dozen horses kicked up dust in the corral. Tents had sprung up, brought along by wagons. Evening cooking fires burned in three locations. Most possemen treated the affair as a riotous holiday, some already feeling the effects of liberal doses of Double Anchor and Pike's Magnolia. Not one suspected a single Tunstall cowhand would ride, alone and unannounced, into their midst.

The sun dropped below the Sacramentos as the rider pulled his floppy hatbrim low to shelter his eyes. Dust-covered and with his dark face, he appeared to be one of the dozen Mexican drovers Dolan recruited to drive Tunstall's herd to the Mescalero Reservation. The sorrel mare wound through the melee, Jethro guiding her first one direction, then another to avoid individuals he recognized, angling always toward the bunkhouse. One man, roaring at a companion's joke, thrust a half-filled bottle toward the rider. The horseman shook his head and continued on. Two blustering invaders, filled with liquid courage and looking for sport, made as if to block his way. But when the rider closed enough for the revelers to make out the pinched face and how the horseman laid a hand on his gunbutt, they laughed and slapped each other on the shoulder and staggered aside.

Jethro saw the elder Beckwith and one of his sons and he put a corral runway between the mare and the two men. At the bunkhouse, he swung casually down, leaving the mare's near-side rein trailing in the dust. In the gathering gloom, no one paid attention to him or his horse.

Jethro drew his Colt as he pushed into the bunkhouse.

Billy Matthews looked up from a game of solitaire. A coal oil lamp, its wick in need of trimming, spluttered nearby. "My God! It's the half-breed!"

James Dolan, his back to the door, started violently, knocking over an inkpot. The dark stain spread across Matthews' cards and the letter Dolan was writing.

"Don't do anything you might regret, Jimmy," Jethro said, closing the door with a foot, eyes sweeping beyond. The room contained two other men: Tunstall's cook and a heavy-set older man Jethro did not know.

Dolan settled back into his chair. "Get something to clean up this mess with," he snapped at the cook.

Gauss leaped to obey when Jethro said, "Let Dolan clean up his own mess if he wants it clean."

Dolan glared with bloodless intensity at the undecided cook. Then his eyes shifted and he said over his shoulder, "This is too much to hope for, Winter—you dropping into our hands, too."

The bronzed man reached behind and threw the door's bolt. The snap of its closing sounded as loud as a rifle's report in the still room.

Dolan tried again: "I'll give you credit for havin' more

gall than anybody I know. There ain't half a dozen people in the world got enough guts to ride in here through fifty men."

"Thirty-one," Jethro said. "I counted them."

Matthews' hands shook, for all that they lay flat on the table.

"You expect to ride out as easily?" Dolan asked.

"Where's Tunstall?"

"Go to hell!" Dolan spat.

Jethro glided forward and in one swift move, laid his gunbarrel solidly behind Dolan's right ear. He holstered the gun in almost the same motion, stared Matthews down, and caught Dolan before he slid from the chair. The newcomer propped up the unconscious storekeeper, dropping his head in the spreading puddle of ink. "Where's Tunstall?" he again asked, this time of Matthews.

Matthews' face reddened. He choked trying to speak. Jack gazed at the man he didn't know, then at Gauss. "Well?"

"They left early this m-morning, Jack," Gauss stammered. "Headed for Lincoln, they was. Tunstall had me stay, and he sent word for Dutch, here, to come r-rep for him."

"Dutch who?" Jack asked, eyes swinging back to the blocky stranger.

"Martz," the stranger said. "Dutch, I am called. I own a ranch. It is from here, east."

"How long have you been here?" Jethro asked Matthews.

Matthews stammered, then choked again. Jethro looked to Gauss.

"A couple hours after Tunstall and the boys left," the cook replied.

"What did Dolan mean when he said it was too good to be true, me falling into their hands, too?"

Matthews eyes darted about.

"Well, they ..." Gauss began, only to be cut off by Jethro's wave. "I want to hear this from Matthews."

"I ... I don't know," Matthews squeaked.

Jethro slid the Colt out deliberately, then stuck the muzzle in Matthews' ear. "Try real hard, Deputy," he said. "Now, on the way in, I don't remember seeing Evans or Baker. I didn't see Hindman, either, or Roberts or Hill. Granted, I might have missed some of 'em, but I find it hard to believe I missed them all."

Matthews shook uncontrollably, but he managed to get out, "After Tunstall."

Jethro holstered the Colt. "Much better. Why?"

"To ... to bring back the horses they took with 'em."

"Which horses?" Jethro asked, looking at Gauss.

"The ones Brady let 'em keep."

Flint-edged eyes flipped back to Matthews. "What do you have to say to *that?*"

"He made me do it!" the deputy cried, pointing at Dolan. "He said it wasn't up to me to decide what the courts are s'posed to decide. Said we had to impound all the stock on the place."

"How many men did you send after the horses?"

"Twelve."

"Evans and Baker and Hill in the bunch?"

"Yes," Matthews squeaked.

"And Buckshot Roberts and George Hindman?"

"Yes. But dammit, Dolan made me send them very ones." The deputy buried his face in his hands.

"Is there anything else I need to know?" Jethro asked Gauss.

"Can't think of anything, Mr. Winter," the cook said, "except I think they was taking the Pajarito Trail."

He backed to the door and drew the bolt. "Matthews, if you come to this door and holler before I'm long gone, it's liable to make me goddamn mad." Then, like a ghost, he faded through the door.

Outside, away from the bunkhouse's sputtering lamp, all was darkness. Showing no furtiveness, Jethro picked up the mare's ground-rein and led her toward the barn. Just before the barn, he switched course toward a near corral, then changed again to move to an end corral. Men still roved about, laughing and shouting to one another. At the last corral, with hair on the back of his neck pushing from his shirt collar, Jethro twisted the stirrup, stuck in a boot, and swung into the saddle, pointing the mare into the night.

———•—•———

Jethro Spring wormed the last few feet to Pajarito Spring on his belly. He'd heard their laughter from a distance and, curious, had tied the sorrel well back to approach on foot, carrying his Winchester.

The posse had no fire, and by the sounds of loose horses rustling around, Jethro guessed they possessed Tunstall's stock. The lack of a fire and excess of banter told him the men were merely resting before continuing back to Tunstall's ranch. He wormed closer. As he did, someone called out, "All right, boys, long enough. Mount up and move out."

Two men who'd squatted near Jethro stood and moved to their nearby horses. One was stooped and walked with a limp. Jethro recognized him as Buckshot Roberts, an old buffalo hunter and wolfer, respected and a little feared by all who knew him. Roberts responded to something said by a man Jethro didn't recognize. The wolfer's voice carried considerable heat: "Could be. Could be. But you can take all the glory far as I be consarned. I take no pride in what they done today."

The other mumbled something Jethro couldn't make out. Then the group was mounted and chousing loose horses onto the trail. Jethro tried to identify as many riders as possible against the starlit sky. None appeared to be prisoners. He lay with sinking heart, unmoving until the posse's sounds faded.

———— ◆ ◆ ————

He found the dead horse an hour before dawn—or rather, the sorrel mare did, stopping abruptly, snorting at something in the darkness ahead, catching her rider dozing in the saddle. When the startled man urged her ahead, the mare only snorted more and shied first one direction, then another.

So he tied the mare to a stubby juniper and slipped down the narrow trail, Winchester at the ready. He sensed more than saw the massive body athwart the trail, it's stench already permeating the air. Tunstall's expensive tooled saddle was still clinched tight to his favorite horse. Seeping blood stained the ground around the bloated bay. Something caught Jethro's eye and he crouched to pull a gray felt hat from beneath the horse's head. Jethro came slowly to his feet, mouth a grim line. He punched John Tunstall's hat back into shape and lay it beneath a spreading Juniper, awaiting daylight and the dread secrets he expected would be revealed.

Jethro awoke to the grim light of dawn peeping over the canyon's eastern rim, momentarily blank until his eyes fell on the dead horse. Pushing stiffly to his feet, he brushed dirt and needles from his clothes and studied the ground in the growing light. Many horses and men had torn the soil around the death site, obliterating much of the story, even to an accomplished tracker. It hadn't erased, however, the second bloodstain that soaked the stony trail ten feet from the horse carcass. The animal's fatal wound told Jethro it died at once, so this other blood was not from that source.

He knelt in the dirt and picked up pieces of bone. Mucous still clung to what he knew instantly were tiny bits of human skull.

Only Jethro's head and eyes moved for a full half-hour, intently studying each horse and human print, searching for a tell-tale feature that would distinguish each. At last, he stood and shuffled in expanding circles, gray eyes still implanting each smudged footprint or shod horse track.

Satisfied he'd memorized all the murder scene had to tell, he walked back up-trail until reaching the place where the posse had ridden pell-mell through the loose horse band, scattering it. He had proof then that return of the horses was not the sole reason for pursuit.

Jethro remounted his sorrel mare and rode uptrail, studying the ground with continued care. Two horses had dashed to the side, shod hooves throwing rocks behind in a wild uphill scramble. Other tracks beelined for a copse of trees, and he decided at least some of his friends had survived the first onslaught. He followed those tracks through the juniper and pine until he spied the boulder pile. Minutes later, picking his way through the boulders, he counted tracks of four horses and four men. He picked up empty shell cases and knew a battle had been fought between those holed-up here and their pursuers.

He breathed easier when he could find no bloodstains among the rocks. Then he tracked the four men and their horses from the rocks for nearly a mile across broken country, down to the Rio Ruidoso. Jethro was back at Tunstall's dead horse by mid-morning.

He worked in ever-widening circles until he found tracks leading uphill. Moments later, he discovered John Tunstall's body hidden among trees and partially covered with leaves and brush. The Englishman had been shot once in the chest, once in the back, and once through the back of his head at close range.

At last, with the sun already well past noon, a bone-weary Jethro Spring lashed his friend's body across the sorrel, leading her down the steep slope to the trail. He took one last look at the dead bay, then hiked downtrail. He'd reached the Ruidoso and wiped dust from his face and neck with a wettened bandanna when a wagon, followed by four grim-faced riders, rolled down to the ford.

"Be best if we laid poor Mr. Tunstall out in the wagon box," John Newcomb said, "and cushioned him up some, wouldn't it, Mr. Winter?"

Chapter Eighteen

Death was palpable about the wagon carrying John Tunstall's body. It was manifested in the sad and somber surrounding riders carrying their rifles like battle standards, with rifle butts propped on thighs, muzzles skyward. Neither riders nor driver interrupted the dismal sound of the wagon's creak, or the clip-clop of horse hoofs on the sunbaked road. Death was there, too, in the sickening-sweet odor of decaying flesh; of death too long unburied.

Jethro Spring tasted it in the bile rising in his throat each time he remembered his friend in life, remembered his nobility, remembered the rape of the man's dreams by cowardly curs not fit to lick his boots.

It was well after dark when the wagon rolled into Lincoln and halted before the home of Alexander McSween. There, a large crowd was gathered to await the arrival of the Englishman's body. It was a sullen and subdued crowd; a marked contrast to the unruly, boisterous Dolan-Riley mob at Tunstall's ranch on the Feliz. It was equally well-armed, however, and potentially more explosive.

"Did you see them, Jack?" McSween asked when Jethro slumped wearily into a chair in McSween's kitchen. "There are well over sixty men out there, and they all swear they're behind me!"

Jethro stared at the floor. "And what are you going to do with your new-found army?"

"Obviously we must avenge John. That must be first."

"And how will you do that? Will you try to kill all those responsible?" He paused. "Or will you use these people to try and establish a just law and order in this godforsaken country—like John wanted?"

McSween sighed. "You are right, Jack. I think in some ways you are ahead of me. Especially in view of the military's position."

"Explain that."

"Word is out Brady asked for and will receive a military guard around the Dolan-Riley store." The barrister spread his hands in a gesture of helplessness. "We asked for help last night when Widenmann and Bonney first came with news of poor John's murder. Widenmann rode directly on to Fort Stanton carrying my personal request for aid in apprehending his murderers."

"What did they say?"

"Purington said he was indisposed to intervene in civilian matters."

Jethro grimaced, but became stone when McSween whispered, "The military detail will be around their store by tomorrow morning, so our informant says. It's now or never."

"What would John want?"

McSween's humorless smile returned. "You're right. Law is our only course."

"That decided," Jethro said, "what can we do?"

"I've already had Brewer and Bonney appear before Wilson and swear affidavits against the men they recognized. Wilson has issued warrants. They're in the hands of Constable Martinez, who is certainly no friend of Brady."

"You're assuming Brady will not move?"

"He dares not, Jack. They were all his appointed posse. To move against them would be admitting their criminality."

Jethro's eyelids fluttered and he caught himself sagging in his chair.

McSween said, "You're tired. The house is pretty full, but we can probably fix a pallet in the sitting room."

Jethro came to his feet. "No need. I'm going down to Wortley's for my regular room."

———•◆•———

James Dolan sat at breakfast as Jethro paused prior to entering the dining room. A strip of gauze, padded behind the ear, wrapped his head. Traces of ink lingered beneath it. Hatred burned in Dolan's eyes when he looked up. Except for that brief visual exchange, Dolan gave no sign Jethro existed.

After a leisurely breakfast, Jethro left Wortley's, heading for McSween's. He scowled at the military detail surrounding Dolan's store. An angry crowd still milled around Tunstall's store and the McSween home.

"They're more angry than ever, Jack," McSween said of the crowd. The post surgeon from Stanton just arrived to help with embalming and to prepare an autopsy. Our information is that Dr. Appel was commissioned by Brady and will receive one hundred dollars for the autopsy."

"That's quite a bit, isn't it?"

"Quite a bit? At a time when a normal fee is ten dollars?"

Jethro shrugged. McSween studied him for a moment, then seemed to come to a decision. He pulled a chair closer to his desk and motioned to Jethro.

"I have something to show you. Night before last, when we first learned of John's death, Riley came to see why such a large group was gathering. He was disgustingly drunk. Afraid we would consider him a threat, he turned his pockets inside out to show he was unarmed. Several items fell out, among them a letter from Rynerson exhorting them to get me, Tunstall, and Wilson."

McSween paused to peer more closely at Jethro. "Another was this account book."

Jethro took the black ledger and leafed idly through it. He turned the pages slower and slower. "Why this documents the fact they bought cattle from Jesse Evans and Frank Baker."

"Exactly," McSween said. "Also that they received shipments of sugar, flour, and coffee from the Indian Agency to their store."

"I see that," Jethro said, "but I can't believe Riley would be dumb enough to carry something like this."

"He was drunk."

"If this is real, he damned sure was."

"It's authentic. Read on."

Jethro did. Soon he muttered, "Hmm. Interesting. A code for friendlies and for enemies. You are 'Diablo'."

"Yes," McSween said. "Note also that the Stanton quartermaster is 'Warwick' and Indian Agent Godfroy is 'Hampton'."

"Jesus, this reaches pretty high, too. Rynerson and the territorial attorney general have nicknames, too."

"Jack, that book is conclusive evidence that a 'ring' does, in fact, exist."

Jethro handed the book back. "What will you do with this?"

McSween rubbed his hand across his face. "I don't know," he mumbled. "I'm reluctant to move with it in a territorial court; the evidence will simply disappear and so will any proof it ever existed."

McSween leaned back in his chair and sighed. "John was an English citizen, Jack. I've written his father to push for a State Department investigation. If there is such an investigation, that would seem the opportune time to expose this book."

The barrister had just slipped the book into his desk when Brewer and Widenmann entered the office. Widenmann held out his hand. "We hated leaving John's body, Jack, but hell, they had us boxed. Wasn't nothing else me and the boys could do."

"I'll be having nightmares over that one for a long time," Brewer mumbled.

"He died instantly, Dick. It's certain they had you sewed up tight. I would've done the same."

Brewer's smile was faint. "I doubt that." Then he turned to McSween. "The results of the coroner's jury is in, Alex. It named Evans, Baker, Hill, Hindman, Dolan, and Morton as Tunstall's killers."

"Dolan was at the ranch," Jethro said. "I saw him there."

"He ordered it, though," Widenmann retorted.

"Responsible, certainly. But he could hardly have fired the bullet. By naming someone who couldn't have been there, don't you cast doubt on the whole verdict."

"Bullshit," Widenmann said. "We don't get Dolan on this one, we don't pull their teeth ever."

Jethro sighed. "A level-headed thinker, aren't you, Bob?"

A thin, red-faced man in a black broadcloth suit and string tie loomed in the doorway.

"Come in, Dr. Ealy," McSween said. "Please do. Have you met Jack Winter?"

The man shook his head. "I believe not. You are Mr.

Winter?" He extended his hand to Jethro, who looked to McSween for an introduction.

"Dr. Ealy and his family had the misfortune to arrive in Lincoln yesterday, Jack, at the height of our knowledge of the tragedy. They are Presbyterian missionaries answering a need for a church and school. They came at my behest. Dr. Ealy is also a physician. At the present time, his family occupies the west wing of our home."

Jethro shook the doctor's hand, liking what he saw.

"Jack discovered the body," McSween said by way of introduction. "He, too, was an employee of Mr. Tunstall."

"I see."

"Is the autopsy complete, Doctor?" McSween asked.

"Yes, but there are some things I do not understand, Mr. McSween."

"Such as?"

"The post surgeon wrote of only two bullet wounds in Mr. Tunstall's body—I saw his report. He said both bullets entered from the front."

"Yes?"

"Mr. McSween, Mr. Tunstall was shot three times, and two of those bullets entered from the rear."

———·•·———

Constable Martinez, accompanied by Bonney and Fred Waite, went to the Dolan-Riley store at three o'clock that afternoon, ostensibly to serve warrants on the men named by Brewer and Bonney as members of the Tunstall murder posse. Brady met them on the porch and refused to allow the warrants to be served on the grounds that the warranted men were members of a legally constituted posse and therefore immune to arrest. An impressive array of Dolan-Riley partisans, all heavily armed, and protected by a detail of U.S. Army troopers, backed the Sheriff. An argument ensued.

Moments later, George Washington burst into McSween's office. "Brady, he arrested the constable and Mist' Bonney and Mist' Waite. The Sheriff is marchin' 'em to jail right now!"

On Friday, February 22, 1878, in a small plot beside his store, John Tunstall was buried. Dr. Taylor F. Ealy presided at the service crowded with well over a hundred friends and sympathizers. Every man and several of the women carried weapons. Anticipating a clash, Brady sent a request to Colonel Purington for additional soldiers. A detachment of Company H, 15th Infantry, dispatched immediately, kept an uneasy peace.

An impromptu meeting addressed Brady's refusal to arrest, or permit any arrests to be made, of Tunstall's murderers. Probate Judge Florencio Gonzales headed a committee composed of three other of Lincoln County's leading citizens: Isaac Ellis, Jose Montano, and John Newcomb. The committee's instructions were to interview Sheriff Brady and learn his intentions toward the Englishman's murderers.

"Brady seemed vague," the committee reported. Maybe it's something the grand jury better look at when they meet."

"But that's not until April!" someone shouted.

"What about the arrest of Waite and Bonney and Martinez?" McSween asked. "Did he say why they're in jail?"

"We asked," Ellis growled. "All he'd say was, 'Because I have the power.'"

"Also, we asked about your bond, Senor McSween," Florencio Gonzales added. "The Sheriff, he said he will not take a bond from you, Senor, of any kind, or in any amount."

The following day, Widenmann, following instructions

from McSween, presented three six-month old federal warrants to Colonel Purington. The warrants charged Evans, Baker, and Davis with stealing government horses from the Mescalero Agency at South Fork. Widenmann formally requested federal assistance to serve those federal warrants. Purington could not refuse.

Shortly thereafter, to the consternation of other troops guarding the very same facility, a cavalry detachment under the direction of Deputy United States Marshal Robert Widenmann surrounded the J.J. Dolan & Company store in Lincoln. Widenmann, accompanied by a handful of civilian deputies on temporary duty, entered and searched the building for the three warranted men. Failing to find either Evans, Baker, or Davis at the Dolan store, Widenmann led his military detachment to the store of J.H. Tunstall & Company, where he arrested the five Dolan-Riley guards and marched them to Judge Wilson's court. There he presented them without any formal charge.

Perplexed, Wilson had no recourse but to immediately free the men. But in the brief interim, twenty-two McSween-faction men occupied the empty store. The Dolan men prudently left the building alone.

Alexander McSween, on the advice of Dick Brewer and Jethro Spring (who considered him the next logical Dolan-Riley target), left Lincoln for the safety of nearby hills. Though he was still in the custody of Barrier, that deputy was relieved to take his charge away from volatile Lincoln.

Shortly after McSween and Barrier departed, Jethro leaned against a porch post, talking to Antanasio Salazar. Dick Brewer came from inside Tunstall's store. "Jack, you got a minute."

A sizeable group was gathered in the back room. Jethro nodded at Doc Scurlock and Charlie Bowdre. To Fred Waite, he said, "Brady let you out, huh, Fred?" Then he asked John Middleton, "What's going on Mid?"

Billy Bonney, closing the door behind Jethro, said, "We're organizing."

"We are?" Jethro asked, nodding to three or four others he vaguely knew.

"All right," Brewer said, "I guess that's everybody."

Jethro looked around again and asked, "What's going on?"

"Regulators, Jack," Brewer said. "We want you in on it."

"Fine," Jethro replied. "What are we regulating?"

"We're going after them that killed Tunstall."

"Just like that? If you don't have legal authority, you'll be hunted down like coyotes."

"We've got legal authority, Jack," Brewer said. "Wilson appointed me constable and I'm deputizing them as has asked to go along."

"Brady will never recognize you."

"Brady's a big part of the problem, Jack. Look, I know what you thought of John and his feelings about the law. All of us who worked for him know that. But dammit, you got to know if something ain't done soon, them bastards're getting away scot-free."

"So you plan to gun them down?"

"Hell with him," Bowdre snarled. "We don't need him anyway."

"I say we do," Bonney's high-pitched but authoritative voice rose above several agreeing with Bowdre.

Jethro looked at the ring of faces. He turned back to Brewer. "I asked a question."

"The answer is no. We decided we'll only go after someone to bring them back for trial."

"To Lincoln?" Jethro asked. "You'll bring them back to Brady's jail?"

"Nothing else we can do," Brewer said. "Not unless we want to be judge and executioner, too."

Jethro looked at John Middleton. "You're in, huh Mid?"

"Yup."

"And you, Doc?"

"Tunstall was a good man, Jack. So are you. We need you."

The gray eyes swept around once again. "Where's Widenmann? Why isn't he here?"

Brewer said, "We tried to pick only the best, Jack."

Jethro hesitated.

"We got word the Evans bunch is holed up down at Dolan-Riley's cow camp, below the Penasco," Dick said quietly.

Jethro nodded. "Okay," he said. "Count me in. John wouldn't like it, but count me in."

Buck Morton and Frank Baker, accompanied by two other unidentified hardcases, fell first into the regulators' net. It was while skirting a big patch of riverbottom tules, halfway between Tunstall's Feliz ranch and Dolan's Penasco cow camp, that a wary Jack Winter, riding point, first spotted the Tunstall killers. And it was his strategy that mounted the sudden regulator sweep that surprised the smaller party, heading Morton and Baker off from their outlaw refuges.

Still, the desperate duo made their dash, guns blazing at their pursuers. At last, the two Dolan men accepted a Brewer promise they would be delivered alive and safe for trial in Lincoln.

"Sonofabitch, you can't mean it?" Bonney protested after Morton and Baker were taken. "You know damn well these two bastards are the worst of the bunch. Hell, Morton led the goddamn Posse and him and Baker are two of the four that got there first and shot Tunstall down."

"I gave my word, Billy," Brewer said. "We all did. We said we'd bring 'em in for trial."

"You think Dolan's bunch is gonna let us?" Bowdre growled. "Hell, Dick, two others split off when we first jumped these. You think they're not on the wing to Dolan right now? I say put these bastards away, and let's get on with our business."

"Our business is legal business, Charlie. We been legal all along, and we ain't changing now."

"I don't know but what I agree with Charlie and Billy," Doc Scurlock said. "Likely, we ain't gonna have this chance again."

"I gave my word. If any of you don't like the decision, speak up with more than words. Let's have it out."

The men eyed Brewer, weighing their position. Each man in the group was better with a gun than the big Ruidoso farmer. However, none doubted that same farmer's courage. The balance was tipped when the man they knew as Jack Winter said, "I'm with Dick on this one, boys, if there's any doubt."

They camped that night at Chisum's cow camp on the lower Pecos, and stayed at the South Spring Ranch on the evening of March 8th. Bill McCloskey joined the party earlier that day, only five miles from Chisum's headquarters.

"Hey, I seen you guys from up on the ridge, and see you got them two bastards. I says to myself, 'Bill, there's some boys who knows exactly what they're doin' and you ought to join in.' Where you taking 'em?"

"Lincoln," was Brewer's terse reply.

"I was on my way to Lincoln, anyway. Mind if I ride along?"

"You're here," Brewer said.

Later, Jethro said to Brewer, "You reckon McCloskey was watching Chisum's place? He was in a mighty fine place to do it from." When Brewer said nothing, Jethro added, "Some of the others don't trust McCloskey. They say he was with the Dolan posse. That he's a Dolan spy."

Brewer shrugged. "I don't trust him, either. But I'm not

for trusting all our boys, not when it comes to delivering Morton and Baker in one piece. Having McCloskey along can't hurt there."

Jethro nodded. It made sense.

They were preparing to leave South Springs the next day when Jim Highsaw passed along word one of his cowboys carried from the Roswell Post Office: "Don't know if it's true or not, boys, but there's a rumor that the Dolan-Riley bunch is makin' up a posse in Lincoln to rescue Morton and Baker. Look sharp for a bushwhack."

As a result, Brewer decided on a different route to Lincoln, reasoning the high Agua Negro trail through the Capitan foothills would bring them into town after dark, and by a different route than expected.

The sun shone directly down when Jethro dropped back to ride alongside Brewer. "Billy asked me to see what you wanted to do about a noon stop, Dick?"

Brewer squinted at the sun and said, "Tell him let's go on up to the springs, Jack. We'll be there in an hour."

Suddenly a volley of shots rang out from around the bend.

"What the hell?" Brewer said. His bay and the sorrel mare pounded forward.

"Oh no!" Brewer moaned, plunging from his horse. "Oh, my God. Why?" He looked up at the circle of riders surrounding three bodies lying in the dust.

"They tried to get away, Dick." Billy the Kid played with his rifle. "Morton, he got a-hold of McCloskey's gun and shot him. Then him and Baker made a run for it."

Jethro pushed through the group as Middleton and French galloped pell-mell from the front. Morton lay face down in the dust. Baker died harder, squirming on his side in his death throes. Jethro knelt, examining the bodies. He rose slowly, his face a mask. "Morton's got nine holes by my count, Dick. All of 'em went in the back."

CHAPTER NINETEEN

Alexander McSween returned to Lincoln the day before the three Dolan men were killed in the lonely Agua Negro canyon. His return was prompted by a visit to Lincoln by the Territorial Governor, Samuel B. Axtell.

The governor, responding to a request from his friend James Dolan that he visit the front, spent the night of March 8th at Fort Stanton, then investigated the Lincoln situation for three hours the following morning, all in James Dolan's company.

Governor Axtell declined to interview either those people identified with the McSween faction, or anyone thought neutral. When Isaac Ellis, a respected community member, approached Axtell with some of Lincoln's history, the governor scornfully declared, "I know all about the matter and its cause, and I have already taken such action as I deem necessary."

That action, in the form of a "Proclamation by the

Governor," dated March 9, 1879, was a hammer blow to justice in Lincoln County. The proclamation declared Justice of the Peace John Wilson's appointment by the Lincoln County Commissioners illegal on a technicality, revoked Robert Widenmann's appointment as U.S. Marshal, and announced that the president of the United States approved his request for military support for the Lincoln County sheriff in enforcing the civil process and maintaining order.

Dick Brewer and Jethro Spring were the only members of the regulators to ride into Lincoln late in the evening of March 9—the rest fled to the friendly hills of the Rio Ruidoso. Brewer and Spring, uncertain how to break the news of the shootings, saw a light burning in McSween's office.

"Dick! Jack!" McSween exclaimed as they pushed into the office.

"Didn't expect to find you here," Brewer said.

McSween smiled. "Hiding out just wasn't honorable." Then he said, "I'm told you arrested Morton and Baker and were bringing them in. Was there any trouble with Brady?"

Brewer shook his head. "Morton and Baker are dead."

McSween paled. "Dead? I ... how?"

As Brewer poured out his story, Jethro studied McSween. The strain showed. His face was drawn and unshaven, his wrinkled clothes hung as if on a scarecrow. Jethro grudgingly admired his courage, however.

"So, what's to do, Alex?" Brewer asked. "We got troubles, but dammit, I don't know how to handle them."

"I'm afraid," McSween replied, "you have more troubles than you think." He pushed a copy of Governor Axtell's proclamation across the desk.

Brewer read it through twice and passed it to his companion. When Jethro finished reading, Brewer said, "Way I read that, we didn't have a legal posse."

McSween sighed. "It sounds that way, though I certainly do not agree. You see, I've been doing some research. Let me read this passage to you." McSween picked up a law-book:

> In the event that any vacancy exists now in any county office, or that hereafter may occur in any county, precinct or demarcation in any county by reason of death, resignation or removal or any other manner, the county commissioners of said county shall have the power to fill such vacancy by appointment until an election be held as provided by law.

"Interestingly enough," McSween said, "that is a statute Governor Axtell, himself, signed into law more than two years ago."

"Well, how ..."

"Wait, Dick. Listen to this." The attorney reached for a sheet of paper on his desk. "This is from the minutes of a meeting of our Lincoln County Commissioners, held February 14, 1877:

> James H. Farmer, Justice of the Peace of Precinct No. 1, of this County and Territory, having resigned, giving as reasons for doing so the distance of his residence to the seat of the precinct, and occupations that incapacitate him to faithfully discharge his duties as Judge, his resignation was accepted, and John B. Wilson was appointed in his place, and the Clerk is authorized to issue his commission to that effect to said John B. Wilson.

"My God. That clears us, then."

"Not necessarily," McSween said. "I'm certain you can be legally exonerated as far as your authority went. But the deaths of Morton, Baker, and McCloskey present another problem. Until this proclamation is overturned in court, you have no legal rights whatever—none of us do. My advice is to get out of Lincoln for awhile, until this situation comes into sharper focus."

"You're saying running is our only choice?" Brewer asked. "God, that galls."

"I know. That's why I came back," McSween said. "But I'm leaving again. In the morning I really am going to South Springs. I received word John is being released. I'm going to try and persuade him to join us. It's our only hope."

"I guess sleeping under the stars ain't so bad when a body gets used to it," Dick Brewer said, staring at the remains of his burned-out cabin. "Never did like that cabin site. Think I'll build the next one on that little knoll."

Jethro followed the other's gaze. "Pretty place. Knowing you, it'll be built well, too."

Brewer stuck out his hand. "You'll carry the proclamation word on up the river?"

The gray-eyed man nodded.

"Hate to see you go," Brewer said. "But I don't blame you. If I didn't have ties to the country, I'd pull stakes, too."

"I'm not running out, Dick."

"Hell, I know that. You're just being smart. Good luck."

Bowdre's adobe hut huddled among cottonwoods, close to a bend in the Rio Ruidoso. Jethro reined his mare to the door. "Hello the house!"

"You ain't welcome."

Jethro twisted deliberately in the saddle. Bowdre pointed a Spencer carbine. "You want me to ride out, Charlie, you gotta get out of my way."

Billy the Kid stepped through the doorway of Bowdre's adobe chuckling. "Charlie, you just ain't hospitable at all.

Get down, Jack, and tell us the news of Lincoln town. Can't be all bad if you're still on the loose."

Jethro shook his head. "It's bad, Billy. Bad enough I'm pulling out." He told Bowdre and Bonney of the governor's proclamation.

"So," Bonney said, "that kinda spells it out, don't it? We sure as hell done the right thing with Morton and Baker, didn't we?"

Jethro stared a hole through Billy, then shook his head. "Well, I'll be moving on. I'm stopping off to tell the rest of our bunch on the way upriver."

"I always knowed you for a coward," Bowdre said.

Jethro twisted again to peer down at the farmer. "Shooting a man in the back—is it your idea of courage, Bowdre?"

Bonney laughed wildly. After a moment, Bowdre joined him.

"Hold on a minute," Bonney said after he subsided. "I'll ride along up to Coe's.

"You ain't yellow are you, Jack?" Bonney asked a few minutes later, as the two friends jogged along.

"What do you think?"

"Why you leaving, then?"

"I don't want to be a party to back-shooting."

"Even if they was getting away?"

Jethro's glare was icy.

"Even if they killed a friend?"

"Every man ought to have a chance," Jethro replied.

"They had theirs when we picked 'em out of the tules. They gave up their chance when they throwed down their rifles."

"Brewer gave his word."

"I didn't give mine," Bonney said, grinning.

"What about McCloskey?"

Billy's mood swung in an instant. "McCloskey was a traitor and you know it. So don't try to tell me no different."

The two rode in silence. Finally, Jethro asked, "Where's all this going, Billy? How's it going to wind up for you?"

Billy anger was banked as easily as it flared. He chuckled. "Hell, I don't know. I don't even care, either. All's I know is I got a few things I got to do. Revenge for Tunstall is only one of 'em."

Jethro eyed the frail youth. "What else?"

"Brady. He throwed me in jail for no reason. Made me miss my friend's funeral. He'll die for that."

"Seems to me like 'kill' is a big word in your language, Billy."

"I do what I have to do," the youth replied. "I'm good and gettin' better. I could even take you now."

Jethro checked his mare with a touch of the reins and eyed the smirk on Bonney's face. "You let me know when you can't hold the urge in any longer, Billy. I don't want to catch one in the back."

Bonney laughed until tears came. When at last he halted, the youth gasped, "No need ... to worry ... Jack. I ain't about to try you out for another month or two. No way."

———•—•———

There was a special place in Jethro's soul for the timbered mountain country and he found it pleasant in the high Sacramentos even so early in the year. He paused for the night in a small meadow with an icy-clear stream running through it. A few patches of snow lingered among the big yellow pines. With spring just now beginning, grass was short for the sorrel. But it was enough.

He hobbled the mare, then gathered a few sticks for his fire. Occasionally, the man paused to breathe deeply of the fresh mountain air, expelling with an audible sigh. Soon a cheery little blaze sparkled. He filled a rusty can from his saddlebags with water from the stream and set it on the fire. Finally he took the pouch of coffee and small side of bacon Doc Scurlock had forced upon him, stingily dribbling coffee grounds into the can, then cut and thrust green sticks into the soft ground around the fire and impaled slices of bacon upon them.

After a few minutes passed, Jethro pulled in the decayed remnant of a big yellow pine stump, knowing the pitch-filled roots would burn for hours, warding off most of the high country's nighttime chill.

Leaning back against a pine, the man stared dreamily at a cluster of wild crocus ten feet away. *John,* he thought, *you tried, damn you. But the cards were too well-stacked against you. You had to fight Dolan and Riley and the whole damned Santa Fe ring; and all the while your own best friend is probably a thief. I'd stay, John, but what's the use? Brewer is the only good man in the lot. Bonney is a crazy killer and Widenmann a stupid oaf filled with his own importance. Middleton is okay, I guess, but he only does what he's told and never thinks for himself. None of your allies could really be counted on. The Mexicans' teeth chatter when they think about Dolan and Riley, and Chisum plays his own brand of solitaire to benefit Chisum alone. The Ruidoso boys are tough, no doubt, but they come out only when they feel like it. No, John, we gotta face up to the fact we never did stand a chance.*

One minute he was alone, then the Indian was there! Hair stood on the back of Jethro's neck and he silently cursed his stupidity. The Indian, stocky and bandy-legged, wore a breechclout, knee-high leather leggings and moccasins, and nothing else. The man stood twenty feet away with arms folded, a shiny repeating carbine in the crook of the left arm. He was wide of shoulder and broad of chest, and his bowl-shaped, gray-sprinkled black hair looked as though it'd been bobbed with a jackknife.

He was also the meanest-looking human being Jethro

had ever seen, bar none!

Only the younger man's gray eyes moved. The mare was grazing peacefully. Four feet away, his own Winchester leaned against his saddle. Black eyes flicked to the roasting bacon, then back again. Jethro said "Hello," in guttural Blackfeet, knowing it probably would not be understood. The man continued to stare. Jethro leaned forward to free his hands, then began to speak in the trader's universal sign language.

The Indian watched the hands flow for a time, then shook his head and responded with his right hand.

It was the camper's turn to shake his head. Jethro tried some broken Cherokee; the Indian shook his head. Again the man's eyes flicked to the bacon and back again.

"Well, damn, if I could talk to you, I'd ask you to eat," Jethro blurted.

"And if you would ask, Malvado would eat," came the reply in passable English.

An hour later, Malvado licked his finger, then carefully sucked the last roasting stick before tossing it into the flames. Throughout the meal, the Indian said nothing, his black eyes watching Jethro's every move. Finally, the remainder of his bacon disappeared. So did the precious coffee in can after can of bubbling black brew.

"Mescalero?"

The Indian nodded.

Jethro ambled to his mare. The Indian puzzled him; the impassive face, the staring wide black eyes, the thin mouth that pinched until it appeared cruel. Jethro staked the mare near the fire. His guest hadn't moved.

The pine stump blazed hugely when Jethro threw its remnants on the fire. Both men moved back. In the dancing firelight, Jethro could make out the scar of a bullet wound low on the Indian's right side and two ragged knife scars across the broad chest. A fighting man, sure enough. The

Indian continued to stare impassively at Jethro.

"Well, Malvado," Jethro said at last, "I'm for turning in." He rolled up in his saddle blanket as close as he dared to the blaze, head resting on his saddle.

The other grunted and lay down away from the dancing fire.

Twice during the night, Jethro moved closer to the dying campfire. Each time he saw firelight reflecting from his guest's black eyes.

Pink tinged the eastern horizon when the gray eyes popped open. The Indian was gone. The mare stood contentedly, one hind hoof cocked on its toe. A tiny wisp of smoke curled skyward from a few charred remains of the stump. Jethro threw off the blanket and gazed around in the dawn's half-light, then he rolled to his feet and moved the horse farther out, again hobbling her to graze. He patted the mare's neck, drew up a notch on his belt, and thought ruefully of the breakfast his guest had eaten the night before.

When he shuffled back to his saddle and blanket, the same Indian squatted cross-legged by the whisping ashes.

Jethro grinned. "Sorry. No food this morning." He moved to the tiny rivulet and cupped his hand to drink. Then he splashed water on his face and came back to the smoking embers, gathering sticks along the way. Soon there was a crackling little blaze. He, like the Indian, squatted cross-legged.

"Malvado would talk?" he asked.

"You are the one called the season of the Hunger Moon?"

"Yes, I am known as Jack Winter."

"The ones you seek are beyond the next hill. In the valley of the big tree."

"The ones I seek? I seek no one."

Malvado's dark eyes were fathomless. "The one called Season-of-the-Hunger-Moon," he said at last, "seeks the man with hair the color of dirty snow and eyes of a mountain lake."

Jesse Evans? Jethro wondered. "Malvado is mistaken. Winter seeks no one."

Malvado shook his head. "During the season of Burning Sun, the man called Season-of-the-Hunger-Moon and three others pass here in search of those who drove horses before them." It was not a question.

Jethro nodded. "Last September."

"The one called Season-of-the-Hunger-Moon and others returned. They had no horses before them."

"That is true."

"Two who the man called Season-of-the-Hunger-Moon sought during the season of Burning Sun are camped near here. One is the man with hair the color of dirty snow. They are bad white men. They steal from Mescalero, steal from white men around us. Just this many days"—Malvado held up his ten fingers—"they drive white man's buffalo to Mescalero and take two wagons of Mescalero flour. The Great White Father's agent helped them. White men take from Apache before. This time they give cattle in return."

Jethro sighed, thinking again of his dead English friend. "Where, exactly, are those two, Malvado?"

CHAPTER TWENTY

Their campfire's ashes were still warm; Jethro studied the ground. Two men and their horses had spent the night in a tiny cul-de-sac, well screened from the Tularosa road. Jethro wondered who the second man might be. Tom Hill? If so, the last two of Tunstall's actual murderers were a few hours ahead. But going which way? Jethro studied the tracks until sure Evans and his companion headed for Tularosa.

"Well, John," Jethro murmured aloud, "I'm on my way out of this Godless country. But the least I can do is have a word with the ones who killed you."

At Blazer's Mill, Jethro ate his first good meal in three days. He also purchased supplies: coffee, flour, and another side of bacon. But the Indian Agent Godfroy, Dr. Blazer, nor Blazer's workmen would give information about the two men he followed.

Jethro skirted Tularosa as a hot springtime sun slid

toward the western mountains. As soon as he struck the road, he picked up fresh tracks of two horses heading south. The shoes were badly worn on one horse; the same prints he'd followed to Tularosa.

Scattered sheep bleated in the gathering dusk as far as the eye could see. Jethro Spring wriggled nearer the camp wagon. Off to one side, a young Indian camp tender lay propped against a cottonwood tree. The boy bled from a bullet wound in his lower left leg and a cut across his forehead. Someone threw pots and pans and bedding from the wagon.

Tom Hill thrust his low-browed, stubbled face from the wagon. "Dammit, Jesse, go shake up the Injun again. The Dutchman's money ain't in these trunks. He knows, damn him."

Jesse Evans stood spraddle-legged in front of the boy and Hill leaped down to stand shoulder to shoulder with his partner. "One last time, you little bastard," Evans growled. "Where's the money hid?"

Hill pulled his revolver and spun it threateningly, inches from the young nose.

"*No comprendor*," the boy whispered, sobbing.

Hill stopped the twirling gun and cocked it.

The roar of Jethro Spring's Colt shattered the low-keyed bleating of sheep; its .44 caliber slammed the dying thief alongside the cringing shepherd.

Tom Hill was the first man Jethro Spring had ever shot from behind. The thought—and the merest pause accompanying it—nearly killed him. At the roar of Jethro's gun, Evans threw himself sideways, twisting and jerking at his own revolver. Evans' gun spoke even as he struck the ground rolling. He saw the man who'd shot Hill from ambush stagger, then both guns roared and bucked. A slug ripped through Evans' right wrist, spinning his revolver into the dust. He jerked at his second revolver and scrambling, sobbing, grunting, and shooting wildly, the outlaw rolled beneath the shelter of the sheepherder's wagon.

"Be right with you, Jesse," Jethro Spring called from the gloom, "soon's I punch out these empties and freshen up my Colt."

With nostrils flaring and eyes darting, Evans grabbed a tattered towel to wrap around his bloody wrist. He heard the distant snap of a loading gate latched into place.

"Jesse, I'm ready to talk about Tunstall's murder now. How about you?"

Evans broke and ran. As he dashed away, he fired his last two rounds. Awkwardly snatching up his reins with his left hand and leaping to the saddle, the outlaw steeled himself for a bullet that never came.

Back in the low depression where he'd taken shelter, the gray-eyed man smiled ruefully and cursed himself for his weakness. He grunted with relief—after a final twist on the silk neckerchief around his upper thigh—to see the crimson gush slow to a seep. He glanced into the darkness as Evans' horse thundered away, then tied the knot and hobbled to the wounded shepherd.

The boy cocked Hill's revolver and a chill ran down the hobbled man's spine. "I'll say one thing for you, pardner," he said as he knelt by the frightened lad, "you got grit."

Two hours later, Jethro pulled a silk neckerchief soaked in boiling water through the bullet hole in his thigh. He kept up a running monologue to the Indian who watched in wide-eyed wonder. A clean bandage covered the youth's forehead and a bandage and splint swathed a shattered lower leg.

"Yeah, I near-on bought the deep-six, boy, when I give that Evans the first crack. A man like him, now, he don't—

ouch!—deserve any more chance than—uhh!—a mad dog. Hell, that's what he is, you know." Sweat stood out in huge droplets on the dark forehead as he worked the silk neckerchief back and forth. "Been a inch over, likely I'd have bled to death." Blood flowed freely when Jethro pulled the neckerchief from the wound and again tied it as a tourniquet. Then, in the dancing firelight, he bandaged the wound with clean rags pulled from a boiling pot.

"Then where'd you be?" he continued talking to the boy while he worked. "What with a busted-up leg and a dead man layin' alongside?"

The dark eyes followed Jethro's every move.

"Now it looks like me and old Jesse have a personal thing going, what with both of us bloodied some. I ain't sure where I got him, but he looked funny as hell when he scrambled after dropping his first gun—did you see it? No? Well, he upped with another in his left hand. I could have got him then if I hadn't come empty."

Jethro paused in his bandaging and stared at the ground. "No, lad. There ain't no way out of it—I near blowed that one. Had old Jesse cold to rights when he cut and run. But I let him get away 'cause my pa never taught me it was okay to back-shoot even mad dogs."

Both heard the approaching horses. Jethro tied the bandage off, picked up his rifle and trousers, and hobbled into the darkness. He returned when he saw it was the Dutchman and his two drovers.

Just as he'd done for three days, the dark man, still as a sunning lizard, studied the ranch. He gnawed off another chunk of the Dutchman's jerky and took two swallows of precious water. He knew Evans was in the Shedd place; had watched a man with blond hair and his right arm in a sling walk to the outhouse on two different occasions.

Jethro glanced behind. His mare stood quietly in the shade of a huge boulder. He shook his head. "We'll get him yet, horse," he muttered, "if we can hold out awhile longer."

Evans broke cover the next day. Jethro headed him off at San Augustin Pass, then again when Evans tried to bolt back to Shedd's. Relentlessly, the gray-eyed man drove Evans north, staying between the outlaw and his refuge. Evans lured his pursuer into the shifting white sands to the west of the Tularosa Road. But the pursuer was no novice, and his early years at the side of his mountain man father served him well. He circled like a hunting eagle, and circled again, ground hitching his horse to creep painfully among the dunes in pursuit. Once, a rifle bullet kicked sand into his eyes, and he tumbled backward down a dune to escape. He laughed aloud, though, his voice rolling across the sterile landscape.

"Evans! All I want to do is talk about Tunstall. Why not?"

Jethro twice glimpsed horse and man topping some distant dune, standing out in stark contrast to the blinding brightness of the White Sands. He hurried back to the mare and easily rode around to drive Evans and his tired horse away from Shedd's and back into the dunes.

Evans next exited the shifting sands on the north. It was two hours before his pursuer picked up the tracks. But the worn animal Evans rode had crossed and recrossed the white land too many times without water or rest and was simply too exhausted to carry the outlaw to safety. In a side canyon of the Sacramentos, Evans demonstrated his own special cunning by abandoning the worn mount; scrambling over terrain too difficult for a horse to follow, heading for high, rocky crags.

Without the painful wound, Jethro Spring could easily have run the outlaw to ground. With it, he could only limp in painful pursuit. That's why he decided the next best thing was to wait for Evans at Tularosa.

Two days later, the blond outlaw, sure the demon who followed was between the mountains and the Shedd Ranch, crippled to the town on blistered feet. But an uncanny sixth-sense saved Evans once again—on the outskirts, the cagey outlaw stole a horse at gunpoint, then surprised his pursuer by heading north, away from Shedd's. His lead was short-lived, however, as Jethro took up the pursuit with two rested, well-grained saddlehorses: his own sorrel mare and the steeldust gray Evans had abandoned in Marble Canyon.

Evans came to bay in the early evening of the seventh day of their chase. He'd been forced to flee up yet another side canyon, striking toward the towering whiteness of Sierra Blanca. The exhausted outlaw fled from his second horse, darting from shelter to shelter along a boulder-strewn hillside, bullets spanging and whining about him.

"Jesse!" a voice floated from below. "I'm not quitting until you and me, we talk about John Tunstall!"

Evans poked his Winchester between two boulders, swallowing panic. The throbbing arm tortured him, its white bandage long since begrimed and torn. He squeezed off a shot, cursing beneath his breath.

"That's plumb unhospitable, Jesse! Is that how you got Tunstall—more or less by accident?"

Evans levered awkwardly and fired again. Though the waning day was turning cool, sweat dripped from his chin. His eyes flicked about and fell on two trunk-sized boulders before him and the man screamed in panic as ancient carved-stone masks stared accusingly back. Heedless, the outlaw leaped to his feet and dashed uphill. A shot sounded behind as the outlaw dove for shelter. Rock fragments cut into his cheek and blood trickled down his face. He stared fearfully at first one boulder, then another. Each of the large, gray-colored stones had a design carved into it: geometric patterns of the sun or moon, circles with dots in the center, beetles or caricatures of people, feathers and angles and handprints carved in stone. Evans buried his face in his good arm and sobbed.

Far below, Jethro Spring also stared about in amazement. He blinked at a crudely carved replica of a bighorn sheep, at another of a bird in flight, and yet another of a beast-head with a human body. Jethro pulled out his boot knife and scratched the surface of one of the rocks and was surprised that it was so soft.

Darkness came with a rush like it always does in desert country. As the last light dulled on Sierra Blanca, Jethro crawled to his feet. He nearly caught Evans at Carizozo Spring. The outlaw fled west into the Malpais—a badlands of black lava and little water. Again he forced Evans to foot in order to escape, but not before the outlaw nearly pulled his own ambush.

As it was, the steeldust threw his head in time to catch a bullet intended for its rider, and the horse went down kicking. Jethro leaped clear, but he landed on the weak leg and tumbled into the dirt, losing his rifle. He rolled and hobbled and crawled to cover as two more bullets whomped the dirt behind him.

"Evans!" Jethro called. "Glad you stopped long enough to talk!"

Another bullet whined from the rock he crouched behind. The rifle lay but a short distance away, but to try for it would be suicide. He cursed silently, knowing he could not get behind Evans while crippled with his throbbing leg, nor could he approach armed with a mere six-gun while Evans held a rifle. At sundown, the outlaw made his play.

Evans had the mobility Jethro lacked. For three hours he circled through the lava, crawling at last on Jethro's lair from the rear, bounding out of the sinking sun, firing as he came.

Although he'd discarded the rifle in favor of the easier-to-handle revolver, Evans was in no condition to confront the man who'd hounded him for days. The first shot at twenty yards grazed Jethro's left shoulder. The second at seventeen thudded harmlessly into the ground where the prone man had lain. At fourteen yards, the third round burned along his quarry's neck just as Spring snapped off his first shot.

It was as though a horse kicked Evans; the outlaw slewed sideways from a hammer blow just below his right-side ribs. Falling to his knees, the desperate man still gripped his revolver and got off two more wild shots as his gray-eyed pursuer scrambled behind yet another knife-edge of lava. Then Evans was up and running deeper into the Malpais.

Meanwhile Jethro Spring tore off his shirttail and thrust it beneath his neckerchief, stemming the flow of blood along his neck. He shrugged off the other near-miss and the blood seeping from his shoulder as unimportant. He waited the few minutes until dark, then worked his way back to the sorrel mare. Then he circled into the Malpais until he picked up his quarry's trail.

Jesse Evans' bold bid to escape was testimony to the outlaw's stamina and courage. With a serious wound in his lower abdomen, a bullet-smashed right wrist and complete exhaustion from being harried for days with little sleep and less to eat, Evans did the one thing Jethro Spring thought him unable to do: he walked out of the Malpais on a beeline to Carizozo Spring. The outlaw's luck turned as he reached the first tiny spring along the Malpais' eastern edge; there he stumbled upon a cavalry patrol searching for twenty-three reservation-jumping Mescalero Apaches.

The troopers stared in disbelief as Jesse Evans staggered into their camp, babbling about being pursued by a devil. Usually nattily dressed and well-groomed, Evans was ragged and blood-soaked. His hat was gone and a dirt-streaked, scraggly beard covered his face. He'd lost thirty pounds during the three week ordeal. Haunted blue eyes stared from sunken sockets. He began sobbing.

Jethro Spring, also haggard and gaunt, followed the patrol's trail to Fort Stanton. At high noon, April 1, 1878, the day following the patrol's arrival, he crossed the Rio Bonito bridge and reined to a halt. With Jethro Spring's name on WANTED posters for killing an army officer, he hardly wished to enter the fort. So he tied his horse to a cottonwood sapling and, avoiding the fort gate, limped to a parade ground where a group of recruits drilled. A young lieutenant raised an eyebrow at the ragged man's approach.

"Excuse me, sir," Jethro said.

The lieutenant's gaze returned to the parade ground. "Yes?"

"That patrol—the one that came in yesterday from Carizozo Spring—apparently they picked up a man over near the Malpais?"

"So?"

"The man's name is Jesse Evans. He's wanted. I've followed him for two, three weeks. I caught him robbing a sheep camp south of Tularosa."

The lieutenant's gaze switched to Jethro. "Are you a peace officer?"

"No, sir, I'm not. But I know who he is. That man is a horse thief and murderer. He shot an Indian boy at that sheep camp. He's also wanted for the murder of John Tunstall."

"And what is it you wish me to do?"

"I hope you'll be kind enough to convey this information to the commandant."

"The gate is open," the lieutenant said. "I'm sure you could get an audience with the adjutant about any important matter."

Jethro stared at the imposing Fort Stanton walls, then back at the lieutenant. "Sir, I know I don't look like much. I've been on the trail for three weeks. I'm really too ragged and dirty to formally appear before the commandant or his adjutant." He tried to make his tone engaging and condescending.

"What did you say your name was?"

"Winter."

"Winter what?"

"Jack Winter."

The lieutenant took the other's measure. "All right, Mr. Winter. I'll convey your message. But I must ask you to remain here in case my superiors require more information."

Lieutenant Milford Atkins was accompanied by two sergeants carrying sloped carbines when he returned.

"Colonel Purington would like to talk to you, Mr. Winter."

Jethro eyed the two black sergeants, then the lieutenant. "What did he say about Jesse Evans?"

"Colonel Purington is well aware of Mr. Evans's reputation. In fact, Mr. Evans turned himself over to our patrol because of remorse at his escape from jail."

"And?"

"Mr. Winter," the lieutenant said, "I repeat—Colonel Purington wishes to talk personally with you."

"I'm really not in condition ..."

"I'm afraid I must insist!"

"Of course," Jethro mumbled. "I'll get my horse." Jethro pointed. "Down by the bridge. See? Standing by the bank."

Atkins hesitated.

"Look, lieutenant, I'll just get her and lead her into the compound. I didn't realize it was going to be this complicated."

"All right, Mr. Winter. Sergeants Randolph and Davis

will accompany you. I'll wait at the gate."

The sergeants snapped a brisk salute. One said, "This way, suh."

Jethro marched between the two blue-clad soldiers. He knew he was being taken into custody and had just begun thinking how he could take both men out when the sergeant on his right whispered, "Don't go into that fort, Mr. Winter. They's planning to th'ow y'all in the stockade."

Startled, Jethro said, "How can I help it?"

"Y'all just get on that horse like you planned to ride along into the fort. Then you feed him spurs. We'll play act and shoot a couple rounds, but we'll miss."

They were halfway to the sorrel mare by now. Jethro asked, "Why do they want me?"

"You ain't heard of Sheriff Brady?"

"What about him?"

"Gunned down this morning in Lincoln. Him and another man."

Billy? he thought. Then he said, "I had nothing to do with it."

"You a danger to 'em, suh."

"But what is the charge?"

"They'll think of something. You got to ride, suh. And don't never come back."

As the three men approached the sorrel, Jethro asked, "Why are you doing this?"

The taller black sergeant said, "I'm Jefferson Davis, suh. I'm the one Frank Freeman tried to kill before you stopped him. We all owe you this, Mr. Winter."

Jethro yanked the halter rope free and moving deliberately, swung into the saddle. Taking no chance, he buried his heels and drove between the two sergeants, knocking them away. Two desultory shots followed.

The fugitive fled back along the Carizozo road, circled, then laid a trail to confuse even an Apache tracker. Dusk

found him in the one place no one would think to look—
within hailing distance of the fort.

While resting there, Jethro Spring saw Susan McSween
for the first time in almost four months.

The road curved around Jethro's hiding place atop a low
ridge. Four soldiers came first, then the wagon guarded by
two others. He pushed aside the juniper branches to better
see. Three men and one woman sat in the wagon. Jethro recognized Susan immediately, then her husband and Bob
Widenmann. By the way the bluecoats surrounded the
wagon, he understood that its occupants were under arrest.

CHAPTER TWENTY ONE

This time Antanasio Salazar was surprised. When the soft voice came out of the darkness, the old man stiffened, then just as softly, he returned the greeting. "And *buenas noches* to you, too, Senor Jock."

When Jethro said nothing else, the old man added, "It was I, Antanasio Salazar, who was wrong, *mi amigo*. The senor does indeed see and move as a cat."

It was almost an hour before Jethro again spoke. Only then did he sigh and say, "Antanasio, my friend, these few quiet moments that pass in companionship between us are all I've had since coming to New Mexico." Jethro was dimly aware the other nodded. "So tell me, when will it all end?"

"This village is not safe," Antanasio replied softly. "Not for one who does not belong to Senor Dolan and Senor Riley."

"They arrested McSween and his wife."

"This I know, Senor Jock. The *jurisconsulto*, he gave

himself up to the *soldadoes*. The Senora went with the Senor."

"I can't believe they killed Brady."

"No senor. Those were not even in Placito when it happened," Antanasio said. "They only arrived later."

"How, then, can they be arrested?"

"In this place, justice is a feeble thing, Senor Jock."

"Will it ever come?"

"Si. Little more than one week away, the grand jury will meet."

"Will they help?"

"The grand jury, she is but the people. When she speaks, it will be the people speaking."

Jethro stared into the night. "Tom Hill is dead," he said at last.

"Word has come that Senor Hill was killed while robbing a camp of poor sheepherders beyond the Tularosa."

"And Jesse Evans has been wounded. He is at Fort Stanton, in custody."

Si. Was it only yesterday we heard of the *loco hombre* who wandered out of the Malpais and gave himself to the army patrol? It is said such a man was pursued by an army of devils."

"Now Brady. Who else, Antanasio?"

"Senor Hindman."

Jethro rubbed his eyes. "That about completes the picture, doesn't it? Except for Evans."

"And except for Senor Dolan and Senor Riley. They still have their boots upon our necks."

"I was thinking of Tunstall's killers," Jethro muttered.

"Senor Jock, we must think beyond even such a bueno hombre as Senor Tunstall. We must keep our eyes upon what is good for our children, or their children. As long as Senor Dolan and Senor Riley control our lives, none have gained."

It amounted to a long speech for the old man. Again, Jethro rubbed his eyes. "I was leaving—going away. I ran into Evans and Hill. They had a young Indian boy propped against a tree. They'd shot him. Aw, hell! Why am I back?"

Antanasio nodded in the darkness. "Because you are helpless to do anything else, Senor Jock."

"Who shot Brady?"

Antanasio Salazar was silent for several seconds. "I will tell you how he was killed, senor. I will tell you who was in the corral where the bullets that killed were fired from. As to who fired the bullets? *Quien saber?*"

"Tell me only what you know."

"Senor Bonney and Senor Middleton, they were in Senor Tunstall's corral. As was Senors Macnab, French, and Brown. It was nine o'clock in the morning of the day before this one. All Fool's Day."

Jethro listened quietly as Antanasio Salazar spun out the story of yesterday's double murder; how Brady, Hindman, Matthews, Peppin, and Long left the courthouse to walk back to the Dolan-Riley store. He heard how a volley of shots rang out from behind the walls of J.H. Tunstall & Co.'s adobe corral; how Brady died instantly, while Hindman sprawled in the street, moaning for water. He listened as Antanasio told of crossing gunfire; of the wounding of Billy the Kid, Jim French, and Jack Long; how the McSween partisans at last rode from Lincoln while Dolan and Riley prepared their store for a siege.

When Salazar fell silent, Jethro asked, "What about Brewer? Was Dick Brewer here when Brady was killed?"

"No, Senor Jock. Senor Brewer has remained upon his farm since the affair with Senors Morton and Baker."

Has that only been a month? Jethro wondered. He came to his feet.

"Where do you go now, *mi amigo?*"

Jethro sighed. "To Dick Brewer, Antanasio. Where else?"

The old man grunted. "Senor Brewer will need your

help, Senor Jock. These killings yesterday was a bad thing. Now with Senor and Senora McSween and Senor Widenmann arrested, all the more weight will fall on Senor Brewer."

"He's a good man. A strong man."

"*Si.* Now he must be stronger than ever. These *hombres* are no longer under his control, or they would not ambush even such a bad sheriff." Antanasio paused before adding, "Never has Senor Brewer needed you more."

There was no reply. His visitor was already gone.

———— • • ————

Jethro caught the "regulators" two days later at Blazer's Mill. He was amazed at their numbers, augmented by the last of the Ruidoso farmers. Fifteen strong and led once again by Dick Brewer, the group had set out for the Shedd Ranch, where many of John Tunstall's cattle were reported to be. Near noon, the party rode up to the building owned by Blazer and leased to the federal government as headquarters for the Mescalero Indian Agency. Here, they ordered dinner from Mrs. Godfroy, the agent's wife, who operated an eating place for travelers.

When Jethro swung from his horse and walked into the dining room, he was greeted boisterously by his friends. Another chair was offered and another plate set.

"Suppose you heard about Brady and Hindman?" Doc Scurlock asked.

"I heard. And if what I heard was true, I ain't too proud."

A chair sounded unnaturally loud as it scooted along the puncheon floor. Bill Bonney laid down his fork. "What is it you ain't proud of?" he said, biting off each word.

Jethro took out his belt knife, picked up a fork and began to eat. With a mouthful, he pointed the fork at Billy and said, "I'm not proud of gunning down anyone from behind an adobe wall. Not even someone who hates my guts."

"They killed Tunstall!"

"Brady didn't. I doubt he even had any idea it might happen. Even so, he didn't deserve to be bushwhacked. Nobody does."

Bonney's chair slid further and he came to his feet. "Funny. I heard Tom Hill was gunned down in the back? Me, now, I'm looking at you. You want to do something about me?"

Jethro forked another bite of meat into his mouth. "Yeah, I do, Billy," he said at last. "I want your promise it won't happen again."

"And what if you don't get it?"

"I already have it, Jack," Brewer broke in from the end of the table. "The whole damned bunch of us swore we'd use only legal methods from here on out."

"My God! Here's Roberts!" Scurlock cried.

Jethro leaned forward to peer out the open doorway into blinding sunlight. He saw the stooped old wolfer, Buckshot Roberts, hobbling toward Godfroy's.

"Roberts?" Bonney whispered. "Buckshot Roberts?"

"Yes!" Scurlock hissed. Chairs scraped back, and men reached for rifles that leaned on roundabout walls.

"By God, he was part of the posse that killed Tunstall," Billy blurted. "He's mine."

A coldness seized Jethro. He recalled how he'd crawled near the murder posse at Pajarito Spring and how, as the possemen mounted, Roberts growled, "*... you can take all the glory far as I be consarned. I don't take no pride in what they done today.*" Now, the crippled old wolfer walked alone and unsuspecting toward a building holding fifteen of his enemies!

"This is too easy," the Kid said, peering around the doorjamb.

"Hold it!" Brewer hissed. "What the hell do you bastards think you're doing?"

Bonney glanced toward his leader. "It's Buckshot Roberts, Dick."

"I know that."

"You got a warrant for him in your pocket."

"I have a warrant, yes," Brewer said. "But a warrant is no license to kill. I asked what you're going to do?"

Roberts sensed something and paused fifty feet from the door.

"Don't you understand, Dick? He killed Tunstall."

"Bullshit," Brewer said. "He was in the posse."

"Same difference."

"Shut up, Billy!" Brewer shoved past the youth. "We'll take him in, just like we said we would. At least we'll give it a try." Brewer's big frame filled the opening. "Hello, Buckshot," he called.

Roberts peered from beneath shaggy eyebrows. He swung his head to eye the corral. Through its gate, he spotted the regulator horses, still saddled; until then hidden by the corral's adobe walls. "What you want?" he asked.

"We want to talk about Tunstall, Buckshot."

"Talk away," the wolfer said. "I didn't have nothin' to do with it."

"Ain't that for a jury to decide? I got a warrant to take you back. Throw down your guns and give up. I'll promise to see you safe to Lincoln for the grand jury."

Roberts stood his ground. "Nope, Brewer. I won't do it. I don't know who all's in that buildin', but I know some of 'em's not to be trusted by man nor beast. If I'da seen yore hosses ahind them walls, I'da never stopped and that's a fact. Now that I'm here, I ain't a-throwin' myself on yore tender mercies."

"Fifteen men, Buckshot. No, sixteen. You don't have a chance."

"Don't make no difference. I ain't a-throwin' down my guns, and that's that."

Brewer hesitated. He turned to look around the room. "I'd rather talk than fight. You're friends with him, Frank. Will you go out and talk to him?"

Frank Coe nodded. "What do I say?"

"Just talk him into giving up if you can." Brewer turned back to Roberts who backed toward his horse. "You can't get away, Buckshot. But we'll talk it out with you. Will you talk to Frank Coe?"

The old wolfer paused in his retreat. "I trust Frank," he said.

Brewer motioned to Coe. "Okay, Buckshot. You and Frank walk around the corner to Blazer's office and talk. Just remember, though, we'll have it covered. You can't run, so don't be a fool."

As soon as Roberts and Coe disappeared around the building, Brewer turned, still blocking the door with his big frame. Bonney said, "You're a goddamned fool. We had him dead to rights."

"Is that what you do, Billy? Shoot first, then talk?"

Time passed at a snail's pace to the men gathered in the dining room. Meanwhile, Coe and Roberts talked in the doorway of Blazer's office. "I'll never give up while Bonney is with you," the wolfer spat. "Don't I know what happened to Morton and Baker."

Coe told Roberts that the posse was after some of Tunstall's cattle at the Shedd Ranch, but if Roberts would give up, he would persuade Brewer to let him and his cousin George and maybe one other man escort the wanted man back to Lincoln for the grand jury deliberations.

"Who'd be the other?" Roberts asked.

"How about Winter?"

Roberts nodded. Then he said, "Lemme keep my Colt."

Inside, Bonney blurted, "The bastard took Frank hostage."

"Maybe," Brewer said. "Maybe we better send somebody around to check."

"I'll go," Jethro said.

"Not you, Winter. I need you here. Let's see, Mid, why don't you and Bowdre and George see how things stand?"

Coe and Roberts had just finished talking when Bowdre leaped around the building's corner, clawing for his gun. "Throw up your hands, Roberts!" he cried. Middleton and George Coe followed, guns drawn.

"Never!" Roberts leaped to his feet, swinging up his Winchester. Frank Coe dived for cover.

Bowdre fired first. The round tore into Robert's stomach and knocked the old wolfer into the room's inky darkness. Roberts held his rifle as he fell. He cursed and started firing methodically out into the blazing noon sunlight. His targets were better. Roberts' first shot grazed Bowdre. His second smashed into Middleton's chest. His third caught George Coe's hand. His fourth nicked Billy the Kid as he rushed to join the fight.

During a lull, Roberts dragged a mattress across the open doorway. Then firing became general, with a hornet's nest coming from Blazer's office. A half-hour later, Bowdre, crouching behind a lumber stack, cried, "Where in hell is he getting all the ammunition?"

Brewer crawled to Bowdre. "Blazer says he's got a Springfield in there—and a thousand rounds for it." Slowly, Brewer raised his head to better view Roberts' refuge. The big Springfield barked from a hundred and fifty yards away and the regulator leader collapsed without a sound, a hole through the center of his forehead, the rear skull blown apart.

———•———

All fight vanished from the regulators upon Brewer's

death. Within minutes, they'd left Blazer's Mill, borrowing a wagon to haul the wounded John Middleton.

All save the one known as Jack Winter. The dark-faced man had watched them mount as he leaned against the corral gate, chewing a grass stem. "Reckon we should bury Dick first, boys?"

Bowdre asked, "How we gonna get to him with that bastard coverin' the yard?"

"Don't you think we should try?"

Bonney jerked his horse's head around. "Buryin' him won't bring Dick back."

"He was a good man," Jethro said stubbornly.

"Better'n most," Bonney agreed. "Not too smart, though. If he'd let me pick off Roberts when first we seen him, Brewer'd be alive yet."

Jethro opened the gate. "Billy, there's still a few things you don't understand."

The posse left and the dust settled. Jethro walked out into the yard. When he neared the lumber pile where the body lay, he called: "Roberts! Brewer's dead. I'm going to bury him."

A voice floated back: "He was a good man. Go ahead. Dig two holes while yore at it. I ain't gonna make it neither."

<hr />

The spring term of the Lincoln County Grand Jury began April 8, 1878. It was composed of Joseph H. Blazer, foreman; Juan B. Patron; Crescencio Sanchez; Vicente Romero; Camilo Nunez; Wesley Fields; Robert M. Gilbert; Francisco Romero y Valencia; Desiderio Zamora; Jerry Hockradle; Andrew Wilson; A.M. Clenny; Juan Jose Lopez; Ignacio de Govera; and Francisco Pacheco. The jury began deliberations with a charge by Third Judicial District Judge Warren Bristol related to Alexander A. McSween's embezzlement case. Bristol's charge to the jury was little more than a partisan argument seeking to prove McSween guilty before the jury had even heard the case, let alone deliberated on its merits. Bristol's tirade against McSween took more than three-quarters of the charge; Tunstall's murder only one short paragraph.

Despite Judge Bristol's bias, and attempted intimidation by District Attorney Rynerson, the grand jury results exonerated McSween entirely. In fact, the grand jury went even farther, officially finding that the proceedings against McSween had been a deliberate persecution by his enemies.

Tunstall's killing, the grand jury found, was a brutal murder and a number of indictments were brought.

Indictments were also found against the murderers of Sheriff Brady, but McSween and Widenmann were both cleared in that regard.

In addition, a great number of indictments were returned against many individuals for cattle theft and receiving stolen cattle.

The Dolan-Riley defeat appeared total. Accused by association of receiving stolen cattle, and by implication of stealing from Indian and Army, James Dolan took newspaper space announcing the temporary suspension of business at the J.J. Dolan & Co. store. His "card to the public" stated, "... business will resume when peace and quiet shall take the place of lawlessness ..."

There was reason to believe there might be more to Dolan's announcement than met the eye since District Attorney Rynerson was overheard telling Dolan at the close of court: "Don't give up. Stick to that McSween crowd. I will aid you all I can, and will send you twenty men."

Shortly afterwards, a posse headed for Lincoln from Mesilla's Rio Grande Valley. It was composed of ex-military mercenary John Kinney and fifteen members of his hard-bitten band. The group was augmented with seventeen outlaws from the Seven River vicinity. Ostensibly, the "Rio Grande posse" proposed to offer assistance to newly appointed Lincoln County Sheriff John Copeland. Copeland, an appointee of District Judge Bristol, was less sympathetic to the Dolan-Riley faction than supposed. It was hoped the appearance of Kinney's "posse" and the Seven Rivers contingent would reverse Copeland's attitude.

Just west of San Patricio, in late afternoon of April 30th, Kinney's irregulars rounded a road bend and met Frank Macnab, Frank Coe and Ab Sanders, who jogged unsuspectingly toward Sander's farm on the Rio Hondo. Macnab and Sanders fell in the initial fusillade, with Macnab fatally riddled and Sanders seriously wounded. Frank Coe took refuge in a shallow arroyo and staved off his attackers until running out of ammunition. Then he surrendered to Bob Olinger, a friend among the Seven Rivers men.

Frank Coe's hour-long defense against impossible odds served to buy time for the unsuspecting McSween men in Lincoln. They were alerted when Ramon Trujillo galloped into Lincoln with word of the San Patricio battle—and that a hostile mob was approaching.

—— ◆ ◆ ——

After burying Brewer, a melancholy Jethro Spring stayed on at Blazer's Mill, sitting beside the dying Buckshot Roberts until the man's eyes glazed. Roberts suffered in silence, except for a final burst just before his death rattle: "There ain't no winners in Lincoln County, boy. Get out while you can. That's where I was a-goin'."

After burying Roberts, Jethro fled to the solitude of the high Sacramentos. He drifted aimlessly south, pausing to camp at each likely spot that contained water for his needs, grass for his horse, and fuel for a fire. Sometimes he moved only a couple of miles in a given day. The mare quickly recovered from the long Jesse Evans chase. So did her master, losing his gaunt hollowness, putting on lost weight and regaining his strength. He tested his wounded leg with long hikes and practiced incessantly with his Colt. Most of all, he debated his course in the bloody dispute that was coming to be known as the Lincoln County War.

There was no doubt where he would be if Tunstall still lived. And he'd returned after his running battle with Evans to fight alongside Dick Brewer. But Tunstall and Brewer—the two men he most respected—were dead. And he couldn't forget Buckshot Roberts's dying words: the safest—and perhaps wisest—course was to quit the county; leave both factions to fight their no-win war.

But what about Antanasio Salazar and the country's "little" people? Forget Billy the Kid and Charlie Bowdre. They were no more than mad dogs racing with an otherwise steady pack of solid men. Doc Scurlock, like Brewer, was a courageous, hard-working farmer. So were the Coe cousins and Jim French. What of them?"

He was convinced a *Santa Fe ring* did indeed exist, stealing the territory blind, and that Dolan-Riley was a local manifestation of the "ring." He was also convinced its powerful tentacles stretched into the military.

But what could he do? What *should* he do?

Susan McSween decided it for him. His head told him not to think of the married woman, but his heart said otherwise. There was simply no other answer—Susan needed all the help she could get.

He rode into the outskirts of Lincoln on April 30th, just as night was winning its struggle with daylight. As chance had it, he was only minutes behind Ramon Trujillo and his message about the approaching mob of irregulars.

The ripple of Jethro's return preceded him down Lincoln's street. Little knots of men stopped their dashing to-and-fro to shake his hand and tell him how glad they were to see him. For his part, the quiet man was bewildered.

By now, all Lincoln County knew of his exploits. By now the Tularosa sheepcamp fight was common knowledge as was the legendary three-week chase of Jesse Evans and the outlaw's subsequent reduction to a quivering wreck. Known, too, was Winter's recent escape from Fort Stanton arrest and his heroic confrontation with Dolan at Tunstall's ranch amid—by now—a hundred posse members! Also remembered was the face-offs with the insane outlaw, Frank Freeman, and how the badman's horse packed Freeman's corpse, like a sack of grain, into San Patricio.

But the exploit most admired was not one of chase or fight or stealth or flight, but the one where he'd stayed on to bury Dick Brewer after Brewer's other friends deserted him in death; how he'd sat beside the old wolfer until Roberts died, and how he'd also buried his fallen enemy. All were acts of courage and responsibility that seemed almost beyond the ken of ordinary men.

And in all Lincoln County, it was probable that he was the only person not grasping his stature in the minds of others.

Billy the Kid lounged at McSween's hitchrail, grinning broadly, as though nothing had happened between them. "Am I glad to see you, Jack. Hell's about to pop and I can't think of nobody I'd rather see turn up."

Jethro took the Kid's hand coolly. "What's about to happen, Billy?"

"There's a mob on the way. John Kinney and his pack from over to the Rio Grande and a bunch of Seven Rivers bastards. They'll be here in a few minutes."

"What's it about?"

"We control the town. They don't like it."

"How did you get control?"

"We, Jack," Billy said. "You're one of us. We got it when the grand jury returned their indictments." Bonney's cackle rippled in the moonlight at Jethro's hanging jaw. "Christ, haven't you heard?"

"No."

"McSween is scot-free. So is Widenmann and most everybody else. The Dolan store is closed up tight. We got us a new sheriff. Hell, everything's coming up roses."

Jethro shook his head like a man coming out of a dream. "McSween inside?"

"Go on in, Jack boy," Bonney said. "We heard you was coming up the street. He's expecting you."

McSween bounded across the room in giant strides, both hands flung wide in welcome. "Jack! Thank heavens you're here. Just in time, too."

Jethro stood barely inside the threshold, twisting the floppy hat around and around. Then Susan ran breathlessly into the room. "Have you heard?" McSween boomed, grabbing Jethro and pulling him forward. "They are starting a counter-offensive. They'll be here almost any moment. Until you arrived, we were leaderless. As soon as I heard you were back, I sent out word that you'd be along to plan defenses. Why in heaven's name did you wait so long? Were you scouting the enemy? Have you heard about the fight at San Patricio? It's imperative that we ..."

Jethro said, "Hello, Susan."

She came with a rush, laughing and crying, throwing her arms around him and burying her face against his chest. Then she stepped back, hands on his arms. "Oh, Jack," she sobbed. "Thank God you're here. We were so afraid. Dick's death. No one knew where you were. Some even said you'd lost your courage. But I knew better."

"Jack," McSween said, pushing a hand between his wife and Jethro, "what will we do about Kinney and his mob?"

Jethro brushed away the hand and stared down at Susan McSween. "Tell 'em to go to hell," he replied.

⇒ Chapter Twenty Two ⇐

Thrust into unwanted leadership, Jethro Spring made his dispositions in four fortified strong points: the outskirts home of Isaac Ellis, Jose Montano's store, the Tunstall & Company's building, and the McSween home. The defenders shuttered and barred windows and doors and mounted rooftop sandbag battlements. The town appeared so quiet and sinister that John Kinney's invaders declined battle during the night, contenting themselves with sending a message to Copeland offering to help serve warrants.

Copeland's response was to dispatch a request for military support to a new Fort Stanton Commandant, Colonel N.A.M. Dudley, who'd replaced Colonel Purington only days before.

Few slept in Lincoln that night as battle lines were drawn and barricades strengthened. During the nighttime quiet, a conference took place in McSween's kitchen.

"A tremendous victory, Jack. Tremendous!" Alexander

McSween strode back and forth before his table, waving his hands in a flush of excitement. Susan perched demurely in a straight-backed chair, hands folded, eyes shining as she watched her husband.

Jethro Spring slumped in another chair, cradling a coffee cup between both hands. His raven hair lay askew, the dark face drawn. "What did the grand jury find with Morton and Baker?" he asked.

"Completely exonerated, Jack. No indictments returned. Morton and Baker died trying to escape after killing McCloskey."

A muscle twitched in the dark cheek. "There had to be some sort of an indictment for Brady's murder."

"Oh yes," McSween replied. "Four. Bonney and Middleton and, let's see, Waite and Brown.

"Bonney, Brown, and Waite are in Lincoln right now."

"Yes, and grateful I am with that Seven Rivers mob here."

Jethro shook his head. "What I meant was why don't the new sheriff serve the warrants?"

McSween stopped pacing. "Against *our* men?"

"Yes, dammit. If there's reason to believe they shot Brady and Hindman from ambush."

"But they're *our* men," protested McSween.

"Law is law, isn't it, Alex? Isn't that what you used to say. Is Copeland any better than Brady if he overlooks guilty people from either side?"

"I dare say some of Tunstall's murderers are in town with Kinney's mob."

"The law should apply equally. That's a truth you, above all, should support."

McSween wagged his head and turned his pasted smile upon the other. "The law certainly hasn't been equally applied before, Jack."

"Are you saying that's reason enough to gun somebody

down from ambush?"

"This is a struggle for survival."

The gray eyes swept past Susan, then fell to the table. In a far-away voice, he said, "Survival will come to everyone in Lincoln County only when everyone is equal before the law."

The attorney paced furiously. "I don't understand you! At last, things are going our way. You want to throw it aside. What justice can you expect from Dolan and Riley? For heaven's sake, man, don't be a fool. If we permitted our best fighters to be arrested, we would be sheep before wolves. To even consider such a thing is insanity."

"What happened to your resolve to do things legally? Having a fair and impartial sheriff seems to me to be in our best long-term interest, Alex, rather than having one so blindly on our side that he creates a Santa Fe backlash."

McSween threw up his hands. "I'm going out to check our men at Tunstall's. That seems like it would be more productive than arguing a point I consider moot." He paused at the door. "Care to come?"

The other shook his head. After her husband left, Susan poured more coffee. "He's wrought, Jack. Forgive him."

Lost in thought, Jethro studied the knuckles of his clasped hands.

"Of course you're right," Susan said, "and Alex is wrong. He knows it, too. That's why he became so emotional. But surely you cannot believe now is the correct time for Sheriff Copeland to begin serving papers on men from our side?"

He said nothing.

Sensing his mood, she said, "I've missed you."

He raised his head, brow wrinkled, mouth twisted.

"You cannot know how heartsick I felt when I thought I might never see you again." When he still failed to reply, she asked, "Didn't you miss me a teensy bit?"

"You're why I came back," he whispered.

"Jack, can we forget that Las Vegas thing? I don't know what got into me and I'm sorry. I know you are a man of high moral principles. I knew it then. Believe it or not, I have some myself."

"I know that."

"There's no denying there's a certain attraction between us, and there's no denying that we'll both have to work at checking our impulses, whatever those may be."

"True," he murmured.

"But"—pools welled in the hazel eyes—"I cannot bear to lose you altogether. We must remain friends, even though we dare not give rein to our emotions."

He hesitated so long, she whispered, "Please."

He nodded. "That's the way it has to be, I guess."

Her face radiated. "Wonderful. You are so wonderful."

His voice became metallic. "Do you remember the last question I asked you in Las Vegas?"

The light slowly faded from her eyes, the smile from her lips.

"Well, I still want to know."

Susan's pupils sharpened to coral specks. "That is a despicable question. Alex was exonerated by the grand jury. You know that."

"I know. But I still don't know what happened to the money."

"What makes you presume you have any right to know?"

"Because he is asking me to lay my life on a line for something I'm not sure I believe in. You trust John Chisum. I don't. You'll see him leave us all hanging. The Fritz money question leaves me wondering about your husband. You ask what gives me the right to ask? What gives you the right to question my rights when you're asking for such sacrifice?"

Her face softened. She whispered, "Believing as you do, why, then, are you here?"

"Because of Antanasio Salazar and Doc Scurlock and the memories of Dick Brewer and John Tunstall. Because I have no doubts about what they are—or were—fighting for. And God help me, because I can't keep thoughts of Susan McSween out of my godrotted mind!"

She came to him and pecked him on the cheek. "Bless you," she said. "You must believe in Alex. His objectives are noble."

Scattered firing began at daylight. "Dutch Charlie" Kruling, one of the Seven Rivers men, was the only casualty. All shooting stopped at noon with the arrival of troops from Fort Stanton, under command of Lieutenant G.W. Smith. Kinney and his "posse" immediately surrendered to the custody of the military detachment. The raiders were taken to Fort Stanton and confined for two days, then released on their own recognizance by the new Commandant.

———•◆•———

An uneasy peace settled over Lincoln County for the next four weeks, with McSween and his adherents firmly in control of the seat of county government. The lawyer busied himself preparing for re-opening Tunstall's store, while most of his farmer/warriors scattered to their farms, convinced they'd triumphed.

The axe fell on May 28, as Governor Axtell issued a proclamation removing John Copeland as sheriff under the thinly veiled guise that Copeland had failed to file bond, as provided by law. That the county commissioners had yet to set the amount of taxes upon which the sheriff's bond was based proved of little consequence to the decision.

Instead, Governor Axtell appointed rabid Dolan-Riley partisan, George Peppin, a member of Tunstall's murder posse, as sheriff of Lincoln County.

Governor Axtell also made an official request to

Brigadier General Edward Hatch, United States Army Commander, District of New Mexico, for federal troops to be placed at Sheriff Peppin's command.

Consolidation of Lincoln by Peppin was rapidly accomplished, augmented as it was by a visible military presence. Dolan felt secure enough to re-open his store June 5, while McSween shelved plans to re-open Tunstall's.

Peppin's and Dolan's preparation for moving against their enemies was forestalled by the surprise arrival of a special investigator, Judge Frank Warner Angel, commissioned to look into the Lincoln County matter for the United States Department of Justice.

Judge Angel arrived under instructions to concentrate on two matters: the murder of John Tunstall, and the improper management of the Mescalero Indian Agency. His appointment resulted from two factors: (1) diplomatic pressure from England to investigate a flagrant death of one of its citizens; (2) a persistent deluge of protest letters from Lincoln County to both U.S. President Rutherford Hayes and Interior Secretary Carl Schurz.

Angel's research was thorough. He spent several days in Lincoln gathering affidavits from all who were in any way implicated in either matter. Although the testimony was conflicting, the investigator was able to narrow it in a report that turned out to be a study in diplomacy.

Angel's report disclosed that John Tunstall was honest and straightforward in his business transactions and "had almost overthrown a certain faction of said County who were plundering the people thereof."

The report went on to say, "He had been instrumental in the arrest of certain notorious horse thieves. He had exposed the embezzlement of territorial officers. He had incurred the anger of persons who had control of the county and who used that control for private gain ... and to the enmity of his competitors can be attributed the only cause of his death."

The report delved into the circumstances of Tunstall's murder:

"… said deputy … assembled a large posse among whom were the most desperate outlaws of the territory … they came up to Tunstall and his party with the horses and commenced firing at them … Tunstall was killed some hundred yards or more from his horses…. There was no object for following after Tunstall except to murder him, for they had the horses which they desired to attach before they commenced to pursue him and his party."

However, Angel's conclusion was: "I report that the death of John H. Tunstall was not brought about through the lawless and corrupt conduct of the *United States officials* in the Territory of New Mexico."

As to Judge Angel's second charge, the conduct of management on the Mescalero Agency, there were three angles: First, had the agent Godfroy disposed of government property to individuals or firms? Second, had he knowingly accepted flour of lower grade than contracted for? Third, had he "padded" the rolls in regard to the number of Indians receiving rations?

Angel's findings, based largely on John Riley's lost account book, were: Yes, irregularities had occurred. But here again, the judge was inclined to think leniency might be shown since Godfroy seemed to be controlling and training the Indians better than most agents.

Angel's investigation was completed by mid-June and he left Lincoln on the 17th. On the 18th, Peppin and Dolan moved. They were supported by John Kinney's mercenaries and by Company H of the 15th Infantry.

The strike was inconclusive, however, because Jethro Spring again persuaded McSween to vacate Lincoln for San Patricio, where recruits poured in daily from the Ruidoso and the Rio Hondo.

Finally, on June 28, Peppin's forces, slowed by their infantry component, marched belatedly on San Patricio, only to discover McSween had withdrawn to Chisum's South Spring Ranch.

It was while encamped at San Patricio that Dolan's and Peppin's forces were dramatically reduced with the effect of a new federal law prohibiting use of the military against United States citizens except in specific, congressionally approved, cases.

July opened with McSween and his adherents at the Chisum Ranch, Dolan-Riley forces—including Kinney's "Rio Grande posse"—split between Lincoln and Seven Rivers, and a frustrated military shackled to Fort Stanton.

CHAPTER TWENTY THREE

Jethro Spring threw a rock at the corral's snubbing post in disgust. "Goddamn it, Alex! When are you going to get it through your head that you can't count on Chisum?" He and Alexander McSween stood amid gathering gloom in one of the many corrals of South Spring Ranch.

"Jack, he had to go east for treatment," McSween said.

"Yeah. For treatment of a knee a horse kicked ten years ago."

McSween shrugged. "Isn't that beautiful?" he asked, changing the subject to a flaming sunset tingeing the distant western hills.

Jethro ignored the sunset. "Doesn't it strike you as strange that when things get tight in Lincoln County, Chisum picks that very goddamned minute to go away to get an old injury worked on?"

"You're reading things that aren't there, Jack. You'll see."

"Am I? The old sonofabitch was hiding in a Las Vegas jail when Tunstall really needed him. Now, he's out of the Territory when you need him. Maybe I'm seeing things. Maybe it is a coincidence. Maybe it isn't, though. And what if it's not?"

McSween smiled at his lieutenant. "We are receiving a full measure of the famed Chisum hospitality. Perhaps you'd not agree, but I believe their sheltering our little group of vagabonds fully commits them to our side."

"I'll agree only when I see 'em fling a couple of rifle balls."

"Feeding and supplying fifteen men and their horses for two weeks is no small expense, Jack."

"It doesn't compare with spilling guts into the sand."

McSween sighed. "Shall we go in for supper?"

Susan McSween, Pitzer Chisum, and Jim Highsaw waited in the main dining room. "Well, now, here's them two," Pitzer boomed. "We thought you might have hied on up to Lincoln town." The cattleman alone guffawed.

During supper, Jethro studied Chisum's younger brother. Like a big child, crude, clumsy, and slow-witted though the man appeared, Jethro sensed it a front.

Highsaw said, "You gonna know Pitzer when you see him next time, Jack?"

Though Highsaw said it half in jest, Jethro didn't smile. His gray eyes flicked to the cornstalk-lean, no-nonsense foreman, then returned to Pitzer. "Does your outfit have a position in the Lincoln County War, Mr. Chisum?"

"Shore," Pitzer affably replied. "We're roomin' and boardin' you boys, ain't we?"

"Does that mean you'd send Jim and fifty men with us if we started back to Lincoln tomorrow?"

Pitzer chuckled. "That's quite a leap, from passing out a grubline meal to goin' to war."

"Some folks have already been to war for you," came the

thin reply. "Tunstall and Brewer died fighting rustlers and for your beef contracts."

Chisum's face grew red. He shook his head, timed to the beat of a nearby pendulum clock. "They was good men, too. A real loss to the county."

"Never any doubt about those two, Mr. Chisum," Jethro said stubbornly. "The question is, where do you people stand when the chips are down?"

"Jack!" McSween exclaimed.

"No, no," Chisum broke in. "I understand, and if it'll make Jack feel a little easier, I'd like to be the one to tell him the Jinglebob is plumb behind you folks clear down to the end."

Susan clapped her hands in glee and McSween's pasted smile was broader than ever. "Of course," the attorney said. "I knew it all along."

A muscle twitched in Jethro's cheek as his gray eyes met Highsaw's. The Jinglebob foreman looked away and Jack returned to stare at his plate.

Moments later, the somber, dark-faced man excused himself and strode into the night. But he was back unannounced within the hour. All four of his supper companions still chatted sociably at the long table. Pitzer and Highsaw puffed cigars and cradled whiskey-laced coffee. Susan and Alex sipped from glasses of sherry. All looked up as Jethro hurried in.

"You said you were with us, huh, Chisum?" he asked without preamble.

"Jack, for heaven's sake!" Susan cried.

McSween threw a linen napkin on the table and thrust back his chair. "This is inexcusable!"

Pitzer puffed his cigar rapidly before leaning back in his chair and measuring Jethro. "I ain't sure what it is you're after, boy, but I thought I gave it to you."

McSween laid a hand on his lieutenant's arm. "Come

along outside, Jack. It is past time we had a discussion about manners."

Jethro threw off McSween's hand just as Highsaw interrupted, "Hold it! Why do you ask, Winter?"

"Because," Jethro said, a sardonic smile playing across his lips, "a pack of Seven Rivers boys are surrounding your ranch right now." He had the grim satisfaction of seeing McSween's dismay when Chisum ordered his foreman to keep their cowhands out of the fight.

Jethro posted most of his sharpshooters behind roof parapets on the main house. The rest he scattered below. Desultory skirmishing came at daylight as both groups settled into secure positions while Chisum's main-ranch cowhands stayed pinned to their bunkhouse.

At noon, Seven Rivers leader, Buck Powell, deputized by Peppin, sent in a message under a flag of truce....

"He says he's got nothin' agin us," Pitzer Chisum said, handing the note to McSween. "But he says he's got some warrants he's trying to serve on your people."

McSween scanned the note. He looked up at Chisum. "Surely you don't think we'll surrender?"

Chisum chewed on a moustache end. "He says we could be guilty of hiding wanted outlaws if we allow you to use our house to fight from."

"It makes a good fort, Chisum," McSween's lieutenant said.

Pitzer ignored him. "Dammit, Alex," he pleaded, "John never gave no authority in this kind of trouble."

McSween's gaze wandered around the room. "Well, Pitzer, you certainly cannot cast us out. You know what that would mean."

"I can't let you stay, neither."

"Turn your cowboys loose, Chisum, and the battle would be over five minutes after you did," Jethro said.

Highsaw nodded tightly, but Pitzer again ignored Jethro.

"No," Chisum said, biting off the words. "No way out of it, Alex. I'll have to ask you and your men to leave."

A stunned silence fell over the room. Then Jethro Spring said, "You can ask, Chisum. But I'm not leaving."

Chisum stared through him, a pained expression twisting his features. Highsaw said, "If it comes to it, Jack, I'll throw my irons on Jinglebob's side."

Jethro grinned. "I expected that. I expect, too, you know where to find me, 'cause I'm sticking damned close."

"Have we come to such a pass?" McSween asked in dismay.

"'Fraid so," Chisum muttered.

Jethro reversed a dining room chair and straddled it. "Everybody in the room, sit down," he ordered.

All obeyed.

"Now," Jethro said to Chisum after they were seated. "Let's call a spade a spade."

Chisum glared at him.

"You got orders from John not to do any shooting, don't you Pitzer?"

Still, Chisum glared.

Jethro's voice snapped, lashing through the room. "That's why your brother left, wasn't it? He figured his outfit could avoid the fight if he wasn't here to be forced into a decision."

"That's about enough, Winter," Highsaw said, coming to his feet.

Jethro's hollow laugh echoed down the halls. "Tell Jim to back off, Pitzer, or there'll be a shootout right here in this room and you'll not have obeyed your brother's orders."

"Sit down, Jim," Chisum said.

After Highsaw had again sank into a chair, Jethro said, "Now, you and John never figured the Seven Rivers bunch for enough gall to hit your main ranch, did you?"

Every eye in the room locked on the mute rancher.

"Well, they got some sand," Jethro continued, "but that's not the reason they're here. They're here to force the Jinglebob to take sides. If they can, then they'll get warrants against this ranch and strip it like wolves, won't they?"

Pitzer said, "Go on."

"You and John are smarter than the rest of us, Pitzer. You figured out a long time ago that the safest course for the Jinglebob would be not to get in on the shooting, but to keep on encouraging Dolan haters. That's why John is gone each time the goin' gets tough and why you don't ever seem to have any authority."

Pitzer smiled grimly. "If what you say is true, Winter, then we got no choice 'ceptin' to ask you people to leave, do we?"

"Yeah you do, Chisum," Jethro shot back. "For two reasons: The first is because we're not leaving without a fight, which will force the Jinglebob to do just what you don't want to do—choose your enemies. After all, we might win in the end."

"And the second reason?"

Jethro smiled. "Because there's a way out for both of us."

"How?" McSween and Chisum asked in unison.

Jethro let them hang for several ticks of the Jinglebob's pendulum clock. At last, he said, "The way it stands, this ranch is a fort. Hell, them Seven Rivers boys can never touch us, even without your help, and they know it. I doubt there's any more of them out there than us in here. But remember, their real objective is to force you off the fence."

"I still don't see how ..."

Jethro, his mood even darker than his features, leaned forward conspiratorially....

<hr />

Pitzer Chisum led two-dozen Jinglebob hands from South Spring Ranch in mid-afternoon, evicted, so he claimed, by fourteen McSween partisans who moved freely throughout the buildings.

The Seven Rivers posse left the following morning, retreating down the Pecos with nothing to show for their trouble.

During the last night of the siege, Alexander McSween stalked the dining room while Jethro Spring lounged, watching in silence from a high-backed chair, one leg draped over an arm. "We can't stay here. That seems quite clear," McSween said. "I simply do not know what's become of John. Surely he's been subjected to poor counsel."

McSween halted, spread his arms dramatically and said, "I believe we should return to Lincoln and have it out with Dolan once and for all."

"You can't mean that, Alex," Susan said. "You haven't enough strength."

"Those new War Department orders may well balance things out."

"What if it doesn't?" Jethro asked.

"Eh? What if what doesn't?"

"What if you commit yourself to a battle in Lincoln and Fort Stanton still decides to take a hand?"

"How could they?"

"They could either ignore orders, or they could interpret them different from the way you do."

McSween faced his lieutenant, face haggard and drawn. "I'm tired of being a fugitive, Jack. I want to go back to my own home and have it out, once and for all."

"That could be a fatal decision."

"What are you suggesting, Jack?" Susan asked.

"Avoid a fixed battle at any cost," he said. "Right now, it looks bad. But things in Lincoln County have a way of flip-flopping. A month ago, it looked good. A month from now, it might again."

"What is there to hope for?" McSween demanded.

"The governor's catching hell over Peppin's appointment. Maybe he'll change it again. What about Angel's report? There were some things that should stir folks up back east. I always consider survival a pretty important part of success."

"I'm tired of mere survival," McSween muttered.

"You're wrought up over the Chisum defection, dear. And you shouldn't be. Jack predicted it all along."

McSween sank into a chair, nodding wearily. "How could he? How in the world could he do such a thing to us? He stands to gain more than anyone."

"Only if he and his ranch survive," Jethro said. "He figured that out long ago. Give him credit for that much."

"Still, there's such a thing as loyalty."

"There's not much profit in looking at hands already played. We've got to play the cards we're dealt here and now."

"If not home, where shall we go?" McSween asked.

Jethro shrugged. "To the hills. To the Ruidoso, maybe. That's not too far from Lincoln and most everybody there— the ones who aren't already with us—are sympathetic. Hell, we could even go up to Colfax County. The people around Cimarron have no love for the ring either."

McSween seemed lost in thought. "Listen to Jack," Susan said. "So far, his advice has been eerily accurate."

McSween's head sank to his chest. He sat so long with his head down and eyes closed that Jethro and Susan both thought he'd fallen asleep. Then he raised his head to stare at first one, then the other.

"I'm going to Lincoln as soon as the devils surrounding this place leave. Neither of you need go if you do not wish to do so."

CHAPTER TWENTY FOUR

In the wake of Alexander McSween's decision to return to Lincoln, Jethro Spring busied with strategic planning. He dispatched Doc Scurlock and Jim French to the Ruidoso with a call to arms. Joe Bowers made a similar journey to the Rio Hondo, while Tom O'Folliard carried a carefully composed note to Antanasio Salazar. At dawn, Billy Bonney, Charlie Bowdre, and Henry Brown left South Springs to make a diversionary raid on Dolan's cow camp on the lower Pecos. Jethro led the remainder of McSween's shriveled force up the road toward Bosque Grande, laying a false trail along the way. Fifteen miles north, the party swung toward Agua Negro Spring.

When the sun peeped over the eastern horizon to cast long shadows on Sunday, July 15, 1878, McSween's forces held three strong points in Lincoln: The stout adobe-walled homes of Ellis and McSween, and Montano's store. In addition, key riflemen from the sixty-strong contingent were stationed in a small warehouse, located in the corral of Tunstall's store.

Jethro's feints up the Bosque Grande road and at Dolan's cow camp had been so successful there were only six Dolan-Riley men in Lincoln. Peppin sent off a frantic letter to the Seven Rivers bunch who were even then scouring the lower Pecos and Penasco regions for the "huge" force of McSween "regulators" who'd swept down upon the nearby cow camp. Kinney and his "Rio Grande posse" were recalled from Bosque Grande, where they searched unsuccessfully for McSween's trail. A third group was summoned from the hills around San Patricio, where McSween was expected to show. It was two days before Peppin's forces came to full strength, their total equalling McSween's and exceeding them in desperate fighting experience.

Peppin stationed men strategically around the town. And as darkness fell on July 16, the second day, scattered rifle fire erupted between the groups.

Susan found Jethro crouched behind a roof parapet corner. She handed him a steaming cup of coffee.

"You shouldn't be up here," he said.

"Do you think a woman should be spared all risk?" she asked, spreading her skirt to sit upon the roof, leaning back against the parapet. •

He laid his Winchester on the battlement and sank beside her. A cool breeze fanned a lock of hair hanging from beneath his hat. She lifted her hair from the back of her neck to let in the fresh air.

"You are in risk enough by just being in Lincoln," he said.

"Nonsense. Alex and some of the others think we are getting the best of it. They are quite sanguine about winning, you know."

Jethro set his cup upon the roof and took out his notebook and pencil stub, squinting in the moonlight.

"Still seeking mind improvement, Jack? Even under these conditions?"

He nodded. "How do you spell it?"

"S-A-N-G-U-I-N-E. It means hopeful or cheerful."

He scribbled for a moment, then folded his notebook and returned it to his shirt pocket. "Well, I'm not as sanguine as they are."

"Why not, Jack?"

"Blood will flow unless the army takes a hand to stop it. Likely, some of it will be ours."

"Is that too much of a price to pay for victory and freedom?"

He smiled. "Who says victory will be ours?"

Her hand stole into his. His entire body jerked, but he made no attempt to withdraw. He did, however, pull off his hat and sail it ten feet away, across the flat roof. Then he leaned his head tiredly against the parapet.

"You still believe Alex made a grave mistake by coming back to Lincoln, don't you?" she asked.

"Yes." he closed his eyes. "But I'll have to admit, I didn't expect he could muster this many men."

She squeezed his hand. "Alex didn't, you ninny. He thinks he did, but all the Mexicans and half the anglos know it isn't true. And so do we."

"We do?" he muttered.

"Don't we? *I* know they came because you summoned them. It was your call to arms that gave us all cause to hope."

He opened his eyes to stare at the Big Dipper. "Whoever is responsible, the last cards are about to fall."

She also tilted her head to stare into the heavens. "There are some indescribable qualities about you."

He said nothing, so she continued: "Like earning the faith and confidence of the Mexicans, so they believe in you when you send them word. I can't understand how you did it in the relatively short time you've been in New Mexico."

He retrieved his hand and rolled to his knees to peer over the parapet. When he again settled beside her, she said, "Alex would like to be able to inspire his fellow-man as you seemingly do without consciously trying. And indeed, he believes he has. But it is to you we owe our chance for victory. Yet few—least of all, you—know you've imbued others with your vision."

He fumbled for his notebook. "How do you spell 'imbued'?"

"Oh bother your notebook!" she flared. Then she said, "Billy Bonney seems to inspire a measure of the same leadership among many. But his is different and doesn't touch as many people. Doesn't it appear some of the Mexicans are devoted to him?"

Jethro nodded, mostly to himself.

"His devotees seem more inspired by his daring—perhaps by his ruthlessness. Your leadership comes from other sources and enjoys a much broader range."

Both were silent for a long time. He broke it when he softly said, "And I may have betrayed them by calling them into a trap."

"We will win," she said, again laying her hand on his."

"Not if the army jumps in on their side," Jethro murmured.

Serious fighting began on Tuesday, July 17. It soon became apparent Peppin's forces could neither dislodge McSween's men from their Lincoln fortresses, nor effectively impede messages being passed between the scattered buildings. A great deal of ammunition was expended before the sheriff sent his best marksmen to the ridge south of town and settled on a tactic of harassing sniper fire. At the same time, he dispatched an urgent request to Colonel N.A.M. Dudley for troops to aid him in serving warrants.

Colonel Dudley regretfully refused, citing his war department orders. But he dispatched an encouraging supportive note, sent by a young Negro courier. As Private Berry Robinson, Company H, 9th Cavalry approached the Wortley Hotel to deliver the message, a single shot was fired in his direction from the home of Dolan-Riley partisan, A.H. Mills. The Mills home was in line with the McSween home, fifty yards beyond. The Robinson "incident" gave Sheriff Peppin an excuse to draft another letter to Dudley, apprising him that McSween partisans had deliberately fired upon a soldier wearing the proud uniform of the United States Army. Sheriff Peppin ended this letter with a request that army troops be garrisoned in Lincoln during the disturbance as a means to "protect non-combatants." Dudley went into immediate conference with his officers.

Evening came. Jethro Spring paced the room like a caged lion.

"Sit down, Jack, for heaven's sake," Alexander McSween said. "You are making everyone nervous."

Jethro spread his palms. "Can someone tell me," he said, "just what it is we're accomplishing by staying cooped up here?"

"Why yes. We're winning a great victory."

"How?" Jethro demanded. "What is it we're doing that has all the honor and glory of victory?"

McSween smiled at Jethro much the same as a schoolmaster would at a dense child. "We're proving to the world that Dolan-Riley hasn't the strength nor the courage to force their will upon us provided we remain firm."

"And what does that gain us?"

"Respect, certainly."

"Does it mean we walk out of here?" Jethro persisted. "Does it mean we'll be winners? Does it mean they'll run for their lives? Or does it mean we eventually starve or run out of water?"

"We're low there, now," Jim French said.

"What I never have got clear, Alex," Jethro continued, "is just what you plan to accomplish with this stand?"

"I want to assert ourselves," McSween said. "We're doing that, too, you know. We've been here nearly four days and we're making our presence known. Look at the way our men came to join us when we determined to hold fast once and for all. Jack, you have no sense of timing."

Jethro slapped both palms flat upon the table and thrust his nose an inch from McSween's. "Alex, have you got a death wish?"

"Certainly not!"

"Well excuse me, but it sure as hell looks like it."

"Are you frightened, Jack?"

"'Frightened'?" Jethro straightened and stared about as if he was choosing a victim to strangle. "Hell yes, I'm frightened. But I'm sure not frightened for you—you're the one got us into this. But I damn sure *am* frightened as hell for some of these other people." Jethro wheeled and pointed to the Mexican dandy leaning indolently against a wall. "Eugenio, why are you here?"

"Because you asked me, senor."

"No, no," Jethro said. "What is the goal you hope to achieve?"

"To break the power of Senor Dolan."

"And do you see how we're doing it?"

"No, Senor Winter."

"Now see here, Jack ..."

Jethro whirled and pointed at Billy the Kid. "Why are you here, Billy?"

"I don't like it, myself," Bonney muttered.

"How about you, O'Folliard?"

Tom O'Folliard shrugged, embarrassed.

Jethro whirled back to McSween. "You see!" he thundered. "There isn't a single damned one of these people who knows why they're here. Not a single goddamned one has any idea how it is you plan to pull off this grand coup at the end, including me! What I'm asking you, McSween, is do you have any plan? If you do, share it. If you don't, damn you, you're taking every one of these men, and maybe those at Montano's store and Ellis's place with you to a glorious death!"

McSween dropped his head.

Jethro again leaned across the table. "Answer me, damn it!"

McSween said, "The Lord will provide."

The dark-faced man pushed erect, scowling. "Road apples," he said. "Even the preacher—the Lord's messenger—and his family left two days ago!"

Susan led her trembling husband to bed. She returned as a clock struck midnight. Jethro Spring tilted a chair against a wall. He stared at a spot on the ceiling.

Joe Smith asked, "Aren't we winning? Really."

Billy the Kid said, "No. But I ain't sure we're losin'."

Jethro's chair thumped to the floor. "I think we should pull out."

"No!" Susan McSween said, her one word cutting with the intensity of a surgeon's scalpel.

"All right, Susan," Jethro said. "You have the pulpit."

She was far more forceful than her husband. "We have three days invested now. Word is going out to all New Mexico about our fight for freedom. If we retreat now, we'll appear little more than bandits who seized a town and held it until law and order expelled us. My husband is right, we must fight and even die here, if need be, in order to prove our cause is just."

"Dramatic," Jethro said. "But what about the army?"

"What army?" she flared. "I see no army. I see only

Dolan-Riley bandits and outlaws out there; faces of wanted murderers and military mercenaries. I see no army cordoned around my home. And if Alex says there will be none, I believe him."

"And if they come?"

"They won't!"

"But if they do?"

"Jack Winter," she said angrily, "my husband plans to die here if necessary. And I plan to die beside him!"

Jethro rose and picked up his rifle. "Where are you going?" Billy the Kid asked.

"Up on the roof," Jethro replied. "This discussion is over. We'll all stay, you know that. There's not a man here will leave as long as this woman shames us into staying."

Jethro lit one of his rare cigars. It was a foolhardy thing to do, standing upright in the darkness. He blew out the flame and moved three feet left as two rifles cracked simultaneously from across the street. The man felt the whisper of bullets whipping past his head before he heard their bark.

"That was stupid," Susan McSween muttered, coming up beside him.

He jerked her down behind a parapet.

"I had to come talk to you," she said. "You must understand there is some reason for this madness."

He took a long pull on the cigar before saying, "You just condemned a lot of good men to death."

"Nonsense. The army won't interfere."

He sighed.

"And I thought you were so strong," she said. "So brave."

His white teeth lit the darkness. "Tell me, Susan. You gave no better answer than Alex, aside from some vague notion that all the territory thrills to our just cause—which I doubt. What I want to know is what's the grand design? Are we supposed to attack in force, kill the sheriff, take over the town, raze Dolan's store, storm Fort Stanton? If so, we should have done it the first day, when surprise was in our favor. We've lost the initiative now. Whether you and Alex like it or not, we're under siege. Way I see it, a lot of things can happen, and they're all bad."

She shifted uncomfortably and he surprised her by draping an arm across her shoulders. She stiffened, then relaxed as he began talking again. "We've got some good men here, and lots more of them at Montano's and Ellis's. It's like you said last night, they depended on me. I gave 'em bad advice."

She turned in his arm to better see him. He drew deeply, holding the smoke for an eternity.

"You're not frightened at all, are you." It was not a question.

He blew the smoke out then turned his head as if on a ratchet. Then he bent and jammed his lips against hers so hard their teeth grated. The surprise was total. A shock of excitement raced through her.

"Well!" she said breathlessly when he finally broke off. "How long I've waited."

He held out his cigar. "Hold this for me, will you?"

She took it without thinking, fingers still-tingling.

He jumped to his feet, picked up the rifle and leaped from the parapet into the night!

CHAPTER TWENTY FIVE

Guns barked from three sides as Susan flung open the trap door screaming, "Stop shooting!" She half-clambered, half-fell down the ladder, screaming over and over, "Don't shoot! Don't shoot!"

Bonney raced into the room.

"It's Jack!" she sobbed. "He leaped from the roof!"

Other faces crowded into the room. "Jack!" she sobbed. All ears were cocked to the staccato chatter of rifle fire from the surrounding buildings.

"Sounds like he's running right at 'em," Bonney said.

The gunfire dwindled and died. "I didn't figure him for a coward," Jim French said.

"He ain't," Bonney snapped. Then the youth stared curiously at Susan's hand where a tiny wisp of smoke curled toward the ceiling.

"I ... he asked me to hold it," Susan said, staring down at the cigar. "Then he ... he leaped from the roof." She looked around at the bewildered faces around her. "Why?" she asked.

"Senor Winter is one smart *hombre*," Francisco Zamora said to no one in particular. "Without him, this house turns cold."

Eugenio Salazar snorted. "*Mi padre*, he trusts Senor Winter. Can I do less?"

———————

Jethro Spring hit the ground rolling, the Winchester cradled across his stomach. No sooner had he hit and somersaulted than he was on his feet, legs pumping. Four steps and he dived over the picket fence, rolling again and coming to his feet in the moonlight. The first burst of gunfire came from the Cisneros house, across the street. Jethro ducked low and zig-zagged toward it crying, "Don't shoot! Don't shoot!" Then a rifle barked behind him, then another. Gunfire winked from the Wortley Hotel and Ham Mills home. A bullet tugged at his shirt sleeve and another furrowed across his cheek. He dove to the ground and rolled once again as a steady drumbeat of gunfire rolled toward him from McSween's house.

Jethro's cry not to shoot and the roll of flashes from McSween's threw Peppin's men into confusion. Then, firing abruptly stopped from McSween's. Before the Dolan-Riley men in the Cisneros home could once again throw down on the elusive target, the zig-zagging figure darted past, digging hard for the rear. Guns from the nearby Stanley home continued to rattle at the wisping figure. Billy Matthews and Jim Reese rushed out of Cisneros's back door, rifles at the ready. Once they thought they saw a shadow rounding the corner of Judge Wilson's home, but neither had a chance to shoot. Later, rifles chattered along the ridge above.

———————

The following evening, Jethro tied a bay gelding with a "US" brand in a thick patch of willows behind Wortley's. He moved cautiously downstream until he was behind the McSween home. The first picket was easy. The man was just below the bank's rim, a little to the right. Jethro lay still as a rock until the second man shifted uncomfortably. That man lay to the left, along the bank top. Both pickets concentrated on the house before them.

Jethro wriggled between the guards, then lay unmoving until the first dropped below the bank's edge to work his way to the second. "Hey, George," the man whispered. "Let's have a smoke."

George—whomever it might be—dropped down to his companion and Jethro eased forward. He paused behind a cottonwood, searching the stable and corral for sign of a guard. Taking a deep breath, he crawled to the corral fence, then eased along it until he reached the stable. "Francisco," he whispered. "Joe!"

"Who is it?" came a muffled reply.

"Winter. I'm coming over the wall."

Harvey Morris opened the stable door and said, "By God, it is you. We thought you'd run out on us."

Jethro's return swept from room to room like wildfire. Six men were already gathered in the McSween kitchen when Susan rushed breathlessly in to embrace him. "Jack! Oh Jack! We were so afraid you'd gone."

McSween hurried in seconds later, no less enthused.

Billy the Kid lounged against a doorjamb, shaggy straw-colored hair dangling beneath his hatbrim. He grinned wryly at Jethro and said, "Your impulses come sudden, friend. You're lucky we didn't put you under ourselves."

"Just wanted to know could you shoot, Billy. You can't."

"Why did you leave?" McSween asked, wringing the gray-eyed man's hand. "We've all been frantic."

Jethro gazed around. "Things been pretty quiet?"

"Quiet ain't the word for it," Joe Bowers said. "It's been plumb boring."

Jethro took a deep breath and said, "We've got to get out of here. And we've got to do it tonight."

"What?" McSween exclaimed. "Impossible. Don't you see, we're winning. No one in his right mind would leave now."

A babble broke out within the room. Billy the Kid's youthful voice lifted above the others. "Hold on!" When the noise subsided, Billy asked, "What do you know that we don't?"

"The army is taking a hand. They'll be here in the morning."

"How could you know that?" McSween demanded.

"I spent yesterday at Fort Stanton. They're preparing a unit to march. Around forty men. I saw a Gatling gun and a mountain howitzer being prepared, as well as supplies and rations for what I heard was to be three days."

The news stunned the room's occupants. It was a measure of respect for the dark-skinned man that most never questioned his information. Only McSween asked, "How do you know, Jack? Perhaps marauding Indians ..."

"They're *infantry*, Alex."

"Do you know they're coming here?"

"Positively."

"Well, that does it," O'Folliard said.

"So what if they do?" Susan McSween asked.

Her husband grasped at the straw. "Yes, how do we know they'll choose one side or the other? They may just be coming to see that justice prevails."

"Do you believe that?" Jethro asked.

"I don't see why not?" Susan replied. "We are citizens, too, you know."

"Yes, that's right," McSween said. "If the army intervenes, it is duty-bound, by law, to favor neither side in a territorial matter."

"Well," Jethro said, "you can believe what you will. We're still leaving. Nobody's going to die a martyr's death because of me. I had something to do with getting us into this. Now, I'm getting us out. You can argue the rights or wrongs of it later."

"How'll we get out?" Billy asked.

"There's two pickets in the willows behind the bank. I think we can take them going out and ..."

"I'm not going!" Susan McSween's voice was shrill. "I intend to stay and live or die alongside my husband. His cause is right and just. His cause is our cause and it will prevail."

"Your husband isn't staying," Jethro growled. "Neither are you."

All eyes fastened upon Alexander McSween. The attorney betrayed a tremor as he swiped a hand over his eyes.

"I know Alex!" Susan's voice rang with authority. "Though the rest of you may not, I know he has courage. We'll both stay and we'll both die if need be."

"Susan is right," McSween said haltingly. "I came home intending to live or die here, and"—his voice became firm—"by heaven, I'll do it!"

"You have no right to take others to the grave with you," Jethro growled.

"All those who do not believe in the righteousness of our cause are free to leave," McSween replied.

"Righteousness be damned!" Jethro roared. "We're talking about bullets and cannons and flesh and blood. How can you two stand there and mouth that high-sounding bullshit when we're all faced with the wrong end of a Gatling gun?"

"The army will not take sides," McSween doggedly repeated.

An awkward silence fell on the room. Jethro broke it moments later when he said, "I'm for packing them out, bound and gagged."

Another silence descended. Susan said, "It seems, Mr. Winter, that we have two very different opinions. My husband and I will stay, even if it means death. I would suggest those who wish to leave with you can move to the far side of the room."

No one moved, no voice was raised in protest. She pushed her advantage: "In other words, gentlemen, we should vote. Those who are with Alex and me should stand as they are. Those who wish to save their lives—but lose their honor—leave."

Jethro's eyes narrowed to slits.

Billy the Kid looked at his one time mentor. "Well, gen'ral," he said, voice dripping with sarcasm, "what's the next move?"

Jethro walked to a chair and sat down. He smiled faintly at the red-faced men around him. "Not a thing, boys, not a thing. Unless we all get over being skirt-whipped before morning, we'll be seeing our last sunrise."

The men started to drift to their posts when Susan said, "There still may be some things we could do to ensure victory."

"What's that?" her husband said.

"John Chisum," she said. "He's back now, I think. Didn't Pitzer say he was due back on the 18th? John still holds the balance of power."

"Not against the United States Army," Jethro interrupted.

"Assuming they are neutral!" She bit off her words, particularly for his benefit. "John Chisum could swing the balance of power. True?"

A bemused smile locked Jethro's face. This martial Susan was new to him. She'd never been more bewitching, and she used her beauty and sex to ruthlessly seize command. He shook his head, thinking it a pity it all had to end on the morrow.

"At least it's a chance!" the woman continued. "Someone should ride for South Springs and ask John to come to our aid."

The men considered it. Jethro finally said, "It's no use, Susan. It's sixty miles to South Spring. The best could be done, even if Chisum would come, is Saturday. The army will be here in the morning."

"Jack Winter, will you shut up! If Fort Stanton joins our enemies, John Chisum cannot help at any rate. But if, as Alex believes, the army will maintain its neutrality, Chisum's men can carry the day."

Jethro jumped to his feet, overturning his chair. "What makes you think he'll come now? The bastard wouldn't before. Are you people so blind you can't see how he works? He plans to sit the fighting out, join neither side, then pick up the pieces."

"Susan is right." It was Alexander McSween, his tone at first halting. "We should try."

Jethro picked up his rifle and started for the roof.

"All right," McSween said, "that's decided. Now, who shall go to Chisum?"

"There's really only one here who's qualified," Susan said. "Jack must go."

Jethro paused, his hand on the ladder. "What? Me? Are you out of your mind? I don't even believe in such a thing." Every eye was on him: Bonney's, Salazar's, O'Folliard's, everyones'.

"For one thing," Susan continued, "you are very persuasive. For another, John Chisum likes and respects you. I would trust you to present our case better than anyone, except perhaps Alex or me. Yet neither of us are strong enough for such a ride. You've shown you can do it by riding on several similar missions. You're familiar with Pitzer and Highsaw. Most of all, you just came from the river. You know where their pickets are located."

"Do you think there's a chance I'd even *think* of going?"

"You *must!*"

McSween cleared his throat. "This could be the most important service you could ever do for our cause, Jack."

"NO! No, goddammit, and that's that!"

Susan McSween slipped an arm around her husband's waist and began to sob. Alexander McSween cupped his hand beneath her chin and wiped away a tear with a forefinger. At last he straightened and said, "Jack, would you be kind enough to repair with me to the study? I do believe we need discuss some things in private."

Jethro's hostility bubbled just below the surface as he glared at McSween and Susan in turn. Then his gaze swung around the room to the others and he nodded.

———•◦•———

Alexander McSween closed his study door behind Jethro, and locked it.

Jethro whirled at the click of the lock, but McSween's smile was, as usual, disarming. He gestured to a chair and the dark man shook his head.

"Please do."

Jethro thought it odd that McSween's voice turned crisp, business-like, holding none of its previous whine. "We have some things to discuss, Jack; things too long left unsaid; things others need not hear. So sit down and let's lay all the cards on the table and be done with it."

Susan! He knows about me and Susan. He sank to the chair.

McSween shuffled papers on his desk before looking at his lieutenant. "I've come to believe our situation is indeed desperate, Jack, but I'm as committed as ever to remaining steadfast. Susan is right, you know. The entire territory does thrill to our cause."

Jethro's eyes rolled to the ceiling and his mouth corners curled into a sneer. "I thought that was your idea."

"Hear me out, Jack. There is more to this. Susan is also right that our best chance lies with support from John Chisum and you are the only one to convey a letter from me to him."

Jethro made to rise but McSween stopped him by abruptly changing subjects:

"Now, about the Fritz estate money...."

The younger man settled back to the chair.

"I've always admired your response to the question of who killed Frank Freeman, and I've decided to employ that strategy when the Fritz estate money question is raised. My answer is clear enough, isn't it? I have it in a safe place and when I can be assured it goes into the right hands, I'll produce it." McSween paused. There was a hint of a smile.

Jethro shook his head. "Not good enough, Alex. Not after what happened to Tunstall and Brewer because of it. Not after what's going to happen to everybody in this house, and at Montano's store, and at Ellis's."

Still the hint of a smile.

Jethro leaned forward. "Let me see it. If you really do have it, let me see it."

McSween's pasted smile spread into place as his head wagged. "It's in a safe place, that's all I can tell you." McSween sank farther into his chair and added, "But what if it isn't?"

"Is this some trick?"

"What if I did temporarily use the estate money, Jack? Surely you, nor anyone else, would believe I'm intending to do anything else but borrow the money. Do you?"

"Wait a minute! Are you saying you did take it?" Jethro reached out to grip the edge of McSween's desk.

"Not at all. I'm saying precisely what I've said all along:

I have the money in a safe place."

Jethro leaped to his feet, moving around the desk. His face was livid. "You sonofabitch! Tunstall and Brewer and a hell of a lot of other good men died because of you! I ..."

McSween raised a hand to the other's anger, broad, pasted smile in place and unwavering. "Let he who is without sin cast the first stone."

McSween's biblical quote momentarily stopped Jethro. Then he pointed a finger and snarled, "You yellow-bellied ..."

"And are you without blemish, *Jethro Spring!*

Everything became suspended in time; Jethro's face turned to a mask. Later, he would swear the clock even stopped. He sank back into his chair.

"We all have our skeletons, don't we, Mr. Spring?"

"How did you find out?"

McSween opened a desk drawer while saying, "Sheriff Copeland asked for legal assistance in straightening out his new office. While doing so, I came across this." He held up a wanted poster from the drawer, just out of Jethro's reach.

"So you've known for ..."

"A month. Give or take a day or two."

"Why didn't you turn me in?"

This time it was the attorney's eyes that rolled. "Don't be absurd. For the same reason I resisted your suggestion for Copeland to serve warrants on our other fighting men." The wanted poster disappeared into the desk. "You have no value to me, sir, hanging from a Fort Stanton scaffold."

Jethro's eyes flicked to McSween's hand as the lawyer pushed the drawer tight. There was a tiny "click" of a lock falling into place. Then the gray eyes again lifted to the barrister's face.

"Does she know?"

McSween shook his head, chuckling at Jethro's cupidity. "Anybody else?"

"My dear sir, surely you know an attorney's confidence

is his chief asset."

Jethro sighed. "And what do you intend to do with this revelation?"

"Why it should be obvious." When Jethro's hypnotic eyes continued to grip him, McSween said, "Trade. I'll trade your life for mine."

"How?"

"You'll carry my message to Chisum. Then you can continue out of the territory." When Jethro said nothing, McSween added, "You could come back if you wish, of course, and I would consider our mutual obligations discharged. However, you may think it a matter of uncertain trust."

Jethro gazed around the room, as if seeing it for the first time. The eyes fastened on the door. "What makes you think I'd deliver your message after leaving here? I could ride in any direction."

"Honor. You are an honorable man—that much I know. You see, Jack ..." McSween's use of his alias did not go unnoticed as Jethro's eyes swung back to the attorney. "... I trust you implicitly, even though you do not accord me the same honor."

Jethro considered his choices. McSween was ahead of him.

"You are wondering what would happen if you refuse."

No reply.

"Just remember, a secret becomes less a secret in direct relation to the number of people who share it."

Gradually Jethro's thoughtful stare turned to flint.

McSween, too, appeared thoughtful. "Why am I choosing to reveal this to you now? Frankly, I planned to keep the notice for some unknown future need. But if you're right, I have little future and therefore can have no further use for the knowledge than to utilize it in a last roll of the dice to survive, no matter how vain?"

McSween cleared his throat, then added, "Permanently separating you and Susan would be a peripheral benefit."

"Write your letter," Jethro said. "It won't help you, but from now on I don't give a damn if you don't understand that Chisum is a bigger and smarter bastard than you."

The letter took two hours for McSween to draft. All the while, Jethro's eyes never left the attorney. Not once did he shift position or utter a sound. At last, McSween blotted the last page, folded the foolscap and sealed the envelope. Then he handed the letter to his lieutenant.

Jethro carefully buttoned the letter into his shirt pocket, then held out his hand. "The wanted notice," he said.

McSween leaned back in his chair, smile once more in place. "Surely you must see it's better to remain where it is, Jack. You could lose it on your way to South Springs and someone might find it who has less regard for you than I."

Jethro looked down at his upright palm, then back into the brown eyes of his one-time friend. He smiled, but there was little warmth in it. "You know, barrister, you're working your way to the top of my hate list."

McSween clucked, still leaning back in his chair. "Alongside Dolan and Riley? Think nothing of it. All we merchants are alike."

⇒ Chapter Twenty Six ⇐

Jethro Spring burrowed his cheek into baked earth beneath the single cottonwood tree. He lay in no-man's land, half-way between McSween's adobe corral and the riverbank willows. Where were the pickets now? He cocked an ear. Was that music? Yes! Susan McSween played the piano. He smiled as the pounding beat of *Camptown Races* wafted through the chill night air. He lifted his head to study the willows. There! A man moved, dropping below the bank. He waited ten seconds, then crawled from his cottonwood shelter.

The two pickets murmured together as he slithered past: "That little bitch beats all, a-playin' that piano like that. She's got more guts than most men I know."

Five minutes later, Jethro reached the Rio Bonito. Ten minutes after that he untied the stolen army horse. A half-hour later, Jethro led his saddled mare out of Ellis's corral, talking earnestly to Doc Scurlock. An hour and a half later, he pounded past San Patricio on his way to Chisum's, the stolen bay galloping behind.

Riding at the head of his column and with all Fort Stanton's officers serving as his personal escort, Colonel N.A.M. Dudley was an imposing sight. The body of troops marched behind in a dusty fog, a limbered Gatling gun in mid-column. Pack mules carrying a mountain howitzer trailed behind.

Dudley halted his column in front of the Wortley Hotel where he made a pompous declaration that his troops came not to join the fray on one side or the other, but to protect non-combatants throughout the village. Dudley made the same declaration to anxious watchers in McSween's home, then ordered his detachment to camp in a vacant lot directly across the street from Montano's.

Billy the Kid ran into the kitchen. "They're setting up right between our three strong points!" he exclaimed.

McSween sat with his head in hands.

"Goddammit, Alex," Bonney said again, "they're pinning us down by setting their tents there."

McSween raised his head. "It just looks that way, Billy."

Dudley mounted his howitzer facing Montano's building. Then he sent word to the body of McSween's men there, again saying he came only to protect non-combatants. *But*, if any of his troops were fired upon, or appeared to be fired upon, he'd order the cannon to level the building.

Similar threats were sent to the men at Ellis's.

Dudley's order had its intended effect on the Mexican partisans gathered at Montano's. The entire body evacuated at noon, fleeing to their horses in the Ellis corral. The opposition let them go; McSween was the one they wanted. Panic bred panic and ten minutes after Dudley's threat caused the exodus from Montano's, all McSween partisans, except for the dozen trapped in the McSween house, fled Lincoln.

Peppin lost no time closing the cordon. Gunfire drove away the first attempt to set fire to the building. The second attempt was more successful; two daring deputies kindled a fire against the west wing's back door, using coal oil, wood chips and planks torn from the stable roof.

The beleaguered combatants tried desperately to put the fire out, but a hail of gunfire from the stable and the two houses to the west drove firefighters to cover. They were also frustrated by a shortage of water. At last the McSween followers gave up and let the blaze run its course. Their sole hope was the flames would take several hours to work eastward through the largely adobe building against a strong wind. The flames crept on, feeding on rafters, flooring, doors and window casings, furniture.

Susan McSween left the house in mid-afternoon to appeal to Colonel Dudley. When the woman stepped from the house, all firing ceased. Dudley at first refused to see her, then made sport of McSween's plight, earning Susan's undying enmity. When she returned to report her failure, a council met to choose a course of action. Suffering for want of a clear leader, the council began awkwardly. Though youngest of the group, Billy the Kid stepped into the breach:

"We can stick it out if the fire don't burn any faster. What we want to do is wait 'til dark. Some of us are bound to get hit, but most can make it across the river. It's only a few hundred yards. If we run fast and shoot faster, we can hold the bastards off."

There was general agreement with Bonney's plan. Then Billy turned to Susan McSween. "I expect, ma'am, you'd best leave. A dress ain't very good to make a run in."

"Billy, I can't," Susan said. "I must stay by my husband and you men."

Bonney shook his head. "No. We're gonna have to run

for it, ma'am. It ain't hardly fair for somebody to have to look after you. Go on and leave. Nobody'll think bad of you."

Susan hesitated, then nodded. As she left, she heard Billy say, "Okay, here's what we'll do. Me and a couple others will go first and draw fire. Then the rest of you come on."

It was nearly nine o'clock before darkness fell. McSween and his men were holed up in the very last room in the east wing, barely waiting out the encroaching fire. Billy the Kid, Jim French, and Harvey Morris burst from the house, darting toward the corral gate, guns blazing. Morris fell at the first answering fusillade, but miraculously, French and the Kid reached the riverbank willows, plunged through, firing as they went, driving Peppin's men back.

Tom O'Folliard, Joe Bowers, Joe Smith, Jose Chavez, and Tom Cullins burst out direct behind. All escaped to the willows as Dolan-Riley men frantically reloaded.

McSween and the remaining ones waited too long. Faulty timing? A breakdown in courage? No one will ever know. But all firing had died behind the second group when Alexander McSween led Francisco Zamora, Vicente Romero, and Eugenio Salazar from the burning building. The enemy was ready. With the blazing building behind them, the fugitives were prime targets. A hail of bullets cut all four down. McSween's body jerked for several minutes afterward as round after round pumped into his inert form.

Then the victory celebration began....

CHAPTER TWENTY SEVEN

Jethro Spring's grimy hat-brim flopped low over bloodshot eyes as a blistering noonday sun beat down. The sorrel mare plodded past the homes of Isaac Ellis and Octabiano Sales. Jethro glanced at Patron's house, at the jail, then at Montano's store, boarded up and lifeless. He swung his gaze to the military encampment across the street. Gray eyes narrowed at the mountain howitzer, mounted and ready, its muzzle yawning at Montano's door, and at the Gatling gun, limbered and pointed up the street. Several lounging soldiers peered boredly at the dusty rider.

Jethro and his plodding horse moved past the shuttered home of Santurnino Baca, and the "Indian Tower" standing within the adobe corral of Lucius Huff. Across the street was the courthouse; coming up on the left squatted Judge Wilson's home and the adobe of Luis Aguayo. Jethro thought of his wild nighttime dash past both buildings.

He reined the mare to a stop in front of the J.H. Tunstall

& Co. store, shaking his head at the broken windows and smashed door. What had not been carried away lay scattered or broken upon the floor or in the street. Two bolts of yard goods lay upon the porch, half-unrolled, ripped and dirty. A torn blanket draped through a broken window.

Jethro stared vacantly at the old Mexican whose chair tilted precariously against the wall as if it had always been, a huge sombrero at his feet. The two men's eyes caught and held for a moment before Jethro clucked to the mare.

A few feet further, Jethro reined to a halt before the wreckage of what had once been Lincoln's most pretentious home. The white picket fence lay smashed and broken, much of it torn away and used for the celebration bonfire, around which the Dolan-Riley partisans had danced to the death of Alexander McSween.

The adobe walls thrust upward, blackened from the gutting fire, all doors and windows burned or smashed. The roof had collapsed as the fire ate through its supports; the floors and furnishings also consumed. He leaned, palms crossed upon the saddlehorn, lips pinching as he watched Susan McSween move haltingly through the wreckage, a black shawl pulled over her head and across her shoulders.

The woman shuddered and turned away, saw Jethro, gathered up her skirts and ran toward him, lifting up a tear-streaked face. "Jack! Oh Jack, they've killed Alex!"

Jethro cocked a leg around the horn, staring through her, fumbling in his shirtpocket for a cigar. He licked it and bit off one end, the gray eyes flashing a warning to the woman to keep her distance.

"They killed young Harvey Morris, too, and Francisco Zamora, Vicente Romero, and Eugenio Salazar." She began crying.

He blinked at her mention of Salazar and felt Antanasio's eyes boring into his back. He fumbled for a match, struck it across his belt buckle and held it to the cigar, puffed, then pitched the match toward the blackened shell, saying, "Nothing will burn there now."

She stopped crying. "Didn't you hear me, Jack? I said Alex is dead. So are the others. It was horrible. They shot them down like beasts. Billy and some others escaped, but my husband died!"

"I'm wondering why you're still alive?"

"Jack! What has come over you?" She moved near enough to brush his stirrup.

He pulled on his cigar. He took another glance at the blackened ruin, then reached down to grip her shoulder and shake her. "You were the one who said, come what may, you were going to stay. If need be, you said you'd die alongside your husband and every one of his men. That's why they all stayed, because you shamed them to it. They stayed to die when they could've lived to fight."

"But, Jack! They *made* me leave!" A tear trickled down her cheek.

He released her and his voice was toneless. "You knew they'd send you out at the last, didn't you, Susan? You knew your men; knew they'd never allow you to stay and die with them."

"No! No!" she sobbed, grasping his leg. "No, you're wrong. Please."

"I'm curious. What's it like trapped in a house that's burning around you and death as your only option?"

"They made me go-o-o-o-o!"

"And you made them stay." Jethro uncurled his left leg from the saddlehorn and picked up the reins.

The woman darted forward to grasp the mare's head-stall. "No! Please! You can't go!"

"Turn her loose, Susan."

"Please, Jack. What about us?"

His laugh might have come from the bottom of a well. "I give up. What about us?"

"But we love each other so. We can pick up the pieces. Now it will be the two of us, Jack. Your strength and mine working together. Alex was weak, don't you see? So was poor John Tunstall. Neither of them understood how strong one must be to survive out here. You are such a man. Between us, we can still destroy Dolan and Riley, as John wished. Surely you can see? Only the strong can succeed, Jack. Together, we will be invincible!"

Jethro prodded the sorrel mare with his heels, but Susan held fast. "Jack, you can't leave. You can't. Don't you understand? I'm offering myself, too."

His eyelids hung at half-mast. "Have you really spent a suitable time in mourning, Susan? Poor Alex, as misguided as you forced him to be, deserves more."

Her face twisted, hardened. "You know what I mean, Jack Winter. I've been yours ever since I first saw you. The more so since Las Vegas. And you've been mine. You can't tell me otherwise."

Jethro leaned forward, forearms folded across the horn, voice flat. "You had it planned all along, didn't you, Susan? You were the one who really sent me to Chisum's, didn't you? You wanted to get me away from the fight, didn't you?"

Her features twisted while tears squirted from clinched eyes. A breeze blew wisps of unbrushed, grime-streaked hair from beneath her mourning shawl. Soiled hands gripped the sorrel's bridle all the harder.

"And all along, I thought it was Chisum who took the cake for conniving. I knew Alex was up to his pants pockets in playing others for fools and that Chisum was way out in front of him. I knew about Dolan and Riley and Rynerson and the rest of the scheming bastards making up their ring. But you! I got to hand it to you—none of the rest of 'em played as cutthroat as it turns out you'd probably planned from the day you kicked the slats out of your baby cradle."

The woman's eyes widened and her mouth formed a silent "Oh!"

"Tell me, Susan," he said without rancor, "did you really figure your husband was going to die? Or did you think it was all a worthwhile roll of the dice, with me held in reserve in case Alex's gamble failed to come off?"

She released her grip. "Go!" she snapped. "Go away! Whatever I saw in you, I'll never know. I hate you!"

Jethro clucked to the sorrel mare.

"Go on! Get out of here! I never want to see you again!"

She screamed insults that followed him past Wortley's, past Dolan & Co.'s brick building, and were still ringing in his ears when his horse rounded the road bend west of Lincoln.

To make matters worse, the woman's insults still rang in the man's ears the next day at Carizozo Spring, and the following week at Tularosa....

Watch For

Lincoln County Crucible

Third in an exciting series chronicling the life of Jethro Spring, a man born of two cultures who fails to comfortably bridge either. Still caught in the coils of a merchant's war he didn't choose, Jethro rides the tale to its exciting and treacherous conclusion.

As you'll see, Billy the Kid continues. So does the beautiful temptress, Susan McSween and the entire surviving cast of the previous book, *Bloody Merchant's War*. But there are newcomers: Sheriff Pat Garrett and Lewis Wallace, the new territorial governor who drops into the "war" while busy creating *Ben Hur: A Tale of the Christ*.

From *Lincoln County Crucible*

Jethro Spring trotted up the sandy bed of the dry arroyo, sheer rock cliffs towered on either side. Once, he glanced behind, suddenly fearful Naiche Tana had abandoned him to his fate. It was a senseless fear—the war chief trotted easily behind, knee-length moccasins only whispering on the arroyo sand.

Much earlier, while the land was still steeped in darkness, they'd left their horses somewhere near the headwaters of the Rio Tulerosa. From there, Naiche Tana led off west, Jethro following, climbing a rocky defile where no horse could travel, into the mid-April snows clinging to these eastern slopes of the highest Sacramentos.

Jethro was sure they'd left the reservation boundary shortly after they'd trotted across the high summit, Naiche Tana leading. They then began a laborious descent along a treacherous game trail that followed a narrow cliff slash. At the bottom, the two men again set out at a steady ground-eating trot down canyon, to a fork, then up canyon to another fork, then another. Mile after steady mile, climbing now to the east, the two churned on. Sweat ran freely through Jethro's pores and he envied the bare torso and loin cloth of his companion. And he marveled that the chief, at his age, could run so steadily and easily.

In his early twenties, as a well-conditioned middleweight prizefighter known as Kid Barry, Jethro had put in thousands of miles of roadwork. Now, as his lungs screamed and eyes dimmed with fatigue, he was everlastingly grateful for those miles. As it was, all he could do was concentrate on the dark form ahead. Then Naiche Tana stopped. "We rest," the chief said. "Then the gray-eyed-one will go first."

Jethro stared around. They were in a high, rock-walled canyon, only ten to twelve feet wide. He glanced at Naiche Tana and concentrated solely on breathing as easily and shallowly as the old chief.

A few minutes later, with Jethro leading, an Apache warrior fell in beside him! The move was sudden, but so deep and trusting was his faith in Naiche Tana that he gave no hint of surprise. When the next warrior fell in on his other flank, he was prepared. Then another fell in to lead.

They trotted on in that way, Jethro surrounded by Naiche Tana and the three Apache warriors. Gradually the warrior in front increased his speed; faster and faster, until the four Indians and one half-Indian/half-white man pounded headlong up the arroyo. Jethro's lungs were near bursting and his eyes began to dim. Then they rounded yet another bend and the lead warrior stopped. Jethro, rushing pell-mell caromed off the first warrior and bumped into another before he could stop. He staggered, wobbling in a circle as his eyes slowly focused. He was in the middle of a ring of Apaches—warriors all. Dimly he saw Naiche Tana. The war chief stood haughtily outside the circle, his legs spread and arms folded. Just the hint of a smile was on the stocky chief's lips and the black eyes flashed with a mischevious glint.

Slowly, Jethro turned, peering at each warrior in turn. A tall, broad-shouldered Indian with wide, cruel-bent eyes and unruly black hair hanging to his shoulders said, "I am Victorio." He spoke in English.

Jethro still panted, fighting for breath. He studied the man as he did. Victorio, Jethro decided, had an uncontrolled fierceness about him that seemed foreboding—actually a wildness. "Greetings," he said in halting Apache. "I am Jack Winter. I am called the gray-eyed-one by your people, the Mescalero. I am agent for the Mescalero Apache people on the reservation to the north. I am their friend. I would be your friend."

Victorio rattled something in rapid Apache. Jethro caught only a few words: "Enemy," "white eyes," "kill," among them.

"I do not understand," he said. "I speak Apache poorly. Please speak more slow."

Again, Victorio rattled more garbled Apache. Jethro looked casually around. He was getting his breath now and thought more clearly. Only hostility met his eye. He turned back to Victorio. And this time his voice was flat when he said, "If we are to talk, we must both understand. If we are not both to understand, then Victorio and the gray-eyed-one came for nothing."

"What is it the white man would say?" Victorio said coldly, but slowly.

"I came to ask you to come to the reservation and dwell in peace amongst your people."

"How can we live at peace with the white man who kills us and drives us from our homes?"

"How can the white man live at peace with Apaches who do the same? I tell you, there has been enough war. You are tired. The white soldiers are tired. Would it not be better for both to say we are tired? Can we not live in peace without one defeating the other in war? Those who truly want peace can seek peace with no loss of honor."

"Any who seek peace are women with neither honor nor friend."

Jethro still wore his Colt on his hip. And he, like Naiche Tana, carried his Winchester. There was a knife in his left boot, too. The Mescaleros had deliberately left him armed. But they all carried weapons, too, and at least twenty of them surrounded him. "How," he asked Victorio slowly, putting as much disdain in his words as he could muster, "can I prove to you I am not a woman?"

A look of greater wildness came over Victorio. "All white eyes are women, and women can never prove themselves to be men."

Jethro's breathing had returned to normal. Still, he was tired from his all-night ride and long morning run. He measured his chances and shrugged. Then he bent, laid his Winchester at his feet and unbuckled the Colt from around his waist to lay alongside the carbine. He straightened and stared hard into Victorio's malevolent orbs. Then he bent again, this time to his boot, and removed the small knife. Straightening, he glanced at Victorio then spun the knife to its hilt in the ground between them.

"Many whites," he growled in guttural Apache, "have the courage of Naiche Tana or Victorio. I am one of those. To prove to you this is so, I will fight any warrior Victorio chooses to send against me. But he will be armed with only a knife and I will have only empty hands."

A low murmur swept the circle of Apaches before Jethro

continued: "Or alone and with no weapons, I will fight three"—he held up three fingers—of your warriors, who are also unarmed."

Victorio stared coldly at the newcomer, then barked three names. The three warriors who'd escorted Jethro and Naiche Tana up the winding little arroyo laid their rifles at their feet and divested themselves of pistols and knives.

Jethro backed cautiously until the rock wall was at his rear. As he did, he subconsciously mumbled a prayer to his one-time mentor, Ling San Ho, who'd taught him many lessons in the art of unarmed fighting.

The first Apache to disarm himself—the lithe warrior who'd led their pounding run through the arroyo, leaped to the attack before the other two were ready. He came with arms wide-spread, intending to grapple. It was too easy. Two hard straight lefts, a vicious right to the body and a full left uppercut to the jaw stretched the man full length between his two partners as they advanced. They paused momentarily in shock, then separated and went to a crouch, each advancing more cautiously than had the first warrior.

The man on Jethro's right was first within range. The gray-eyed man's arm snaked out and iron-like fingers clamped on a brown wrist, jerking at once. As the warrior tumbled off balance, a hand edge slammed against the bridge of his hawk-like nose and the warrior tumbled to his knees. It was so skillfully and quickly done that Jethro was set for the warrior on his left when that man made his move. As that third warrior lunged, a soft boot came from nowhere and smashed him full in the face. Then, as the Indian staggered back, Jethro grasped his long hair and jerked him forward and down, while slamming a knee into his jaw, sending the Apache into oblivion.

Jethro wheeled back to the second warrior, who wobbled to his feet. "I am truly sorry, my friend," Jethro growled in Apache just before a measured blow to the man's jaw laid him in a crumpled heap between his two partners.

The quick and violent action had Jethro panting again. He wiped sweat from his eyes with a grimy shirtsleeve. As he did, Victorio chattered a name and instructions and a squat, powerful warrior pitched his rifle to a comrade, whipped out his knife and sprang to the attack. Jethro dodged the first thrust and stumbled over one of the unconscious warriors lying at his feet. The knife wielder was on him in an instant. Still off balance, Jethro knocked the darting knife arm aside once, twice. The second time a dark red stain spread over his lower sleeve.

The warrior paused, then began stalking his prey as Jethro regained his balance and backed against the rock wall. When the warrior thrust again, Jethro was prepared. He neatly kicked the man's pivot knee from beneath him, caught his knife wrist in a vice grip, and kicked his attacker in the crotch. Ignoring the other hand clawing at his face, Jethro threw the man off balance, using both men's full weight to fall upon the knife wrist.

All within the circle heard the snap, but there was only a grunt from the squat warrior. Jethro clambered to his feet, pulling at his shirttail. His eyes widened as the squat warrior picked up the knife with his left hand and crawled to his knees, eyes savagely intent. A measured kick sent the man to temporary oblivion and Jethro tore a strip of shirttail with his teeth. He was wrapping the torn cloth around his bleeding forearm when he heard Victorio snarl three more names.

Three Apache warriors pulled knives and began their advance. He glanced at the squat warrior's blade laying in the sand four feet away and realized he'd never reach it in time. With only one alternative left, he began to back along the rock wall, sidling toward the nearest advancing knife wielder....

Other Books by Roland Cheek

Non-fiction

Chocolate Legs 320 pgs. 5-1/2 x 8-1/2 $19.95 (postpaid)
An investigative journey into the controversial life and death of the best-known bad-news bears in the world. by Roland Cheek

My Best Work is Done at the Office 320 pgs. 5-1/2 x 8-1/2 $19.95 (postpaid)
The perfect bathroom book of humorous light reading and inspiration to demonstrate that we should never take ourselves or our lives too seriously. by Roland Cheek

Dance on the Wild Side 352 pgs. 5-1/2 x 8-1/2 $19.95 (postpaid)
A memoir of two people in love who, against all odds, struggle to live the life they wish. A book for others who also dream. by Roland and Jane Cheek

The Phantom Ghost of Harriet Lou 352 pgs. 5-1/2 x 8-1/2 $19.95 (postpaid)
Discovery techniques with insight into the habits and habitats of one of North America's most charismatic creatures; a guide to understanding that God made elk to lead humans into some of His finest places. by Roland Cheek

Learning To Talk Bear 320 pgs. 5-1/2 x 8-1/2 $19.95 (postpaid)
An important book for anyone wishing to understand what makes bears tick. Humorous high adventure and spine-tingling suspense, seasoned with understanding through a lifetime of walking where the bear walk. by Roland Cheek

Montana's Bob Marshall Wilderness 80 pgs. 9 x 12 (coffee table size) $15.95 hardcover, $10.95 softcover (postpaid) *97 full-color photos, over 10,000 words of where-to, how-to text about America's favorite wilderness.* by Roland Cheek

Fiction

Echoes of Vengeance 256 pgs. 5-1/2 x 8-1/2 $14.95 (postpaid)
The first in a series of six historical novels tracing the life of Jethro Spring, a young mixed-blood fugitive fleeing for his life from revenge exacted upon his parents' murderer. by Roland Cheek

Bloody Merchants' War 288 pgs. 5-1/2 x 8-1/2 $14.95 (postpaid)
The second in a series of six historical novels tracing the life of Jethro Spring. This one takes place in Lincoln County, New Mexico Territory. It was no place for a young fugitive to be ambushed by events beyond his control. by Roland Cheek

Turn page for order form

Order form for Roland Cheek's Books

See list of books on reverse side

Telephone orders: 1-800-821-6784. *Visa, MasterCard or Discover only.*

Visit our website: www.rolandcheek.com

Postal orders: Skyline Publishing
P.O. Box 1118 • Columbia Falls, MT 59912
Telephone: (406) 892-5560   Fax (406) 892-1922

Please send the following books:
(I understand I may return any Skyline Publishing book for a full refund—no questions asked.)

Title	Qty.	Cost Ea.	Total
_____	_____	$ _____	$ _____
_____	_____	$ _____	$ _____
_____	_____	$ _____	$ _____
		Total Order:	$ _____

We pay cost of shipping and handling inside U.S.

Ship to: Name _____

Address _____

City _____ State _____ Zip _____

Daytime phone number (_____)_____-_____

Payment: ☐ Check or Money Order

Credit card: ☐ Visa ☐ MasterCard ☐ Discover

Card nunber _____

Name on card _____ Exp. date ___/___

Signature: _____